D0171412

"Sto

A female voice came from the doorway as Donovan Crow flashed the would-be gunfighter his trademark glare.

Every man in the saloon turned to stare at the stunning woman. Her trim-fitting yellow gown displayed her full creamy breasts to their best advantage. Her dark eyes sparkled with so much inner spirit that Van became lost in their depths.

To his amazement, the alluring woman headed straight to him and positioned herself in front of him like a human shield.

"Mr. Crow and I are going to be married day after tomorrow and I will thank you not to spoil my wedding, sir," she said in a heavy Southern drawl to Van's opponent.

"Married?" The crowd hooted in unison.

Staring down at this stranger's shimmering auburn hair, Van couldn't recall a single instance in his life when he had been struck speechless.

Until now.

* * *

The Gunfighter and the Heiress
Harlequin® Historical #1051—August 2011

✓ ✓ ✓ ✓ 2013

PROPERTY OF ✓
SUMMERPLACE ✓
LIBRARY ✓ ✓

**Praise for
Carol Finch**

"Carol Finch is known for her lightning-fast, roller-coaster-
ride adventure romances that are brimming over with a
large cast of characters and dozens of perilous escapades."
—*RT Book Reviews*

Bandit Lawman, Texas Bride
"Finch has made her reputation on wonderfully realistic
and humorous westerns filled with biting repartee
and nonstop action. She's at her finest with this
action-packed tale of a lawman and a spitfire."
—*RT Book Reviews*

Texas Ranger, Runaway Heiress
"Finch offers another heartwarming western romance
full of suspense, humor and strong characters."
—*RT Book Reviews*

Lady Renegade
"Finch's forte, verbal repartee, is at its best here.
With well-developed characters and a quick pace,
this tale is highly reminiscent of her classic westerns."
—*RT Book Reviews*

McCavett's Bride
"For wild adventures, humor and western atmosphere,
Finch can't be beat. She fires off her quick-paced novels
with the crack of a rifle and creates the atmosphere of the
Wild West through laugh-out-loud dialogue and escapades
that keep you smiling."
—*RT Book Reviews*

The Ranger's Woman
"Finch delivers her signature humor, along with a big dose
of colorful Texas history, in a love and laughter romp."
—*RT Book Reviews*

CAROL FINCH

THE GUNFIGHTER AND THE HEIRESS

Harlequin®

TORONTO NEW YORK LONDON
AMSTERDAM PARIS SYDNEY HAMBURG
STOCKHOLM ATHENS TOKYO MILAN MADRID
PRAGUE WARSAW BUDAPEST AUCKLAND

If you purchased this book without a cover you should be aware
that this book is stolen property. It was reported as "unsold and
destroyed" to the publisher, and neither the author nor the
publisher has received any payment for this "stripped book."

Recycling programs
for this product may
not exist in your area.

ISBN-13: 978-0-373-29651-4

THE GUNFIGHTER AND THE HEIRESS

Copyright © 2011 Connie Feddersen

All rights reserved. Except for use in any review, the reproduction or
utilization of this work in whole or in part in any form by any electronic,
mechanical or other means, now known or hereafter invented, including
xerography, photocopying and recording, or in any information storage
or retrieval system, is forbidden without the written permission of the
publisher, Harlequin Enterprises Limited, 225 Duncan Mill Road,
Don Mills, Ontario, Canada M3B 3K9.

This is a work of fiction. Names, characters, places and incidents are
either the product of the author's imagination or are used fictitiously,
and any resemblance to actual persons, living or dead, business
establishments, events or locales is entirely coincidental.

This edition published by arrangement with Harlequin Books S.A.

For questions and comments about the quality of this book
please contact us at Customer_eCare@Harlequin.ca.

® and TM are trademarks of the publisher. Trademarks indicated with
® are registered in the United States Patent and Trademark Office, the
Canadian Trade Marks Office and in other countries.

www.Harlequin.com

Printed in U.S.A.

Available from Harlequin® Historical and
CAROL FINCH

*The Hawk Brothers

Look for Carol Finch's novella
Christmas at Cahill Crossing
part of the anthology
Snowflakes and Stetsons
Coming October 2011

8/17
PROPERTY OF
SUMMERPLACE
LIBRARY

This book is dedicated to my husband, Ed, and our children, Kurt, Shawnna, Jill, Jon, Christie and Durk.

And to our grandchildren Livia, Harleigh, Blake, Kennedy, Dillon, and Brooklynn. And to Kurt and Shawnna's children, whenever they may be. Hugs and kisses!

Chapter One

Wolf Ridge, Texas, 1880s

"Go away."

Donovan Crow groaned as he dragged the pillow from his head and listened to the persistent knocking at the door of his hotel suite.

"Can't," his friend and business manager called from the other side of the door in the sitting room. "You told me to wake you after you'd had a full day's sleep."

"Changed my mind," he mumbled.

"You told me you'd say that, Van. Now I'm supposed to say, 'Get up and open the damn door and do it now!'"

Muttering, he levered himself onto the side of the bed. He raked his hand through his disheveled raven hair and forced himself to stand upright. Sluggishly, he reached for his breeches. He couldn't remember the last time he'd been this tired. The past few weeks of riding back and forth on the Higgins Stagecoach Express line to stop the rash of robberies had taken its toll on him. Come to think of it, he should have told his business manager to let him hibernate for a *week*.

"Van? Are you up yet?" his friend called impatiently.

"More or less," Van mumbled.

"Then open the blasted door. I have several telegrams and letters offering you jobs."

Van strode from the bedroom to the sitting area to open the door. Bartholomew Collier stared at him all too cheerfully as he invited himself into the suite. Bart was two years younger than Van. He stood five foot eight and had a wiry build and tireless energy. He had curly brown hair, a broken nose and pale green eyes covered by wire-rimmed glasses. Van had saved Bart from disaster eight years earlier and in return he'd acquired a business manager and a friend for life.

Since then, Bart had handled the steady flow of paperwork that arrived at Van's hotel headquarters. He hadn't thought that advertising himself as a gun for hire would bring in so much business, but he was bombarded constantly with jobs.

"You look like hell," Bart observed as he plunked himself down in the chair, then dropped the stack of letters and telegrams on the table near the window.

"Thanks. Sure would hate to look better than I feel." Van strode over to pour himself a glass of water to lubricate his parched throat. He wished it were that easy to cure all the aches and pains caused by bouncing around on the inside of a stagecoach for days on end.

"Oh, almost forgot." Bart bounded up like a jackrabbit and sailed from the room. He returned two minutes later with a heaping tray of food, two cups of coffee and a bottle of whiskey.

Van arched a curious brow as he studied the food Bart set in front of him. "What time is it?"

"You mean what *day* is it?" Bart helped himself to a slice of bacon. "I let you sleep an entire day away, just as you requested."

Van took a cautious sip of steaming coffee. "That last assignment was a bitch." He narrowed his eyes at Bart. "Don't sign me up for that kind of assignment again."

Ever cheerful—damn him—Bart grinned, revealing the slight gap between his front teeth. "You sure about that? Think of all the money you made and the attention you received for arresting those two stagecoach robbers."

Bart always insisted that Van demand high prices because he risked his life as a detective for railroads, stage lines and cattlemen battling rustlers. He also served as a personal bodyguard for the highbrows who traveled through wild country to reach their destinations on the east and west coasts.

Unfortunately, Van was rarely in town long enough to spend the money piling up. He had countless job offers but he didn't have much of a life. Not that many whites invited him to social gatherings. He was the dispensable mixed-breed scout—detective and gun for hire who did his job, but was then quickly dismissed in favor of socially acceptable friends.

"Mr. Higgins is singing your praises to high heaven and you've received publicity in newspapers from Arizona to Louisiana. I should know," Bart declared. "I subscribe to several of those papers so we can keep abreast of what's going on. As for Mr. Higgins, he wants to pay you handsomely to keep you on retainer so you can put the fear of God in would-be outlaws trying to rob his coaches."

Van snorted sourly, then sipped his drink. "Can't stand that much confinement. What other jobs are waiting?" When Bart picked up a telegram, Van flung up his hand to forestall him. "And bear in mind that I am *not* taking *any* assignment until I catch up on my rest."

Bart shrugged and smiled wryly. For the life of him, Van couldn't imagine why his friend—and Van didn't have many of them in white man's society, so he was careful not to offend Bart—looked so amused. Certainly nothing in their conversation accounted for it.

Bart tapped his forefinger against the stack of telegrams and letters. "You have a wide range of jobs to choose from. You can serve as a railroad detective to quell trouble on the line from Fort Worth to points east near the Mississippi River. Several robberies are occurring on the line. Also, you can become a personal bodyguard for some highfalutin politician who wants to inspect the Texas Ranger stations on the frontier."

Bart leaned toward Van. "Personally, I think the Ranger captain is trying to recruit you. He thinks if he can get you to show up at one of their headquarters, you'll cave in and finally agree to join."

"Not happening." Van munched on a slice of bacon, then slathered sand plum jelly—his favorite—on the toast.

"I'll be sure to quote you verbatim when I respond to the Ranger captain and the politician."

Van disliked the Rangers that had swooped down on the Kiowa and Comanche village where he'd grown up. His clan had been in constant conflict with the army and Rangers…until the military had received orders to slaughter Indian horse herds and to march surviving tribe members to the hated reservations in Indian Territory. His mother's people had urged him to take advantage of the fact that his father had been a white trader and to avoid confinement by *becoming* white.

He had fled to begin indoctrination into white society. Now he had his freedom and he received exceptionally high fees for his skills as a hunter, tracker and shooter. But he refused to take any assignment for the Rangers or the military. They couldn't pay him enough to forget the heartache his people suffered at their hands.

"Van?" Bart prompted.

Van shook off the unpleasant memories then sipped his coffee. "Sorry. My mind wandered. What were you saying?"

"Some large ranchers in Colorado are feuding with sheepherders who have slaughtered their livestock…or so they claim. Five big ranchers formed a stock growers association and want to hire you to investigate. You'll receive the usual going rate of two thousand dollars for every conviction, plus reward money and traveling expenses."

Van munched on his tasty meal while Bart listed other assignments that would take him hither and yon, investigating a recent robbery in the no-man's-land between Indian Territory, Texas and Kansas and a horse theft in the Texas Panhandle.

He didn't show much interest in any of the assignments until Bart said, "But I agree that you won't have time for too many new jobs since this telegram states that your fiancée will be arriving tomorrow on the five o'clock train from Fort Worth."

"MY WHAT?" Van croaked—then choked on his toast.

Bart leaped to his feet to whack Van between the shoulder blades until he caught his breath. "That's what *I* said," he remarked while Van wheezed and coughed. "You never mentioned a fiancée."

"That's because I don't have one," Van chirped, then guzzled his coffee to dislodge the toast from his throat.

"Apparently you have one now. Congratulations, by the way. When is the wedding?" Bart asked, and chuckled.

Van leveled a glare at his grinning friend. "I didn't hire

you for your sense of humor," he muttered as he snatched the telegram from Bart's hand. Sure enough, the message stated that his fiancée would arrive tomorrow at five.

Bart plunked down in his chair, pushed his drooping spectacles up the bridge of his crooked nose and stared speculatively at Van. "I've always wondered what your fiancée might look like. Is she Indian or white?"

"I'm not the marrying kind. Not now. Not ever. I don't know who this charlatan is but I damn well intend to find out."

Bart's pale green eyes glinted with amusement as he gestured toward the plate of food. "You should keep eating. Keep up your strength for when the fiancée arrives."

Van gave Bart "The Stare" he was famous for. He'd backed down many a troublemaker with that chilly glare. His friend merely snickered.

"But what if she's really attractive and charming and you decide to keep her?"

"I can't imagine why anyone would pull such a stunt. This has to be a trick." Van shoved aside his plate and poured himself a tall drink of whiskey.

Bart jerked upright in his chair. "You're right! Maybe this has something to do with that threat—" He sorted through the stack of letters on the table and then waved it in Van's face. "I didn't give this warning from the Harper Gang much thought. Outlaws always vow revenge after you wrap up an assignment that didn't end in their favor. But according to this letter the Harpers are out to get you for killing their little brother, Robbie."

Van slouched back in his chair to read the missive. It said:

Eye for an Eye. We will get you for this.

Three months earlier, Van had been on assignment to track bank robbers who'd split up. He'd hunted them individually. He'd been forced to shoot and kill the twenty-four-year-old Robbie Harper, who'd had too much to drink and drew on Van in a saloon in a dusty, no-name little town west of San Antonio.

The drunken fool had tried to make a bigger name for himself. Instead, he'd made the obituaries.

Van had apprehended Georgie Harper, age thirty, Charley, age twenty-eight, and Willy, age twenty-six. He had collected the hefty rewards, but he hadn't had time to recover the stolen money because a high-profile murder assignment awaited him. He'd told the bankers to let the Texas Rangers hunt for the missing money since they worked cheaper.

Unfortunately, the three Harper brothers had escaped from jail and now they were out for Van's blood.

"You must admit this ploy of an arriving fiancée would entice most men to show up at the railroad depot at five o'clock, if only to see what a fiancée of yours might look like," Bart was saying when Van got around to listening. "You're right. This has *bushwhacking* written all over it."

"My thoughts exactly." Van chugged his whiskey. "That's why you will meet the train and *I'll* reconnoiter the area to see if Robbie's vengeful kin are lying in wait."

"Me?" Bart crowed.

"You're the business manager, a practicing lawyer and my spokesman," Van teased as he rose to stare out the window that overlooked Main Street. "In the meantime, I'm planning to catch up on my missed sleep."

"That's it?" Bart huffed. "That's all the forethought you're giving this potential threat? But what if it *isn't* the Harpers who are using a distraction to lure you out and gun you down? What if you really have a fiancée that you conveniently forgot about?"

"I think I'd remember if I had a fiancée." He strode over

to grab the tray and handed it to Bart. "That's not the sort of thing a man like me would forget."

Bart, with tray in hand, headed for the door. "Seems to me that plenty of men conveniently forget about fiancées and wives, in favor of visiting the harlots in Cardinal Row."

Cardinal Row was the red light district that Van and Bart visited occasionally, along with dozens of other local patrons. If Van had approved of blackmail schemes, he could make a killing off unfaithful husbands who frequented the local brothels. Maybe he'd take up that line of work when his lightning-quick accuracy with pistols and rifles failed him in old age. If he managed to dodge the bullets with his name on them for the next thirty years.

Sighing tiredly, Van returned to the adjoining room and stretched out in bed. He'd need quick reflexes and sharp wits at five o'clock the next day if he planned to deal effectively with the bloodthirsty Harper Gang.

"A *fiancée?*" Van chuckled at the preposterous thought. What the hell would he do with a fiancée? Leave her at his hotel headquarters for Bart to tend to while Van took one long-distance assignment after another? Anyway, what sort of female would want to attach herself to a mixed-breed with his reputation as a gun for hire? Women didn't line up to fill a position as his future wife. Never had. Never would.

"No woman with a lick of sense would consider marrying me. I'm the furthest thing from husband material that any man could get," he mumbled drowsily, then promptly fell asleep.

Natalie Blair, alias Widow Anna Jones, craned her neck to survey the landscape outside the train window. Anticipation bubbled inside her as she appraised Wolf

Ridge. The Western community of three thousand residents—more or less—sat on a rise of ground, surrounded by a tree-choked creek known as Wolf Hollow. Even the possibility of this area jumping alive with wolves—and who knew what other vicious predators of the two- and four-legged variety—didn't diminish her excitement.

She had been riding the rails for four long, tedious days. She was about to reach the end of the line—literally—because the railroad was under construction across West Texas. This community was the jumping-off point to launch her into her new life.

The train whistle jostled her back to the present and Natalie stood up to work the kinks from her back. She took her place in line behind an elderly gent who braced his arms against the back of the seats to steady himself as he moved slowly down the aisle.

Beneath the lacy black veil of her widow's digs she had donned to conceal her identity and provide protection, she smiled in triumph. She had succeeded! She had calculated, planned and outsmarted the conniving bastards trying to control her life. She would like to see their expressions of confusion and surprise when they realized she had vanished into thin air like a fleeting phantom.

Serves them right, she mused as she stepped onto the landing. She tapped the gold band on her left ring finger and told herself that her mother was up there somewhere, smiling down on her. *This is for both of us, Mama,* she thought as the conductor offered a hand to assist her down the steps.

With Phase One of her escape plan completed, Natalie surveyed the crowd waiting for arriving passengers. There were a dozen women waiting to welcome home their menfolk. There were several older men waiting to greet women passengers.

But there was no knight in shining armor waiting to help Natalie complete the next phase of her plan.

Disappointment swamped her as she searched for the man she'd hoped would meet her. She had been so certain her provocative telegram would produce the wanted results.

Although she wasn't sure what Donovan Crow looked like, because she didn't have an accurate physical description, she knew him by reputation. She had read every article she could find in the newspapers. The legendary thirty-two-year-old gun for hire—known from Louisiana to Arizona and points north—had been the subject of her research for the past three months.

Refusing to be discouraged because her heroic knight wasn't waiting for her, Natalie stepped to the ground. She searched the gathering crowd once again, while the porter retrieved the luggage.

She fixed her gaze on a rough-looking character with a scraggly beard. Unkempt hair poked from beneath his oversize sombrero. Surely *he* wasn't her gallant knight.

Next she focused her attention on a thin, wiry, scholarly looking young gent who kept pushing his wire-rimmed glasses up the bridge of his nose—a nose that looked as if it had been broken sometime in the past. He was well dressed and reasonably attractive. He glanced this way and that, as if he were expecting trouble. Then he whirled around and strode past the depot to disappear from sight.

"May I help you with your luggage, ma'am?"

Natalie pivoted back to the porter, who looked to be in his mid-fifties. "I would be most grateful if you could direct me to the best accommodations Wolf Ridge has to offer," she said in an exaggerated Southern drawl. "It has been a long, tiring ride and I am most anxious to rest."

The frizzy-haired porter with a pot belly and thick

shoulders smiled kindly at her. "That'd be the Simon House. The restaurant adjoining the hotel serves fine food, too."

Natalie clutched the hem of her black dress to keep from dragging it in the dirt street and tramped off behind the porter, who lugged her oversize suitcase and tattered carpetbag. She paid close attention to the row of stores facing each other on Main Street. This town—the last civilized outpost on the Western frontier, and the end of the tracks—boasted a livery stable, blacksmith shop, billiard parlor, three hotels, several cafés and two general stores.

She noticed a gunsmith shop—which she intended to visit first thing in the morning—a newspaper office, boutique, bank and three saloons named Road to Ruin, End of the Tracks and Last Chance. She frowned disapprovingly at the three bordellos that set apart from the businesses and residences. A covered walkway connected the upper story of the billiard parlor to the more elaborate-looking brothel.

The town couldn't match New Orleans in architecture, accommodations or extensive selections of supplies or luxuries, but it looked like heaven to Natalie. This was the Promised Land. This is where her freedom and independence began—if only she could locate the legendary gun for hire that could help her achieve her long-held dreams.

She reminded herself that Donovan Crow might be on assignment, in which case he wouldn't have received her telegram. Which would explain why he wasn't waiting at the depot to meet the woman who claimed to be his fiancée.

It could very well be that she might have to wait a week or two to meet him. If that proved to be the case, she would spend her time equipping herself for the next leg of her journey—a journey that would be a hardship for the two conniving bastards who would likely try to overtake her.

When they arrived at Simon House, Natalie paid the good-natured porter and then turned to the hotel clerk who looked to be a few years older than she was. He was blessed with thick blond hair, round face and barrel-sized chest. Without delay, he spun the ledger for her to sign, then handed over a key to her room.

"Will you be staying long…?" He glanced at the name. "Missus Jones?"

"That depends," she drawled. "I'll pay for two days and check on my travel arrangements. In the meantime, a bath would be most appreciated."

The clerk snapped his fingers and two teenage boys lounging against the door to the restaurant came to attention. "Take Missus Jones's belongings to her room and fill the tub," he ordered.

While the boys scurried off, she glanced back at the clerk through her concealing veil. "Would you happen to know if Donovan Crow is in town?"

The clerk's hazel eyes widened in surprise. "Why, yes, he is. Just returned two days ago, in fact."

Natalie told herself it was possible the gun for hire hadn't taken time to collect his mail. Perhaps that's why he hadn't shown up at the depot. Either that, or he suffered from a shameful lack of curiosity.

No matter, she reassured herself as she ascended the steps behind the young boys. Donovan Crow would know who she was and what she wanted very soon. She had come to strike a bargain with him and he could name his price.

Van rose from a crouch atop the roof of the train depot. Then he holstered his pearl-handled peacemaker—or widow maker, depending on the outcome of potentially deadly situations. He'd scanned the area around the depot but the vicious Harper Gang was nowhere to be seen. And neither was his supposed fiancée. The only woman near his age had hurried off the platform to greet a waiting sodbuster who hugged the stuffing out of her.

If the telegram announcing his fiancée was someone's idea of a joke, Van was not amused.

Apparently, Bart had come to the same conclusion about the hoax telegram for he halted behind the depot to peer up at him.

"No fiancée." Van walked over to the eave, then shimmied down the gutter pipe.

"Not that I could see," Bart said as he monitored Van's descent. "The only unattached female was a widow in mourning." He frowned pensively. "That odd telegram still bothers me. If I were you I'd watch my back—just in case."

"Exactly what I plan to do. Come on, Bart. I'll buy you supper," he invited.

"Let me stop by my office and close up for the day, then my time is yours. Later, we can decide which assignment appeals to you and I'll send off a correspondence soon."

"I'm not going anywhere for at least a week," Van reminded Bart sternly. "I damn well intend to sleep in my bed instead of a flea-bitten way station or on the hard ground."

On the wings of the declaration, they strode off. Van didn't give another thought to the disturbing telegram from his so-called fiancée.

The next morning, after a surprisingly tasty meal at the hotel restaurant, Natalie returned upstairs to discard her disguise. She hoped to make Mr. Crow's acquaintance and negotiate a price for the assignment she had in mind for him.

Anxiously Natalie appraised her reflection in the smoky cheval glass that stood beside the plain dressing screen and bathtub. The modest gown she selected didn't hint at the wealth her parents had amassed in New Orleans. That was nobody's business and she didn't approve of flaunting wealth the way her stepfather and former fiancé were prone to do.

However, she hoped to look partially rested and presentable when she met Mr. Crow.

She wondered if Crow was holed up at one of the brothels, tripping the light fantastic after completing his most recent assignment. She didn't want to have to march into a bordello. Yet, as of three months ago, Natalie had cast off the burdensome yoke of proper behavior and protocol demanded by the upper class. Now she was alone in the world and vowed to do whatever necessary to make a new, unrestricted life for herself that didn't involve those two devious bastards she'd left behind.

"First things first," she told her reflection as she fluffed the wrinkles from her bright yellow gown. "Purchase a weapon to defend yourself from trouble. Then locate Mr. Crow and strike your bargain."

As she descended the staircase, she noticed she was receiving far more attention than she had while dressed in widow's digs. Since she had moved her mother's wedding band to her right hand, the three men exiting the restaurant made note of her ringless left hand. They gave her a thorough once-over. Their blatant interest was an annoying reminder of the hassle she encountered in New Orleans where adventurers and gold diggers, familiar with the Robedeaux Blair family name, congregated around her like pesky flies.

Although the men in the hotel didn't know who she was, nothing could change her cynical opinion of the male species. To date, she hadn't met a man who proved to be reliable, trustworthy or honest—certainly not all three at once!

Especially not those two sneaky bastards who sought to destroy her life—and would have if she hadn't spirited away from New Orleans when she did.

Natalie walked straight up to the clerk and said, "Could you tell me where I might find Donovan Crow?"

Shocked, the clerk leaned close to say confidentially, "Ma'am, I wouldn't want to be seen with him if I were you."

"Why ever not?"

"Most dignified ladies avoid him whenever possible. He has an infamous reputation, you know. He's also half Kiowa."

"Oh? Which half?" she asked straight-faced then pivoted toward the door. She wanted to ask the clerk for a physical description of Donovan Crow, but that would invite too many questions since she planned to marry him immediately.

"Ma'am? Are you staying at the hotel?" the clerk asked as he perused the ledger.

"I'm Anna Jones," she informed him.

His blond brows shot up his forehead and he glanced owlishly at her.

"I used the widow's digs as a protective disguise during my trip. It worked amazingly well."

The three men who overheard her conversation with the clerk fell into step behind her. Natalie rolled her eyes in annoyance when the men followed at her heels, showering her with effusive compliments.

Change of plans, she thought to herself. She would purchase a pistol to scare off the men who wouldn't take the hint of being ignored and leave her alone. *Then* she would wander around town, hoping she would know Donovan Crow the moment she laid eyes on him.

The night after Van's supposed fiancée failed to show up at the depot, he lounged against the bar in the Road To Ruin Saloon. He threw back a drink and let the strong whiskey burn its way down his throat. He was feeling considerably better after sleeping most of the day away— again.

"There's a saddle tramp in the corner who's been eyeing you for ten minutes," Bart murmured quietly.

"I noticed him. Spoiling for a fight is my guess."

"He's consumed enough liquor to assure himself he can outdraw you and make a name for himself."

"That's exactly how I ended up with Robbie Harper's three brothers gunning for me," Van grumbled. "The little fool couldn't clear leather nearly as fast as he thought."

"Whiskey makes a man reckless with his tongue and far braver than he actually is," Bart agreed.

When Van heard the sound of a chair being scooted across the planked floor to clank against the wall, he pivoted to face the glassy-eyed, peach-fuzz-faced kid toting double holsters and shiny pistols.

He flashed the would-be gunfighter his trademark glare. "The last drunken fool who decided to draw down on me is wearing a marble hat."

The kid had drunk enough bottled courage to make him defiant. He jutted out his pointy chin. His hands hovered over his pistols. "You're the one who'll be wearing a marble hat, Crow. You worthless half-breed," he slurred.

"No one is going to become a permanent resident in the cemetery," came an unexpected female voice from the doorway.

Startled, Van—and every man in the saloon—glanced at the stunning female who stood five foot six and looked to be about ten years younger than he was. Her trim-fitting yellow gown displayed her full creamy breasts to their best advantage. Her eyes were black as midnight and sparkled with so much inner spirit that Van became lost in their depths—and he wasn't alone. The woman had captivated the male crowd with her arresting beauty and her daring.

He dragged his gaze from the enticing display of cleavage to survey her curly auburn hair. The highlighted red-gold strands seemed to dance like flames in the lantern light. To his amazement, the alluring woman headed straight to him. Then, to the shock of every man—including Van—she pivoted to position herself in front of him like a human shield.

"Mr. Crow and I are going to be married day after tomorrow and I will thank you for not spoiling my wedding, sir," she said in a heavy Southern drawl to the drunken kid. "You, of course, are invited to the festivities, along with everyone else. I've decided to hold the ceremony in Lobo Park so we can have a town-wide reception."

"Married?" The crowd hooted in unison. They gaped at Van, then their bewildered stares bounced back to the enchanting female, dressed in bright yellow—who had burst into the saloon like sunlight breaking through storm clouds.

Van clamped his sagging jaw shut as he stared down at the crown of her shiny auburn head. Despite his vast and varied experience, he couldn't recall a single instance in his life when he had been struck speechless.

"So...this is your mysterious fiancée," Bart murmured, his green eyes dancing with amusement. "Excellent choice, my friend. You have my stamp of approval."

Chapter Two

Now that Natalie had thwarted the gunfight and had gained everyone's undivided attention, she pasted on a smile and pivoted to study Donovan Crow. At six foot two, he towered over the crowd. He was two hundred pounds of brawn and muscle and he had a rugged, earthy appeal Natalie found intriguing.

Crow was dressed in dark breeches, a dark shirt and scuffed black boots. The thick, dark stubble on his face indicated he hadn't been near a razor for at least a week. His eyes were an intriguing shade of blue that appeared silver in the flickering light. His shaggy raven hair could use a clipping, she noted. He was nothing like the cocky men who strutted around her social circle in New Orleans. Thank God!

She decided Donovan Crow would suit her purpose perfectly. His formidable reputation warned sensible men to take a wide berth around him—with the exception of the young cowboy too drunk to realize how foolish he was. According to the circulating legend, Crow was as good with his fists as he was with pistols and daggers. You did not tangle with the man hailed as one of the fastest—if not *the* fastest—gunfighters west of the Mississippi.

Not unless you had a death wish.

Or you desperately needed Crow's expertise to protect you from the two conniving bastards who would breathe down your neck and do bodily harm if you didn't watch out.

While she still had a captive audience in the saloon—and more specifically the attention of the man she'd spent the day trying to track down—she pushed up on tiptoe and looped her arm around his broad shoulders. Then she kissed him right smack-dab on his chiseled lips. He stood like stone and stared her down with those eyes that were the color of blue ice.

She dropped down on her heels and stepped back to flash him a blinding smile. "I've missed you like crazy, my love," she said with her exaggerated Southern drawl.

Turning her back on his frosty stare—and she could still feel it boring into her spine—she passed her most dazzling smile around the saloon. "Drinks are on me, gentlemen."

Natalie placed money on the scarred bar, then glanced at Crow, who was still watching her like a hawk. His stare was unnerving, she did admit, but she marshaled her courage and slipped her hand into his.

"I expected you to meet me at the train depot, darling."

"I'll just bet you did, *sweetheart.*"

The endearment he growled in her ear sounded more like a curse. She was pretty sure that's the way he meant it. But she was a woman on a mission and she wasn't about to let something as insignificant as a curse deter her.

Clutching his hand, she tugged him toward the door. The patrons parted like the Red Sea when she zigzagged around the tables. "Sorry for the interruption, gentlemen," she called out to the slack jawed customers. "But I haven't seen my fiancé for such a long time and we have arrangements to make."

She was surprised the legendary gunfighter allowed her to tow him outside. Thankfully, he waited until they were standing on the boardwalk before he wheeled her around to face his dark scowl.

"Who the hell are you and what was that melodramatic little scene about?"

"You're welcome for me saving your life," she countered nonchalantly, hooking her arm around his elbow and guiding him across the street.

He expelled a snort. "You didn't save my life, sunshine."

To her surprise, he didn't yank her to a halt in the middle of the street and commence raking her over live coals.

"You saved that drunken *kid* who picked a fight with me," he muttered.

She nodded and smiled approvingly, despite his unsettling glare. "Confidence. I like that in a man."

"Now what's this nonsense about a wedding that *isn't* going to take place day after tomorrow?" He eyed her warily. "And why did you send the telegram from Fort Worth, claiming you're my fiancée? Which you are not." He gave her that hard, bone-chilling stare again. "Whatever game you're playing, you need to know that you picked the wrong groom."

Natalie disagreed. When it came to selecting the perfect husband, Donovan Crow met her specific requirements. Her brilliant scheme would teach those sneaky bastards not to plan her marriage or her life. By damned, she was in charge of her own destiny. She would never, *ever,* be a man's pawn again. This was her Independence Day.

Nothing, not even a surly, reluctant groom, was going to stop her now.

"Do you need my help, Van?" came a cultured voice from behind them.

Natalie glanced over her shoulder to see the studious-looking gentleman standing on the boardwalk outside Road To Ruin Saloon.

"I can say no to her by myself, Bart," Crow said without taking his icy glare off her.

"We'll be in my room, having a discussion." He glanced at Bart. "Bring me the bottle I just opened at the saloon."

For a split second, unease skittered down her spine. The prospect of being shut in his room brought all sorts of unpleasant scenarios to mind. A moment of doubt tried to accost her. She didn't know Crow except by reputation. He was a hard-edged, hard-nosed gunfighter who never failed an assignment. He was relentless until he brought his missions to satisfying conclusions.

She wondered if he dealt the same way with women—especially one who made the public announcement they were getting married.

She quickly reminded herself that Crow had permitted her to tow him by the hand. She took it as a good sign since he hadn't tossed her in the dirt and stamped all over her. She inhaled a bolstering breath and shored up her floundering resolve. Short of physical abuse—and she had a two-shot derringer tucked in her pocket so she would be prepared for that—she told herself she could hold her own with the brawny gunfighter.

Natalie had spent three months diligently preparing for this moment. She wasn't backing down. She knew exactly what she wanted and needed and she planned to get it. She needed the toughest, most dangerous gun for hire she could locate and Donovan Crow was it.

After all, she reminded herself, Donovan Crow could be *bought*. That's another reason she had selected him.

The hotel clerk tossed Van a speculative glance while he led the bewitching female in yellow across the lobby and up the steps. Thanks to her startling announcement in the saloon, the town was abuzz with gossip and speculation. But very soon, Van would squelch the preposterous notion of an upcoming marriage and he'd get to bottom of Miss Sunshine's theatrical performance. Yet, he had to hand it to this daring chit. She had walked boldly into a saloon full of men, thrust herself into the middle of a potential showdown, then dropped the bomb that left him momentarily thunderstruck.

When the woman reached the head of the steps and veered right, he tugged her to the left and led the way to his suite.

She blinked in surprise as he ushered her inside. "You have a two-room suite. How did you rate that, Crow?"

"It's where I live when I'm not on assignment." He made a stabbing gesture toward the settee in the sitting room. "*Sit,* sunshine."

She didn't obey immediately, just tilted her chin stubbornly and met his hard stare. Now why wasn't he surprised?

"Fine. Stand up if you want, but I'm sitting down." He sprawled carelessly on the sofa. "I've just returned from a long, exhausting foray. I'm tired and I'm cranky. You can either tell me what this wedding nonsense is about or leave me the hell alone. I really don't care which. But you should know there will be no wedding, no matter what you say."

Her cautious gaze darted speculatively to the empty space beside him and then to the door. She expected him to pounce on her and she was calculating how fast she could reach the door to escape his evil clutches.

Van swallowed a grin—and realized he didn't have reason to smile often. She was a refreshing change in his routine. And yes, he did admit that veering into the bedroom to catch up on the lack of intimate activity he'd suffered lately held tremendous appeal. But caution overrode temptation. He was curious to know what sort of plot the auburn-haired beauty was trying to embroil him in.

His thoughts scattered like a flock of geese when someone—Bart, judging by the precise knock—rapped on the door. Sunshine nearly leaped out of her fetching yellow gown but she composed herself quickly and spun toward the door.

"It's me," Bart called out, then burst in without awaiting invitation. He set the whiskey bottle on the table near the window, along with three glasses.

"This is Bartholomew Collier, my business manager and local lawyer," Van introduced. "Bart, this is…" He waited for her to fill in the blank.

"Anna Jones," she supplied smoothly as she extended her hand to Bart.

She graced Bart with a dazzling smile that all but melted him into a gooey puddle. When he collected himself, he doubled over her hand, then pressed a light kiss to her wrist.

Although Bart had taught Van white society's social nuances, he bowed to no one—man or woman.

In Indian culture, to do so was a sign of weakness.

"It's a pleasure to meet you, Miss Jones," Bart murmured against her wrist.

Anna Jones? Ha! Van inwardly scoffed. Before the evening ended, he vowed to discover the woman's real name and find out what she really wanted from him. Bart could play all the senseless social games he wanted but Van had survived well enough for thirty-two years without bothering with the white man's social posturing and protocol.

"Thanks for the whiskey and glasses," Van said dismissively. "We'll talk later, Bart."

Bart glanced at the bottle and glasses Van scooped up, then stared pensively at Anna Jones—or whoever she really was. Van inclined his head toward the door, directing Bart to make himself scarce—and do it fast.

When Bart exited reluctantly, Van set a glass of whiskey in front of Miss Jones. "Drink up, sunshine."

She sat down beside him on the settee but she didn't reach for her drink. He took her hand and wrapped it around the glass. Her dark eyes popped when he touched her and he found himself swallowing another grin. Sunshine wasn't as bold and daring as she'd let on in public. He guessed she was a tad bit afraid of him. Good. He preferred to maintain an edge with clients and antagonists.

He still wasn't sure which one Little Miss Sunshine was.

Van sipped his drink and urged her to do the same. When she didn't, he said, "In negotiations, which I figure this must be, Indians pass a peace pipe. White man's policy is to discuss the assignment over a glass of wine or whiskey." He didn't mention that peace pipes usually contained ingredients that had the same effects of liquor. "This is the only white protocol I usually follow. I leave the hand-kissing to gentlemen, which I am not and never plan to be."

He half turned on the couch to face her directly. "Now what is it that you really want from me, sunshine?"

"The name is Anna Jones." She took a cautious sip and gasped to draw breath.

"No, it isn't." Van whacked her between the shoulder

blades to prevent her from choking. When she could breathe again, he pushed the glass back to her lips, insisting she take another sip. She did, reluctantly. "My friend calls me Van," he informed her, then chugged his drink.

"Friend?" she questioned then took another dainty sip.

"I just have the one," he informed her then smiled wryly. "Two, now that the whole town thinks you're my fiancée. Drink up or I'll fetch the peace pipe and we'll do it Indian-style."

She clamped her lush lips shut defiantly when he tried to force her to take another drink. "You are not going to get me inebriated and take advantage of me, Mr. Crow."

"Van," he corrected. "Then start talking. Unless you want to end up on your back in the bedroom and to hell with whatever scheme you've hatched by declaring we'll soon be wed."

That threat should get her talking, he predicted. Bold as she was, he sensed she didn't trust him. Smart woman. Van wasn't sure he trusted himself with the mysterious, alluring woman who had him entertaining all sorts of illicit fantasies.

When her gaze darted to the door again, he shook his head warningly. "You'll never make it, sunshine. Plus, screaming won't do you any good because no one would dare to venture in here. Except maybe Bart and you'd feel *just awful* if I had to kill my only friend because of you."

She fiddled with the folds of her skirt and he noticed the outline of a derringer she had tucked in the pocket sewn into the seam of her gown. She stared at him in annoyance.

"All right. Fine," she muttered. Then she sent him a mocking toast, grimaced and took another drink. "This stuff tastes awful. Maybe I'd prefer the peace pipe and powwow."

"Another time perhaps." He inclined his head toward her drink. "Trust me, sunshine, whiskey gets better with each glass. Take another sip."

"One thing you should know, Crow," she said, staring at him from beneath impossibly long, curly lashes.

"What's that?"

"I never trust men."

"Neither do I. Most of them try to cheat you or kill you. Sometimes they try to do one right after the other."

"Which is why I'm here to bargain with you, Mr. Crow."

"As Bart is fond of saying, bargain with the devil and you end up in hell. Some folks claim that's where you are when you deal with men like me. So tell me why you're here. What sort of bargain did you have in mind, sunshine?"

He watched her inhale a deep breath. His gaze reflexively dropped to the enticing display of cleavage he'd tried—and failed miserably—not to notice several times already.

"I have decided to take complete control of my life," she burst out hurriedly, then took another sip.

"I'll drink to that." He poured himself—and her— another glass. "Who's trying to stop you from taking control?"

"My stepfather and the unfaithful fiancé he selected for me. They concocted a tidy business arrangement that is financially beneficial. *To them.* They will see to it that I don't live too long. A year at the most, since I'm a defiant inconvenience to both of them."

"So you're hiring me to dispose of the two men before they do unto you?" He shook his head. "Sorry, sunshine, I'm not in the extermination business...unless I'm left with no choice."

"I didn't come here to hire an assassin." She sipped the whiskey more eagerly than before. "I refuse to let them off the hook that easily."

He swallowed another chuckle—and wondered why it came so easily around her. Must be the whiskey mellowing him.

"Ah, a woman who intends to get even," he said, and grinned—again. Amazing! "I like that about you. Not enough to marry you, of course…. Go on."

"My real name is Natalie," she said in a slurred voice.

The liquor was beginning to work like a truth serum. Which, of course, was the whole point of this deceptive exercise.

"You'll always be *sunshine* to me," he replied.

His betraying gaze roamed over the yellow gown that accentuated all her feminine assets. And she had plenty of them, he noted. His well-honed powers of observation were working against him, causing an unwanted distraction. He was painfully aware of his physical attraction to the mysterious Natalie, alias Anna Jones. But he supposed most men—him included—would have to be dead a week not to be affected by her fascinating appeal.

She set her empty glass on the coffee table, then twisted sideways to stare at him. Van refilled her glass, then replaced it in her hand. He found himself taking more time than necessary to wrap her fingers around the glass.

He liked touching her and he took advantage of the excuse. Her skin was as soft as satin. That, in addition to her arresting figure, her bewitching facial features and her devastating smile kept sidetracking him. She also was smart and daring. He admired both qualities, which were highly praised in Indian culture.

Donovan Crow was nothing if not Kiowa at heart.

She cocked her head and studied him for a long

moment. "Are you trying to seduce me, Crow? If so, I must warn you that I've been propositioned by the most experienced rakes and adventurers that New Orleans has to offer."

"Good for you." He was excessively pleased she had now let her first name and her hometown slip. "I'm only trying to get you to tell me the details of this potential assignment. I assume it isn't really marriage to a man like me."

She shook her head and several long, curly strands that were piled atop her head tumbled down and bounced around her temple like springs. He itched to pull the pins from her hair and comb his fingers through those dark, flaming strands. He wanted to watch them tumble across the pillow on his bed while they were naked in each other's arms…

Van snapped to attention, shocked at how quickly his wayward thoughts left him hard and aching. He usually had more self-control. But Miss Sunshine tempted the most self-disciplined of men—and he liked to think he was one.

"You are very much mistaken if you think I wasn't serious when I announced our wedding plans."

He noticed her heavy drawl changed and the slur in her voice became more pronounced. Despite the glassy glaze in her obsidian eyes, she still sounded intent and determined.

"I will pay you handsomely to sign your name on a marriage license. You will receive a substantial fee for the use of your name. I will have the ultimate revenge on the two bastards trying to manipulate my life. No man will ever do that again. My new life of independence and adventure begins after the ceremony…" *Hiccup.* "'Scuse me."

Natalie frowned at the sluggish sound of her own voice.

She stared into the contents of her glass and decided Crow was right. The whiskey didn't taste as offensive as it had earlier. Plus, it took the edge off her nerves. She supposed that was important because they *needed* to have this heart-to-heart talk so they could reach an agreement. As he'd said, this was part of the business negotiation ritual.

Her fuzzy gaze settled on his raven head and she marveled at the thick strands of his hair. Truth be told, she noticed everything about the dynamic man who would never fit into the well-to-do social circle in New Orleans. And that made him ideal for her—except there were two of him now. How odd. She shook her head in attempt to clear her blurred vision.

Donovan Crow didn't spew practiced lines of flattery or flaunt polished manners. He didn't project an air of self-importance that she disliked so much. He was what he was—a seasoned warrior tested and hardened by danger. His training in Indian culture provided him with a keen understanding of how to survive in the wilderness.

"Now I get it," he said, jostling her from her meandering thoughts. "You want me to marry you before your other fiancé shows up. That way you can take control of your life so he and your stepfather can't interfere."

"Precisely. I began this process three months ago when my mother died." Her voice wavered but she gathered her composure and continued. "Mama had been ill for years. She couldn't counter my stepfather's scheme to marry me off and swindle me out of my inheritance. She encouraged me to become free and independent."

He stilled, watching her much too closely with those piercing silver-blue eyes. "How much inheritance are we discussing, sunshine?"

She shrugged lackadaisically. There were some things Donovan Crow didn't need to know. She refused to break her hard-and-fast rule that no man could be trusted explicitly. "Enough to provide him with a modest monthly stipend for the next several years."

That wasn't true. Her stepfather coveted the *generous* stipend that would outlast his lifetime. Natalie's maternal ancestors, the Robedeauxs, were royalty in France who had escaped the revolution and moved their shipping business to New Orleans to provide merchants with unique and valuable products from all over the world. Her father's family held English titles and established several banks in Louisiana and in towns up and down the Mississippi River.

Which is why she traveled under an alias and refused to divulge her last name since it was so well known.

Crow's intense, probing stare bore into her but she waved him off. "The point is those two bastards—" She covered her mouth when the foul names she'd given Avery Marsh, her stepfather (Bastard Number One), and Thurston Kimball III, the philandering fiancé (Bastard Number Two), popped from her lips.

Rather than frowning in disapproval, as she expected, he threw back his head and laughed heartily. The deep, resonant sound utterly fascinated her and left a lasting impression, despite her inebriated state. So did the accompanying smile that lit every bronzed feature of his face. Suddenly Crow didn't seem as formidable as he had while he was bearing down on her earlier that evening.

She would have to remember to picture him laughing and grinning the next time he gave her that chilling look that turned his silver-blue eyes to ice and his face to chiseled granite.

"Those two bastards what?" he prompted, then sipped his whiskey. He raised the bottle to her. "More?"

"Please." And why not? she asked herself. They were

enjoying a companionable discussion and negotiating a business deal. It was a man's way so it would become her way, too.

"The two men who're trying to run my life and end it prematurely..." *Hiccup.* "Sorry... They won't have control over me and my...modest...inheritance."

"So we get married. You pay me for the use of my name and then what?" His penetrating stare was back in place—poking and prodding to reveal the secrets in her heart and soul. Tipsy or not, Natalie was determined to divulge as few secrets as possible.

"Then I set off on a great adventure I've dreamed about. I go where I want, when I want and you collect your fee and no longer bother with me."

"So I sign my name beside yours on the document. We part company without the slightest inconvenience to either of us? That's it?"

He was frowning into his glass. She couldn't fathom why.

"Easiest money you will ever make," she tempted him.

"Or so you say." He stared at her suspiciously. "I don't have to track anyone down, investigate a murder or confront bank robbers, train robbers, cattle thieves or ruthless murderers?"

She nodded affirmatively—or at least she thought she did. A strange numbness affected her movements and her senses so she took another drink to cure the problem. It didn't help.

He stared at her over the rim of his glass. "What if you find someone you really want to marry someday?"

"I won't," she mumbled. "I handpicked you and you are perfect for me. I have sworn off men and their conniving ways for the rest of my life. You are the exception. What about you? Will you marry one day?"

"No, I'm not considered desirable marriage material because of my mixed heritage. The only available jobs are as bounty hunters, hired guns and lawmen. None of which appeals to most decent women."

He was silent a moment, then he said, "That's why you singled me out, isn't it? A gun for hire becomes a husband for hire. We conclude our business transaction and go our separate ways." He smirked then drained his glass. "And whites call *me* cold-blooded. There's a laugh, sunshine."

"You're a businessman and I'm a businesswoman," she replied—and wondered what had become of her exaggerated Southern accent. "We strike a bargain that benefits both of us and our business is concluded. Then I head for Denver to see the mountains I've heard described in books. Simple as that."

"And I venture to a brothel to celebrate my marriage?" He scoffed. "Sounds unconventional in every way imaginable."

She tossed him a droopy smile. "Unconventional will be my middle name, Crow. I plan to enjoy all the conveniences and privileges men take for granted."

"Like barging into a saloon on a wild whim?" he supplied helpfully.

She shrugged. "I'll strive to do anything and everything a man can do and I will never be at any man's mercy again."

"And that is important?"

"As important to *me* as I suspect avoiding reservation life in Indian Territory is to *you*." She fought to keep her wits about her while she played her ace in the hole. "*Freedom,* Crow. I want what you have. I think you understand what I mean."

Their gazes locked and she *knew* he understood her, just as she understood him. He, like she, valued independence. She didn't know the specific details of his former life or his mixed-heritage background, but she suspected his white ancestry spared him from the confinement his Indian clan endured.

Silence stretched between them for a long moment. Eventually he said, "Your plan has a few problems that I can see."

"Oh? What's that?"

"Your two bastard friends might track you down and have the marriage annulled...unless we consummate it. Even then, all they need is enough money to bribe a corrupt judge to discard the license. Or dispose of *me* so *you'll* become a marriageable widow."

Chapter Three

Natalie slumped back on the sofa and nearly sloshed her drink down the front of her dress. Her cheeks felt flushed and her thoughts swirled in disarray. Whether from too much liquor or the intimate topic of conversation, she couldn't say for certain.

She shot Crow a sideways glance, wondering if this hard-edged man knew how to be tender with a woman who had no intimate experience whatsoever. He didn't look the least bit gentle. Which was another necessary qualification for this assignment. If Avery and Thurston confronted him, they would think twice about battling a man with a dangerous reputation and exceptional skills.

More likely, she mused, they would hire an assassin to shoot him while he was unaware.

Damn, then she would have his death on her conscience!

Natalie winced at the unpleasant prospect. She tried to tell herself that Crow was in the business of risking life and limb for exorbitant fees. It's what he did. Nevertheless, she didn't want him injured—or worse—because of her.

She, however, didn't feel charitable toward Avery and Thurston. They could go straight to hell—and stay there—as far as she was concerned.

When Natalie took another sip of whiskey, the room spun around her. She was exhausted from her long journey and from three months of diligent planning to escape. Plus, she'd had entirely too many drinks. Darkness closed in and she tilted sideways, unable to muster the strength to push herself upright. Her head drooped against Crow's broad shoulder and she savored his solid strength beside her. For the first time in months, she felt safe.

"Sunshine?"

Crow's deep, resonant voice echoed from what seemed to be a long, winding tunnel. Natalie thought she heard him call to her again as her glass slipped from her fingertips and she tried unsuccessfully to grab it.

Then the world went dark and silent.

Van snatched the whiskey glass from Natalie's fingertips before it sloshed on both of them. He looked down at her exquisite face resting against his shoulder. Her long black lashes lay against her cheeks like delicate butterflies. Her lush lips parted slightly, as if awaiting his kiss.

A jolt of awareness sizzled through him and he yielded to the impossible temptation. Van kissed her, just as he'd wanted to do since the moment she planted one on him in front of a captive audience at the bar. It had taken all the self-control he'd spent a lifetime cultivating not to respond to her in front of all those eagle-eyed men at the Road To Ruin Saloon. He hadn't dared to show the slightest weakness for this mere wisp of a woman. That might place her in jeopardy and put him at a disadvantage.

Ruthless men, after all, used every vulnerability at their disposal when they came gunning for him.

Now that no one was watching, he cupped his hand beneath her chin and tipped her head back. He kissed her softly, enjoying the feel of her plump pink lips. He savored the enticing fragrance of her perfume—it had been tormenting his acute senses since she'd ventured close to him in the saloon.

He reached up to pull the pins from her hair and the glorious strands of dark flames tumbled over his shoulder. He looked down at the creamy swells of her breasts then involuntarily skimmed his forefinger over the satiny flesh pressed against the scooped neckline of her gown.

Desire hit him like a runaway locomotive. He became hard and aching in two seconds flat. Yep, he definitely needed a woman if Sunshine could bring him to his knees after one kiss and caress. And never mind that he had trouble maintaining a professional detachment when she insisted that she had handpicked him and he was perfect for her. It was impossible not to be flattered. What man wouldn't be?

"Well, hell," Van muttered. Natalie was out cold and he doubted substituting a harlot for her would satisfy him. He needed to get her out of his reach but he couldn't take her to her room because he didn't know where it was. He did not intend to troop downstairs to ask the busybody clerk. That would invite too many questions and speculations.

"No other choice," Van told himself as he rose from the settee then scooped her up in his arms.

Her head tilted backward, sending a waterfall of curly hair cascading over his arm. She was dead weight and she didn't stir for even a moment while he carried her into the adjoining room.

Van stood indecisively at the foot of the bed. He hesitated at stuffing her beneath the quilt and wrinkle her gown. He really liked that yellow dress but he figured he'd like it even better if she were out of it.

"Why me?" he asked no one in particular as he contemplated how he could undress her without reacting to the sight of her partially clad body. Then he shrugged. "Why not me? I should get something from this upcoming marriage, shouldn't I?"

His staunch insistence there would be no wedding had fizzled out sometime during their negotiations over drinks—far too many drinks, as it turned out.

Focused on his task, Van angled her unresponsive body over his shoulder, then unfastened the buttons on the back of her gown. He pulled down the fluffy sleeves to her elbows. Then he doubled over to lay her on her stomach on his bed. Taking care not to rip any seams, Van pulled the gown past her waist, hips and feet.

She stirred slightly and her eyes opened to half-mast. Van took advantage of her dazed state and asked, "What's your stepfather and fiancé's name, sunshine?"

"Thurston and Avery," she mumbled before she collapsed.

When Van gently turned her onto her back, he found himself staring at the lacy neckline of her chemise that barely concealed her breasts. He groaned aloud. This was pure visual torment. Grumbling in frustration, he tugged off her petticoats, then shook out her dress and hung it in the wardrobe closet.

When he turned back to his bed, his gaze settled on the long expanse of her legs and the high-riding chemise that barely concealed her hips. While he tugged off her kid boots he kept his eyes on the task, for fear his betraying gaze would drift up to sneak a peek at whatever undergarment—if any—lay beneath that skimpy chemise.

Hungry need hammered at him while he played

handmaiden. But Van accomplished his task, then drew the sheet over her curvaceous body. He wanted to crawl into bed with her, if only to sleep off the effects of exhaustion and a tad too much whiskey.

It was *his* bed, after all, and the settee was too short to accommodate him. His only option was bunking on the floor—which he'd done too damn often the past few weeks during his last assignment.

His thoughts flittered off when he heard the distinct knock on the door. Wheeling about, Van made a beeline through the sitting room to whip open the door.

Bart craned his neck around Van's shoulder. "What did you do to her? And what does she want?"

He shut the door after Bart burst inside. "Do come in," he smirked. "Now which question should I answer first?"

"Let's start with what you did to her," Bart said in an accusing tone.

"I put her to bed."

Bart blinked owlishly from behind his wire-rimmed spectacles. *"Yours?"*

Van ambled over to pick up his glass, hoping the shot of whiskey would cool the hot, unappeased desire clamoring below his belt buckle. It didn't.

"Yes, my bed. I don't know which room is hers and I sure as hell didn't plan to cart her unconscious body door to door to check availability or consult the nosy clerk."

"I see your point." Bart retrieved the spare glass from the table and poured himself a drink. He stared speculatively at Van. "So what is it that she really wants from you?"

Van took a sip, thankful Natalie was asleep and he and Bart could speak freely. "She proposed a no-strings-attached marriage that will give her independence and control of her modest inheritance. I am to receive a generous fee for signing my name on the license."

"You are kidding," said Bart. He stared toward the door of the adjoining room. "She's an extremely appealing and intelligent woman. Why isn't she interested in what most women want? Marriage, security and family?"

"Sunshine isn't *most women*," Van clarified.

"Yes, yes, I can see that, but what do you think motivated this rash scheme of hers?"

"Supposedly, her greedy stepfather arranged her wedding for his financial benefit to her unfaithful fiancé...*if* her story is to be believed," Van summarized.

He'd heard of shady dealings such as this before. The thought of Natalie Whoever-She-Was suffering a similar fate angered him. He admired her for being assertive and taking charge of her destiny. She had devised a way to have her freedom. Just as he had faced the unknown to avoid confinement on the reservation.

"She explained her situation and I got her to name names, though I doubt she'll remember what she told me since I ensured she drank enough to loosen her tongue," Van continued. "She let it slip that she's from New Orleans and her first name is Natalie. Or so she said. She might have more than one alias." He stared intently at Bart. "I don't intend to call her by that name until she confides in me, however. See what you can find out about someone named Thurston or Avery. I don't know if those are first or last names. Also, check those newspapers you subscribe to about a recent runaway bride. I want to know exactly who we are dealing with and if she's telling me the truth."

Bart gaped at him, then shifted his astonished gaze to the bedroom door. "You are seriously considering taking this assignment of marriage?"

Yes, although I don't trust her completely. But I under-

stand how precious independence and freedom are, he mused. Instead, he said, "Why not? She claims it's the easiest money I'll ever earn. I have the extra added benefit of not having to track anyone down or risk being shot at."

"Unless this supposedly enraged stepfather and bitter fiancé show up to make her a widow shortly after she becomes your bride," Bart pointed out.

"I considered that possibility."

"They might even bring along gun-toting reinforcements." Bart stared grimly at Van. "You're good at what you do, my friend, but even a handful of sharp-shooting Texans at the Alamo couldn't hold off Santa Anna and his Mexican army."

"By the time the two bastards discover where she is, she will be long gone and so will I."

Bart sipped his drink and frowned. "I suppose. But still..."

Van flicked his wrist dismissively. "I'll worry about the details tomorrow. Right now I'm tired and I need sleep."

"I keep telling you that the devil is in the details," Bart didn't hesitate to remind him. "I can't believe you're actually considering a marriage the day after tomorrow. And what if she's a fraud and you don't find out until it's too late? And where, might I ask, do *you* intend to sleep tonight?"

Van shepherded his friend across the room, took the glass from his hand and opened the door. "She might very well be a fraud, but I can handle her."

"Maybe so, but I—"

Van closed the door before Bart voiced more objections. He doubted Bart would complain if Little Miss Sunshine had asked him to be the groom. Van's wry smile fizzled out when he reminded himself that he'd be sleeping on the floor tonight...or not...

Hell, it wasn't as if Natalie Whoever-She-Was would know where he slept. She'd be conked out for hours. Van set aside his drink and doused the lantern. It was *his* bed and by damn, he was going to sleep in it!

"Oh...my...gawd..." Natalie groaned miserably.

The room swirled around her and her stomach pitched and rolled like a storm-tossed ship in a hurricane. She was afraid to open her eyes for fear it would make her more nauseous.

Holding her throbbing head in one hand, she levered herself onto a wobbly elbow and tried to remember what she'd said and done last night—besides ingest too much whiskey. Nothing came to mind. Not recalling her actions troubled her to no end. She pried open one eye and then grimaced when glaring sunshine blazed through the window of her room...

"No, that isn't right," she mumbled hoarsely. "This isn't my room."

An uneasy sensation battled the queasy feelings that assailed her as she glanced sideways to survey the spacious, elaborately furnished room closely. To her shock and dismay, she realized she was in Crow's bed. A yellow rose lay in the indentation in the other pillow beside hers. Also, she noticed her chemise was twisted around her like a maypole, exposing one breast and a bare hip.

"Sweet merciful heavens!" she wheezed as the shocking possibility registered in her liquor-saturated brain.

Natalie collapsed on the bed, gulping for breath. Donovan Crow must have taken advantage of her while she was too far into her cups to protest. Anger and resentment boiled inside her. How dare he...! she thought, and then gulped hard, wondering if *she* had seduced Crow into agreeing to marry her while her inhibitions were drowning in liquor. Dear God!

Natalie gathered her frazzled composure and frowned consideringly. Not knowing the intimate details of their encounter spared her awkward embarrassment and whatever pain might have accompanied the act. Well, that was one less thing to fret about, she told herself. Now, if she could recover from the nausea and hellish headache she could set the hasty wedding plans in motion and be done with it.

Her gaze drifted to the yellow rose again. She plucked it up, noting Crow had removed the thorns from the stem. So he did have a tad of tender sensitivity buried beneath that hard exterior, did he? She had wondered about that.

Rising—carefully, in case her stomach flip-flopped— she wobbled across the expensive carpet to find her gown hanging in the wardrobe. Another thoughtful gesture she hadn't expected from Crow. Thurston Kimball III wouldn't have bothered with any such thing. The philanderer was too self-absorbed to be considerate of a woman. It was a tremendous relief that she didn't have to marry that bastard.

Natalie poured water from the pitcher into the basin, then splashed the refreshing liquid on her face. It helped somewhat. When she had dressed, she returned to her own room to change her clothes and brush the tangles from her hair that had escaped the pins.

As if she couldn't guess how *that* had happened.

The thought provoked a blush, but she strengthened her resolve. The deed was done. Crow said he would marry her...or did he? Last night was a complete blur, she was sorry to say.

Natalie retrieved several bank notes that she had stitched into the hem of three of her gowns, then double-checked to make certain her family's heirloom jewelry was still stashed in the secret compartment in the ratty looking carpetbag she'd brought with her. Then she headed to the hotel restaurant to purchase breakfast.

Bart Collier lounged against the café doorway and he appraised her carefully as she descended the steps. "Van asked me to inform you that he will return shortly. In the meantime, I'm to escort you to breakfast. We can have a cup of coffee while we're waiting."

"I'd love coffee." She rubbed her throbbing temples. "Did you lace that whiskey with a sedative?"

"No, ma'am, that tarantula juice they serve at Road To Ruin Saloon is dangerous all by itself."

It had certainly been the road to *her* ruin, she mused. But she wasn't complaining. Better bedded by Donovan Crow than Thurston Kimball III, the philandering bastard she despised.

When they were seated, Bart handed her the morning newspaper and pointed out the front-page article announcing tomorrow's upcoming wedding and town-wide reception she'd promised. Natalie inwardly winced. She might have gone a bit too far with that public declaration. But as in all things, what was done was done. She would arrange for the ceremony and refreshments as she had promised.

She discarded the mental list of upcoming errands and focused her concentration on the studious-looking man who handled Crow's business affairs. She sipped her coffee and wondered if she was supposed to negotiate the fee with Bart.

Later, she decided. Right now, she was curious about the connection between two men who seemed as different as night and day.

"Just how did you and Crow enter into this partnership?"

Bart smiled faintly, then called her attention to his broken nose. "Eight years ago, three drunken saddle tramps roughed me up for sport one night while I was locking up my recently opened law office. They called me 'Sissy Breeches' because I'm from Boston. Then their derogatory comments went downhill rapidly from there."

Natalie waited curiously while Bart took a sip of coffee.

"The drunken goons broke my nose and planned to break the rest of me, but Van arrived to hammer them over the back of their heads with the butt of his pistol. Then he landed a few punishing blows with his fists…. He's very good at what he does, you know."

"So the circulating legends claim," she remarked and silently said grace over the strong black coffee she ingested. She almost felt human again. Except for the headache pounding against her sensitive skull like a sledgehammer.

"I offered to pay Van for saving my life, but he asked me to repay him by passing along my knowledge of books and white man's social practices. He wanted to function effectively in his father's world. In return, he taught me valuable self-defense techniques that he'd learned from the Comanche and Kiowa tribes while he trained to become a warrior."

She smiled wryly. "Essentially you became his project and he became yours. You taught Crow to fit into white society and he taught you to deal effectively with thugs who have no use for educated men."

"Yes, in addition, I had the distinct pleasure of pressing charges and testifying in court against the thugs who served time in the penitentiary for assault and cattle rustling. They were released a few months ago. I hope they learned their lesson and I'm the last person they assault."

"Ah, if only men learned from their mistakes," she murmured under her breath.

"Nowadays I collect the telegrams and correspondences and manage Van's financial affairs while he's away. I also arrange quarterly deliveries of food and supplies to the Kiowa and Comanche reservation in Indian Territory."

She frowned pensively. "I've heard disturbing stories of soldiers and civilians intercepting the goods and selling them for profit instead of doling them out to the Indians."

Bart stared at her pointedly. "If *you* knew the goods came directly from Donovan Crow and you answered for them personally, would you steal from him when you knew he made unannounced visits to the reservation?"

"I suppose not, but the world is full of arrogant fools, Bart. I'm surprised someone hasn't tried to swindle him."

"They've tried. Two in fact."

"What happened to them?"

"One's in jail. The other is in hell where he belongs."

Crow's voice rumbled from so close behind her that Natalie spilled her hot coffee. She shook the sting from her hand as she glanced over her shoulder at him. Her eyes widened in surprise while she, and the other patrons, stared at Crow in astonishment.

Clean-shaven, he was even more ruggedly handsome. He'd clipped his raven hair and he was wearing a stylish three-piece black suit. He looked amazing, and not the slightest bit hung over after ingesting the same rotgut she'd consumed last night.

"Please excuse me, Miss Jones," Bart said politely, then climbed to his feet. "I have business to conduct. You two can hammer out the details of your…er…arrangement without me."

It occurred to her that Crow purposely sat down with his back to the wall at their corner table. No doubt, it was his custom to keep watch, in case trouble came calling.

She would have to remember that when she embarked on her journey through the wilderness...

She snapped to attention when she recalled her conversation with Bart. Of course! Survival training! It's what she needed before she set off to find excitement and adventure on the frontier. It had worked for Bart and it could serve her well, too.

Aware that all eyes were upon them in the café, Natalie smiled at Crow in greeting. Then she reached over to place her hand on his. That should convince the onlookers that she had deep feelings for Crow and this was more than a business arrangement. To add reinforcement to the presumption, she leaned sideways to place a playful peck on his bronzed cheek.

"You look exceptionally handsome," she murmured. "Wish I looked that nice. But this headache from hell won't let up."

He reached into the pocket of his jacket to retrieve a small leather pouch. He sprinkled part of the contents in her coffee cup. When she arched a dubious brow, he said, "Old Comanche and Kiowa remedy."

She swallowed three quick gulps of coffee, expecting an offensive taste. Surprisingly, she detected only a pleasant hint of mint.

"I won't order for you since you intend to become an independent woman of the world," he remarked. "But I recommend the house special. Also, it will help settle your stomach."

She liked that Crow acknowledged her desire to make her own decisions and take command of her life. Unlike Avery Marsh and Thurston Kimball III, who insisted on speaking for her and telling her what to do because they were men and she was merely a witless female.

By the time the steaming food arrived, her hellish

headache had fizzled down to a dull throb. Five minutes later, she began to feel like her old self again. Natalie dived into the meal with all the enthusiasm of a starving field hand.

"Now, about your fee," she said between bites of fried potatoes.

"Two thousand."

She nearly choked on her food. "Two?" she tweeted.

"That's my standard fee for a wedding."

She eyed him warily. "You've been married before?"

He munched on his slice of ham, swallowed and kept her in suspense, the ornery rascal. "No, but if I'm ever asked again, it will be two thousand. Take it or leave it, sunshine."

She glanced speculatively around the café. "I wonder if I could get any takers for one thousand."

"A dozen, who lack skills and experience, I expect," he said with a nonchalant shrug of his impossibly broad shoulders. "As you pointed out with great relish last night, I can be bought." He slanted her a meaningful glance but she noticed his silver-blue eyes twinkled with playful devilry. "But I don't come cheap."

She narrowed her gaze at him. "But I see that you engage in highway robbery." She blew out her breath. "Maybe I will take my offer to Bartholomew Collier since he confided that you taught him to handle himself against brutish adversaries."

His expression turned cool and distant. "Your choice, sunshine. This is, after all, part of your convoluted plan to avoid marriage to the fiancé you left behind."

"I think Bart is a fine man," she insisted.

"I never said he wasn't."

She drummed her fingers on the table while she stared Crow down. He was a magnificent-looking man and he was followed by the kind of reputation that gave other men pause. Bart was not. There was one clear choice. Plus, she had told herself from the onset that Crow could name his price and she would pay it. Still, it was the principle of the matter.

Natalie huffed out her breath. "Fine. I'm sticking with our original arrangement…except I insist upon receiving the self-defense lessons you gave Bart. That, of course, will be included in the two thousand dollars you demand."

He smirked. "That will cost you another thousand, but I don't have time for extensive lessons. Bart is gathering information about other job offers as we speak. If I train you, you'd have to learn fast."

"I will be your devoted pupil," she pledged solemnly. "I do not intend to set off on my great adventure and get killed immediately. I can use all the pointers I can get."

"More coffee, ma'am? Mr. Crow?" the waiter asked politely as he hovered beside the table.

Van nodded, then waited for the man to walk off. "Bart can teach you what I won't have time to do. He learned well. In fact, he delights in having someone pick a fight with him these days so he can sharpen his skills in hand-to-hand combat and with a variety of weapons. He might work cheaper."

She braced her forearms on the table, leaned toward him and said, "I want to be competent in the wilds because I won't have a personal bodyguard watching my back. I want *you* to teach me. After last night, I don't think that is asking so much in return."

He stared straight at her, watching her face go up in flames. "You mean because I partially undressed you so you could sleep comfortably without wrinkling your dress?"

He didn't think her face could turn a deeper shade of red. He was wrong.

"No. Not that. The other thing," she said, then cleared her throat and fidgeted in her chair.

"What other thing?"

She rolled her eyes in annoyance. "Do not make this more difficult than it already is. You know what I mean."

"No, I don't."

"Was it so uneventful that you have forgotten?" she huffed in offended dignity.

He leaned toward her and said quietly, "What in the hell are you talking about?"

She blushed ten shades of red. "Consummating the marriage," she hissed between gritted teeth.

Van barked a laugh that called too much attention to their corner table and earned him another of Natalie's annoyed glares. "You've misjudged me, sunshine. I find no pleasure in dallying with unresponsive women. There's no give-and-take involved in that." He stared straight at her. "You don't remember much about what we said and did last night, do you?"

She shook her head. "No, I don't. But if nothing happened, then what did the yellow rose signify?"

Van shifted awkwardly in his chair. "I don't know. You just looked so…so…beautiful lying in my bed." Damn, he felt self-conscious. He'd never had a conversation like this one before. "I just…hell, I don't know."

She settled back in her chair and flashed such a breathtaking smile that it would have knocked his knees out from under him if he'd been standing.

"That is the sweetest thing a man has ever said to me."

"Doubt it." He dived back into his meal and prayed for blessed silence. He should have known better with her.

"After lunch I'll make the arrangements for refreshments and look up the justice of the peace to preside over the ceremony in the park."

"Fine, but I already spoke to the marshal about cordoning off the park. I contacted local bartenders about delivering drinks. You can speak to all the café owners about food so we don't leave anyone out…" He glanced at her guiltily. "I didn't mean to take over for you. But if you're determined to get hitched tomorrow, arrangements needed to be made immediately."

"No offense taken. I'll have plenty of decisions to make myself when I'm in the wilderness."

He tried to picture her venturing off into the frontier without a clue of what to expect from two-legged and four-legged predators. The woman was insane to think she could survive alone. Van had years of practical experience under his belt. He still ended up in precarious scrapes occasionally. Maybe he did need to spare the time to instruct her. Otherwise, he'd feel guilty if this lovely tenderfoot met with trouble—and she would. It was inevitable in this part of the country.

"Listen, sunshine, I've decided to offer survival lessons. For five hundred. Just the basics."

"You are too generous, Mr. Crow," she said caustically.

He watched her gird herself to negotiate with him. She delighted in haggling over prices, he could tell.

"Two hundred fifty is my top offer," she declared.

"Three thousand for my license signature, the survival classes and I'll pay part of the wedding expenses."

"Done," she said sooner than he expected. She extended her hand and he shook it. Then she smiled wryly and said, "I'd have given four, Crow."

"Then I'll have to find a way to compensate for what I could have had," he countered suggestively.

When her face turned beet-red, he knew that she knew

what he meant. And hell, if she was hiring him as her husband, then she could compensate for being his wife. Fair was fair, wasn't it?

"You are a scoundrel," she muttered at him.

He smiled widely, showing his teeth. "I wouldn't be if you had agreed to the fair price of *four* thousand."

Chapter Four

Natalie spent the day buzzing around town making necessary arrangements for the wedding and reception. She contacted the justice of the peace to schedule the ceremony at seven o'clock the next evening. She confirmed the delivery of refreshments and requested tables to accommodate the partygoers.

After constant activity all day, Natalie decided to make an early night of it. She needed to catch up on her sleep and fully recover from her consumption of whiskey during her initial negotiations with Crow. Speaking of her soon-to-be groom, she hadn't seen him since they'd haggled over his fee at breakfast. He hadn't shown up to collect his money and she wondered how he'd spent the day before their wedding.

The next morning there was still no word from Crow or Bart. Nonetheless, Natalie hiked off to pick up several items of clothing and necessary supplies for her journey on horseback. She hurried back to her room to relax, then bathed and dressed in the simple white gown she had purchased at the one and only boutique in town.

"Business arrangement, pure and simple," she told her reflection when her stomach knotted and a bad case of nerves seized her. Suddenly she was questioning her decision to rush into a marriage to a man she barely knew.

"This is what you wanted, Nat. This is the man you wanted to provide you with a ticket to freedom. Donovan Crow doesn't love you and you don't have to love him back." After all, these sorts of arrangements were commonplace in New Orleans. It's exactly what she would have had with Thurston Kimball III. Only better.

So why didn't she feel completely satisfied with this arrangement? She chalked it up to hasty wedding jitters and fiddled nervously with her coiffure. The staccato rap at the door startled her, assuring her that despite her pep talk she was still very much on edge.

"It's Bart!" he called from the other side of the door. "I'm here to escort you to the park, Miss Jones."

Natalie inhaled a restorative breath and grabbed the yellow rose she had kept in a glass of water—it was all the bouquet she needed. Then she opened the door.

Bart appraised her new gown. "You look exceptionally lovely. You remind me of…"

He broke off suddenly and she wondered if she reminded him of a woman from his past, but she was too nervous and short on time to delve into Bart's previous life in Boston.

"Ready?"

"As I'll ever be."

"That's exactly what Van said. He's exceptionally nervous. He never expected to marry." Bart smiled wryly. "You should know that yours was his only offer."

Natalie chuckled, thankful that Bart was trying to ease her nervous tension. It worked to a small degree. "Thank you."

He arched a thick brow. "For what?"

"For calming me down, as if you don't know. And by the way, like Crow, I only plan to do this once in my life."

"Then you chose well, Miss Jones."

"I know," she said to him, as well as herself.

Donovan Crow met and exceeded every qualification and expectation. She could drop his name from here to Santa Fe and it should be a deterrent for trouble.

Her thoughts faltered and so did her footsteps when she reached the park and saw Crow pacing in front of the circular garden where the justice of the peace waited, along with the whole blessed town! Dear God, what was she doing?

Bart halted beside her, then cupped her chin in his hand, forcing her to meet his solemn gaze. "I don't know exactly what is going on with you. But if you're going to change your mind, do it now. *Not* in front of the entire town. Van has dealt with far too many taunts and insults because of his mixed heritage. I know how it feels to be teased because I look like an out-of-place greenhorn in the West. Although Van is hard-nosed and tough as they come, I won't allow you to embarrass him."

The lecture was all Natalie needed to shore up her faltering composure. "I have no intention of embarrassing Crow," she told him firmly, then flashed a playful grin. "At the high price he commands, I wouldn't think of wasting my money by backing out now. Even though he hasn't stopped by to collect, yet, I'm sure he will eventually."

Bart snickered as he escorted her toward the waiting crowd. "I'm sure he'll get around to it in his own time. And you're right, he *is* expensive."

She squared her shoulders and pasted on a smile as they walked down the makeshift aisle. She was ready to seal this deal that granted her everlasting independence and control of her family inheritance.

Van heard the murmur of voices behind him as he tugged at the cravat that felt like a noose around his neck. Nervous energy roiled through him as he lurched around to greet his soon-to-be bride. His heart slammed against his ribs—and stuck there—when he caught his first glimpse of Natalie being escorted down the aisle by his best friend.

Married? You're getting married? Are you loco?

He could think of a dozen sensible reasons why he shouldn't marry her—and only one reason he should. Because he *liked* her, even if he didn't trust her. He admired her spunk and spirit. He reminded himself—with a certain sense of pride—that of all the men in the world she had chosen *him*.

His all-consuming gaze roamed appreciatively over her formfitting white gown that accentuated her alluring curves and swells to their best advantage. Natalie Whoever-She-Was was stunningly attractive and she had a body made for sin. He knew it for certain because he'd peeled off her yellow gown and put her to bed that first night.

Erotic fantasies had tormented him constantly since then... His thoughts fizzled out as she walked toward him with her shoulders squared and her chin tilted to that determined angle he'd come to recognize in their short but intense acquaintance.

An unfamiliar sensation overcame him when Natalie halted beside him and he noticed the single yellow rose she carried. He wasn't sure what it signified, but it made him feel...well, he didn't know what he felt but it was a pleasant sensation and there hadn't been very many of those in his adult life.

"Last chance, Crow," she murmured. "Do you want to change your mind and make a run for it?"

"No." He tossed her a teasing smile and said, "I bought this fancy suit already. Hate to waste it."

The grin she flashed made her dark onyx eyes twinkle and he impulsively took her hand in his as they turned to face the rotund justice of the peace who was only an inch taller than Natalie and was decked out in his Sunday-go-to-meeting clothes.

Before Van knew what hit him, Natalie had said *I do* and so had he. Then he felt a moment of discomfort when he realized he hadn't bought her a wedding band. But Natalie discreetly slipped him the ring she had been wearing on her right hand and he placed it on her left one at the prompt. Then they reached his favorite part of the ceremony where the justice of the peace announced they were husband and wife and he got to kiss his bride in front of the whole blessed town.

Even if no one in town could figure out why this bewitching female wanted to marry a man like him, a cheer rose up from the crowd. Van vaguely registered the sound because the feel of Natalie's lush body pressed suggestively to his left him distracted to the extreme. The taste of her honeyed lips melting beneath his demanded his undivided attention.

A moment later, he heard Bart clearing his throat and felt a discreet nudge in the ribs. When Van broke the intoxicating kiss he noted his friend was grinning broadly and Natalie looked as dazed as he felt.

The sizzle and burn assailing his body was nothing more than fierce physical attraction, he tried to tell himself. Natalie was breathtakingly beautiful, after all. He'd been without a woman for more weeks than he cared to count. Naturally, she aroused him.

He curled his arm possessively around her as the crowd surged forward to congratulate them. To his amazement, people who usually ignored him took time to wish him well. It was as if he had become accepted and respected because of his connection to the auburn-haired woman he'd married.

Natalie looked sophisticated and poised. She was gracious to everyone who greeted her, though she insisted everyone call her Anna and he wondered why she refused to divulge her real name... Which reminded him...

"We haven't signed the license," he murmured in her ear.

"We can do it as soon as the greeting line trails off and the refreshments are served," she replied.

A quarter of an hour later, the crowd converged on the tables beside the street to partake of food and drink. The local band struck up a lively tune and a moment of panic hammered at Van. The crowd turned in synchronized rhythm, expecting him to take the first dance with his new wife. Van glanced helplessly at Bart who nodded encouragingly.

"I doubt the ceremonial war dances I learned in childhood are appropriate for a white man's wedding," he mumbled self-consciously to Natalie.

To his relief she grinned impishly at him and said, "Finally, something that I might be able to do better than you. This is a waltz and the steps are easy. Slow, quick, quick... One...two, three."

She stood close enough to him that he could shadow the movements of her body while she counted the tempo in a whisper. He must not have looked too clumsy because the crowd applauded and then went back to eating and drinking.

"I must warn you that these dance lessons will cost

you, Crow," she teased playfully. "A thousand should do it."

"Now who's the highwayman?" he countered with a grin.

By the time they completed the second waltz, Van had his dancing legs beneath him and felt confident that he wasn't making a complete fool of himself or of Natalie. In fact, he felt like part of a community for the first time. It was a gigantic step for a man who straddled two contrasting civilizations and never felt as if he really belonged in either one.

Bart ambled across the area cordoned off for dancing and halted beside Van. "May I dance with the bride?"

"Of course—"

Van's voice dried up when a gunshot rang out of nowhere. He reached reflexively for Natalie and rolled with her to the ground. He managed to pin her protectively beneath him before a second bullet whizzed past his head and slammed into Bart's shoulder when he dived to the ground to protect Natalie's exposed left side.

"Ouch, damn. That hurts," Bart hissed as he grabbed his bleeding arm.

Van reached for the double holsters strapped around his hips then remembered he hadn't worn his six-shooters to the ceremony. He cursed under his breath as he reached into his right boot to retrieve the long-barreled pistol. A third shot whistled through the air and the frightened crowd scattered in every direction at once to avoid being hit. Van swore sourly when he noticed the flares of gunpowder and the dark puffs of smoke rising from the roof of the butcher shop. Now he knew where the second two shots had originated but not the first one.

What he *did* know was someone was taking potshots at him. There were two or three shooters, he guessed. Was it the three surviving members of the Harper Gang? Had they come gunning for him during the wedding reception? He was surprised they hadn't ambushed him during the ceremony.

"Damn Harper brothers," he scowled in disgust, wishing he'd spent the previous day reconnoitering the area instead of catching up on sleep.

He was outraged by the interruption at his wedding party and mad as hell that Natalie's white gown was smeared with grass stains galore. But worse, his best friend had suffered a gunshot wound. Snarling, Van bolted to his feet and fired off two shots toward the roof of the butcher shop.

"Curse it, Crow!" Natalie railed at him as she vaulted to her feet. "Don't call more attention to yourself!"

To his disbelief, she thrust herself in front of him, just as she had done that night in Road To Ruin Saloon.

"Stop doing that!" he snapped, shoving her behind him before he pulled the trigger again.

Although he knew his boot pistol was out of range, he doubted his bushwhackers knew it. He fired off one more shot for good measure. It was met with silence. Apparently, his attackers—who had used guerrilla warfare to hit and run, had beat a hasty retreat before he identified them.

Instinct and training urged him to take off at a dead run to track down the snipers. Van was accustomed to facing danger alone—and doing it immediately. However, with Bart down and Natalie unprotected, he hesitated to race off.

"Oh, God!" Natalie gasped as she stared at the bloodstain that soaked the sleeve of Bart's expensive jacket. "Are you all right?"

"Does having your arm hurt like blazing hell count as all right?" Bart asked with a grimace.

"Take off your jacket and let's see how bad it is." She craned her neck to survey the departing backs of the crowd. "Is there a doctor available?"

"I don't need a doctor," Bart murmured as he carefully peeled off his jacket to see the red stains on his left shirtsleeve. "I have Van."

Natalie blinked owlishly as Crow knelt beside his friend. He retrieved a knife from his left boot to cut open the sleeve of the white shirt to assess the injury.

"Four inches to the right and you'd have a serious problem, Bartholomew," Crow said as he blotted the wound with the hem of Bart's shirt.

"Glad my luck held," he panted as he tried to lever himself into an upright position. His face turned white as salt and he wilted back to the ground. "Go find the men who shot at us and give them my regards."

Crow shook his head. "First things first. I'm taking you and Sunshine to your rooms for safekeeping. *Then* I'll track down those bastards."

Natalie swallowed uneasily as her gaze darted up the side of the brick building to survey the place where the shots had been fired. She felt ill, certain the bastards Crow referred to were Avery Marsh, Thurston Kimball and their hired assassins. How had they managed to find her so quickly?

However they accomplished the feat, their gunmen nearly disposed of her new husband and accidentally hit Bart. Or had they been aiming at *her* and missed...?

"Dear God," she wheezed, her blood practically turning to ice in her veins at the awful thought of Crow or Bart Collier dying because of her. In addition, she hadn't signed the marriage license so the fortune was still up for grabs.

"What's wrong?" Van glanced every way at once. "Did you spot someone on the roof of the butcher shop again?"

"No." Natalie inhaled several cathartic breaths and told herself to calm down now that the danger had passed—for the moment, at least. "What can I do to help Bart?"

"Let's get him on his feet after I apply a tourniquet to stop the bleeding."

With the tourniquet in place, Crow clutched Bart's good arm and gently drew him into a sitting position. Together Natalie and Crow hoisted Bart to his feet. He staggered slightly but gritted his teeth and moved forward under his own power as best he could. Natalie and Crow wrapped their arms around his back for additional support as they headed toward the Simon House.

Once the shooting had stopped, the crowd converged to see who had been hurt. Natalie gnashed her teeth when someone in the middle of the crowd commented the shooting didn't surprise him, considering who the groom was.

"What is the matter with you people?" she burst out. "Donovan Crow is a good and decent man and—"

"It's all right, I'm used to—" Crow tried to interrupt but she was having none of that.

"This is my husband and I demand you show him the consideration and respect he deserves—"

"Sun—"

"He travels the country, capturing vicious criminals who prey on all of you and yet you—"

"Sunshine—"

"—went running when trouble arose," she said, talking over him. "Any of you volunteering to help Crow hunt down the bushwhackers? No? I thought not. You cowered behind his gun. But thank you so much for partaking of the free food and drink at our reception, and then running like cowards while Crow covered everyone who turned tail and ran."

Natalie huffed out an agitated breath as she motioned for the crowd to move out of their way. When Bart grinned at her—in between painful grimaces—she glared at him. "Why are you smiling? You've been shot."

"I thought this marriage might be a mismatch," Bart mumbled. "I was mistaken. What Van does with his weapons you can do with words. I'll have to strive to be that animated when I'm arguing my next case in court."

Natalie tried to get past her anger and indignation but it wasn't easy. When she glanced at Crow, he raised his eyebrows and bit back an amused smile. He didn't have a damn thing to smile about, either, but he didn't realize it yet.

She knew Marsh and Kimball—or their hired gunmen—had fired the shots. They had barely missed their mark and Bart was suffering for it. Knowing those greedy bastards, she predicted they would strike again. Soon.

Her guilty conscience beat her black and blue while they shepherded Bart across the street toward the hotel. Crow was on high alert, looking for trouble in the form of another ambush. He stuck to the shadows beneath the porches outside the stores to reach the hotel lobby without mishap.

Natalie managed to keep her trap shut while they ascended the steps to escort Bart into a spacious, expensively furnished suite that rivalled Crow's living quarters.

Then she blurted out, "I'm so sorry! This is my fault and Bart is suffering for it! This is not what I intended."

Both men gaped at her as if she had ivy vines growing out her ears.

"The two men who want to use me for their greedy

purposes obviously located me sooner than expected. I predict they will attack again."

"Nice of you to shoulder the blame, sunshine, but the three men who swore revenge because I killed their little brother in self-defense are the ones who retaliated. Although I put them behind bars, they recently escaped." He walked Bart across the sitting room to the bedroom. "They sent me a note, promising an eye for an eye."

Natalie hurried to the commode to fetch a cloth to dip in water to cleanse Bart's wound while Van eased him into bed.

"I'll fetch the poultice then stitch him back together," Crow said as he reversed direction to hurry off. "Lock the door behind me."

"What three men is he talking about?" she asked Bart when she returned from securing the door.

Natalie eased down on the edge of the bed to clean the jagged wound. She told herself she wouldn't faint. She was headed for the wilderness as fast as she could get there and she refused to be squeamish, whether she treated her own wounds or someone else's.

"The Harper Gang—" He hissed in pain when she touched a tender spot. "Damn, that stings!"

"Sorry." She tried to be exceptionally gentle.

"The cutthroats committed a series of bank robberies and shot tellers and innocent bystanders. Van told the bankers to sic the Texas Rangers on the outlaws when they escaped jail. Apparently they haven't tracked down the Harpers and recovered the stolen money."

Natalie marshaled her determination to have the wound completely prepared by the time Crow returned with his poultice and needle. When she felt the bullet lodged against muscle she pulled a pin from her hair, dipped it in water and gently probed to remove it.

Bart glanced at the bullet she placed on the end table, and then at her. "I'm impressed." His gaze drifted past her when a knock at the sitting room door rattled the hinges. "Get that, will you? I'd do it myself but my arm's blown off."

She rolled her eyes at his exaggeration, then hurried off to unlock the door. Crow sailed past her, carrying a leather pouch twice the size of the one he kept in his shirt pocket.

His medicine bag, no doubt. She wouldn't be surprised to learn this competent warrior was also a shaman. Natalie wished she could acquire half his talents and skills before she rode off to seek adventure and feed her hungry soul.

"No need to bother looking for the bullet. She removed it already," Bart told Van. "I didn't know you'd found time to give her a few survival lessons."

Van glanced over his shoulder and stared pensively at Natalie who hovered by the bedroom door. "I haven't. She must be a natural. Either that or she has skills she hasn't divulged, along with her real name," he added quietly.

He gestured toward the bag he'd set on the floor. "There's a sedative in a silver tin," he told her. "Give it to Bart with a glass of water before I stitch him up."

While Bart munched on the painkiller and sipped water, Van packed numbing salve around the jagged edges of the gunshot wound. Then he stitched the skin together and applied healing poultice. All the while, his conscience railed at him for allowing his best friend to suffer injury from a bullet meant for him. Furthermore, Natalie had come close to being shot, too, and the thought made him cringe.

In addition, she had stood up for him and lectured the citizens on their bad behavior and rude comment. He was flattered and astounded by her daring and courage. Whoever she was, she wasn't short on gumption.

"My, that's a fast-acting potion." Natalie frowned when Bart stopped talking in midsentence and slumped on the bed.

"Peyote," he informed her with a wry grin. "It affects people in varying degrees. I used it on Bart after those hooligans beat him to a pulp. He reacted the same way, then he slept the night away in total oblivion."

"Well, I suppose I should return to my room," she said as she tucked the quilt beneath Bart's chin. "It has been a hectic day, what with last-minute plans for the ceremony and the unnerving bushwhacking ordeal."

Warily, Van watched Natalie shift from one foot to the other. She refused to meet his gaze, just kept casting concerned glances at Bart. He wondered if she was apprehensive about their supposed wedding night or upset because she thought the ambush was her fault. Which it wasn't. It was *his*. Men shot at him all the time. It was a hazard of his assignments. He was accustomed to it. She wasn't.

He had to admit the prospect of having Natalie in his room on their wedding night—whether anything intimate came of it or not—held tremendous appeal. But this was a marriage in name only, he reminded himself. Under the circumstances, it was probably best if all three of them stayed in separate rooms, in case the Harper Gang came gunning for him again.

Bart had been shot because he had been standing too close to Van. Bullets had flown over Natalie's head. It was a wonder one of them hadn't hit her. The thought of stitching up wounds on her flawless skin made him grimace is distaste.

"You can return to your room if you want," he murmured. "You're a woman of independence now. Just stay off the streets, lest you get shot and I have to patch you up."

She finally met his gaze. "I do have my freedom now, don't I? Well then, I'll bid you good night. And thank you for seeing that I am free to go where I want and do as I please. I will always be indebted to you for that and I will pay you tomorrow."

"No rush," he said with a nonchalant shrug.

She swept across the bedroom in her grass-stained white gown. Van got up and followed her into the sitting area. "Stop right there, sunshine."

She glanced at him as she reached for the door latch.

Van shook his head warningly, then pulled her sideways. "Never open a door while you're standing directly in front of it. Especially after a near brush with bushwhackers. They could be lying in wait."

"Good advice. Is that Rule Number One in Crow's Survival Handbook?"

"Top ten at least." He eased open the door to ensure no one lurked in the shadowed hallway, waiting to gun him down.

She hesitated momentarily, then pressed a kiss to his lips. "Thank you for coming to the wedding."

He smiled. "Thank you for inviting me to be your groom."

She opened her mouth and then clamped her lips shut, as if she'd decided against voicing whatever thought was racing through her mind. "Well, good night, Crow."

He watched her cling to the shadows and noted which room she entered, in case he needed to come to her rescue. He strode quickly to the bedroom to check on Bart, who hadn't moved a muscle. Van decided this was the perfect time to change into his everyday clothes, run the important errand he had overlooked after the shooting and then look around town. If the Harpers were lurking about, hoping to shoot the right man the second time around, he vowed to stop them in their tracks so Natalie wouldn't be caught in the cross fire—like Bart.

Chapter Five

Natalie scurried around her room, gathering her belongings and cramming them into her satchel and carpetbag. Disguised in the men's clothing she'd purchased for traveling, she checked that no one was waiting in the hall to pounce on her. She slipped outside the door, then inched down the hall to the metal fire escape and into the alley.

She planned to be long gone by morning and the two bastards and their hired assassins could chase her and leave Crow and Bart alone. No one else was going to suffer because of her, she vowed fiercely.

Leaving her luggage behind the livery stable, Natalie scampered around the corner of the building, then ducked inside. She surveyed the string of horses in their stalls. One powerful-looking gelding caught her attention. He was solid black, except for a strip of white down the length of his nose. The marking resembled an arrow.

Making her selection, she pulled her oversize cap down round her ears then strode toward the door she presumed led to the owner's living quarters. She rapped on the door and waited impatiently before knocking again.

"Hold your horses, I'm coming," the owner grumbled from the other side of the door.

Natalie nodded to the fifty-year-old—or thereabouts—barrel-bellied man who had a sparse smattering of gray hair on his head. His shoulders were as wide as a bull's and his legs reminded her of tree stumps.

"Whad'ya want, kid?" he demanded gruffly.

"Need a horse," she replied in her deepest voice, to throw off the owner so he would mistake her for a boy. "Want to buy the strapping black one and I got money to pay for it."

"Yeah? Stolen money?" he asked, and snorted. "Can't have that one. Belongs to Crow. He pays me damn good money to make sure Durango is well fed and ready to ride when he wants him."

Should've known, she thought. The muscular mount looked as if he could run all day and night without breaking a sweat. The horse reminded her of Crow—tough, powerful and dependable.

"Give me the second best mount you have. I gotta ride west to see my sick mama," she mumbled. "A boy's gotta be there when his mama needs him, ya know."

The owner squinted suspiciously at her. "You sure you got money that ain't stolen?"

"Hard-earned," she insisted. "I'm not a thief, mister."

She must have sounded convincing because the older man finally nodded and lumbered down the aisle to open the stall where a strawberry roan waited. "I s'pose you need tack, too, huh, kid?"

"Yes, sir, I do." She fished several bank notes from her pants pocket to give to the owner.

Within a few minutes, Natalie led her mount around the corner to toss her luggage on the back of her horse. She tied the satchels in place then caught sight of a darting shadow from the corner of her eye. She tried to scream her head off but a man's hand clamped over the lower portion of her face, making it difficult to breathe and impossible to yell for help. He slammed her back against his solid chest and leaned down to growl venomously in her ear.

"Going somewhere? I don't think so. Besides, you forgot something and I'm here to see you get it."

Van jerked the cap off Natalie's head. Wild curls tumbled around her shoulders. He had a good mind to give the glossy strands a yank. Despite her boy's clothing, he'd known by the way she moved that she was female—and he knew exactly which female in particular. His runaway wife.

Hell, they hadn't been married five hours and already she was hightailing it out of town without him.

And she hadn't paid him, either. In good faith, he hadn't pressed the issue. Maybe he should have.

"Good Lord," she gushed when he removed his hand from her mouth and she glanced up at him. "You scared ten years off my life."

"Too bad, sunshine. I'm mad as hell at you for scaring ten years off mine. I stopped by your room and found you gone. I thought the bushwhackers had sneaked in, grabbed you and your belongings and decided to hold you for bargaining power to get even with me."

He got right in her face, bared his teeth and added, "Do not ever do that again. Understand?"

"I'm doing you a huge favor, damn it," she snapped.

"Are you? Doesn't feel like it to me." He displayed the document he'd retrieved from the justice of the peace a few minutes earlier and shook it in her face. "I thought you were in an all-fired rush to get hold of this paper. My name is on it. So are the witnesses. And where's my money for the use of my name? You trying to skip out without paying?"

He wasn't really worried about his marriage fee, but he was irritated and he hadn't liked the unfamiliar feelings of fear and concern that lambasted him when he realized Natalie had vanished into thin air.

"Certainly not," she said in offended dignity. "I would have wired you the money as soon as possible."

"Instead, you can give it to me in person when we return to your room because you are not leaving town without me."

She blinked, startled. "I'm a liability you can ill afford, Crow. My stepfather tracked me here and hired someone to dispose of you. Or me. I'm not sure which and I won't risk your life again. If you take another assignment and leave town, I'm hoping the hired assassins will come after me instead of you."

Van clutched her elbow to quick-march her to the hotel but she stubbornly set her feet and refused to budge from the spot—short of being scooped up, tossed over his shoulder and carried off.

"What about the horse I bought?" she challenged. "I can't just leave him here to be stolen. I'm going to need him. And there's the matter of my luggage—"

His annoyed growl cut her off. Van untied the satchels, dropped them at her feet and then muttered, "I'll be right back. Do...not...move...or else."

He knew the instant the words flew out of his mouth that he'd made a mistake. Her chin tilted to a rebellious angle and her spine went ramrod stiff.

"Good God, I married a tyrant," she sniped.

"Please do not leave without me," he corrected himself in a gentler tone.

She looked down her pert nose at him, then struck a

haughty pose that would have made him grin at her antics if he hadn't been so aggravated by her.

"Fine, dear, since you asked so nicely."

He led the strawberry roan into the livery to contact the owner and concoct an explanation for returning the horse.

"What did you tell him?" she demanded the instant he returned. "I want to make sure we have our stories straight."

"I told him that the kid and I are heading in the same direction tomorrow. I also told him to take care of the boy's horse as well as he usually takes care of mine." He arched a brow. "That suit you, sunshine?"

"Yes, but what is *not* going to suit me is if you are ambushed on my account," she grumbled as he swooped down to grab her luggage.

"I told you that it's *my* would-be assassins who are lurking about, not yours. So stop feeling guilty—"

His voice dried up as he rounded the side of the Simon House to see three horses tethered to the gutter pipe in the alley. Instant concern blazed through him. "Damn Harper brothers," he scowled. "Stay here."

He wasted his breath because Natalie, with her curly hair flying around her, leaped over the satchels he'd left behind and followed him up the metal fire escape. With both pistols drawn, Van eased into the hallway. He felt Natalie's piddly little two-shot derringer jabbing him in the elbow.

"Be careful with that thing," he warned in a whisper. "Don't shoot me by mistake."

"I won't. Just let me know when I can unload my weapon on those two bastards and their hired killer," she demanded.

Just what I need, thought Van. *A trigger-happy bride.*

He definitely had to take time to give her proper weapon and self-defense training before she rode off into the sunset. The way she waved around that snub-nosed pistol, she was going to shoot somebody—and he hoped to hell it wasn't him!

Van went on full alert as he crept down the hall toward his room. He jerked to attention when he noticed Bart's door was standing ajar. Bemused, he tiptoed into the sitting room and pulled Natalie along with him. He heard jeering voices in the bedroom so he motioned for Natalie to remain where she was while he crept to the bedroom to investigate.

He instantly recognized the three men standing over Bart, who apparently had regained consciousness after one of the burly brutes pounded on him. Bart's eye was swollen shut and his split lip was bleeding.

"Toss your weapons on the bed," Van demanded ominously.

When Jonas Potts wheeled around, his weapon raised threateningly, Van fired off a shot. He left Potts with a wound similar to the one Bart suffered. In the meantime, Bart caused a distraction by hurling the spare pillow at the second burly brute who went by the name of Pete Caine. Van pounded him on the back of the head when he tried to retrieve the pistol he'd tossed on the bed. Caine's legs folded up like a tent and he dropped to the floor, unconscious.

Van lurched around to confront the third intruder— Evan Rigsby—but he was a moment too slow. Rigsby plowed into him, knocking him off balance and groping at Van's pistol.

"You ain't gonna save this scrawny little bastard again, Crow," Rigsby snarled. "This time both of you—"

His voice fizzled out abruptly and his gray eyes

widened in surprise. "What the hell...?" Rigsby chirped, and went perfectly still.

Van glanced around Rigsby's thick shoulders to see that Natalie had defied his orders—again—and had crept into the bedroom. She stood over Rigsby with a cloud of auburn hair floating around her face and the barrel of her pistol crammed into the side of his head.

"Can I shoot him, Crow?" she drawled, then got a crazy gleam in her eye that was amazingly convincing.

Rigsby swallowed with an audible gulp.

"I've been itching to shoot somebody all day."

"No," Van snapped, and bit back a grin.

"Why do you always get to have all the fun?" she complained. "I want to draw blood, too, and watch them squirm in pain."

Van shoved Rigsby aside, then gestured toward the injured bully who was clutching his bloody shoulder. "If Potts tries to move you can blast away at him."

He gestured for Rigsby to get down on his knees, then used the ties from the curtain to restrain him.

"Thanks for the help." Bart stared at Van with his one good eye and licked his split lip. "Looks like I owe you again."

"No, you'd have handled these goons easily if I hadn't given you peyote for the pain."

Taking charge of the situation, Van dragged the unconscious Caine into the sitting room while Bart held Rigsby and Potts at gunpoint.

"Sunshine!" Van called from the other room.

She poked her head around the corner of the bedroom door and arched a questioning brow. "You decide to let me shoot one of these hombres for target practice?"

"Not tonight. Please put a cold pack on Bart's eye and

lip and change the dressing on his arm while I march these goons to jail."

"Yes, sir." She gave him a snappy salute. "Anything else?"

"Yeah, don't shoot Bart for practice, either. He's had a rough night."

When Natalie disappeared from sight, Potts stared curiously at Van. "Why'd you marry that hellion? She's plum loco."

"She's the best I could do," Van said with a straight face. "Now let's move. You're disrupting my wedding night."

Natalie dabbed lightly at Bart's puffy eye and swollen lip. "Who were those men? And what did they want with you?"

Bart shifted position and winced in pain. Apparently, the sedative was wearing off. "Those were the bullies I told you about that attacked me when I first moved to Wolf Ridge."

Natalie blinked in surprise. "They retaliated because you made sure they served jail time for all their crimes?"

"Yes, and I am so sorry they targeted me during your wedding reception," he said out the side of his mouth that wasn't swollen. "They spoiled your evening."

"*They* shot you?" she chirped. "Not the men hunting for me?"

"And not the Harper Gang that Van thought had arrived to ambush him and hit me by mistake." Bart levered himself against the headboard and reached for the glass of water on the end table. "Turns out *I* was the original target and I was to die for making those goons spend so many years in prison."

"Eight years is a long time to hold a grudge," she murmured.

"Not if you possess their spiteful mentality." Bart sighed in frustration. "This should have been my opportunity to use the self-defense tactics Van taught me. Instead I was sleeping the evening away."

"A shame they didn't do you the courtesy of contacting you in advance, the way the Harper Gang did for Van. Which is why he presumed *he* was the target of ambush and *I* assumed I hadn't covered my tracks well enough to prevent my stepfather and former fiancé from finding me so quickly."

"There is a very real possibility of that happening to you," Bart forewarned. "Van has the uncanny knack of finding people who plan to stay lost. He might be the best in the business, but there are others less honest who dispose of witnesses or anyone else if the price is right. Hired killers are easy to come by in any part of the country, I'm sorry to say. I've seen to it that several were convicted in court."

Bart stared at her grimly with his good eye. "That is why you need to tell me your real name so we can be prepared for possible ambush that might place you or Van in danger."

Natalie shook her head, sending the curly tendrils drifting around her shoulders. She considered Crow and Bart trustworthy—to a point. But she'd been serious when she informed Crow that she trusted no man explicitly. The Robedeaux-Blair name was a blessing and curse. People often accepted bribes to offer information that might earn them large rewards. It would break her heart if Bart or Crow betrayed her, for she counted both men as friends.

"Anna," Bart coaxed emphatically. "I'm offering lawyer confidentiality. Tell me your troubles. It's for your own

good that I have all the facts. Even better if Van has them, too."

"But it might not be for *your* own good or Van's," she said, provoking his wary frown. She waved him off with a breezy smile. "At any rate, I will be out of your hair very soon and your life will return to normal. I'll conclude my business with Crow and be on my way."

"You saw what happened to me," Bart said somberly. "It could happen to you. A woman alone in an unfamiliar part of the country is an invitation for trouble."

"What could happen to Sunshine?" Van questioned as he suddenly appeared in the doorway.

Natalie sent Bart a silencing stare. "Nothing important. Did you put the bullies behind bars?"

Van's gaze bounced back and forth between her and Bart. "Yes. By the time Bart testifies against those goons, they will be back in the penitentiary for another long stint."

Natalie rose to her feet. "I left my luggage in the alley. I better collect it." And she should have done so earlier, considering the valuables she carried.

"I'll help," Van volunteered.

"You don't trust me not to flit off into the darkness again, do you?" she asked as he followed closely at her heels.

"I've seen one of your disappearing acts, so no, I don't trust you. Do you trust me?"

"No," she admitted, thinking of her conversation with Bart about her refusal to divulge her real name.

"Then there you go, sunshine. And why didn't you stay on the fire escape like I told you?" he demanded irritably.

"I must've forgotten what you said," she said flippantly.

"And when I told you to wait in the hall outside Bart's room?" he challenged.

She tossed him a caustic smile. "Guess I didn't hear what you said."

She stepped onto the landing, then scurried down the steps to retrieve her satchels. When Crow followed her back to her room, she rummaged through her luggage to fish into the hem of her yellow gown.

He arched a thick black brow while he watched her retrieve the money owed him. "Clever. Any other tricks up your sleeve…or hem…as the case happens to be?"

"No, just the one." She counted out two thousand dollars and said, "I've decided not to take survival lessons because I want to be far away from here before my stepfather and ex-fiancé locate me."

"Too bad." He pulled another thousand from her hand. "A deal is a deal. I don't give money-back guarantees in my line of work. Plus, I'm going with you, just until you get the hang of fending for yourself in the Texas badlands. You'll get a crash course and I will earn the fee we agreed upon."

She pulled a face. "Fine. Keep the money but don't come with me."

He shook his raven head as he loomed over her like a thundercloud. She could understand why he intimidated people. He could look exceptionally formidable when he felt like it. But Natalie conjured up the vivid memory of Crow tossing back his head and laughing. It prevented her from wilting beneath The Stare and quaking in her boots.

She decided to catch him off guard by looping her arms around his neck and pushing up on tiptoe to kiss him full on the mouth. "Our business is concluded, dear husband. Signed, sealed with a kiss and paid in full. Now go away and have a nice life."

He studied her with those penetrating silver-blue eyes that could hypnotize if you stared into them too long.

"What are you hiding, sunshine? What is your real name? And who are your stepfather and ex-fiancé? Do they even exist? What is it that you don't want me to find out?"

"That I've fallen completely and madly in love with you and I want to leave before you break my heart in two."

"All the more reason why you aren't leaving town without me. As it happens I'm crazy in love with you, too, sunshine," he countered, mimicking her lovesick expression. "I can't let you go because it would break *my* heart in two."

"Cute," she muttered sarcastically.

He flashed a teasing grin. "Thanks. I thought so." His expression hardened and he shook a lean finger in her face. "If you dare leave without me I promise to hunt you down. I will not be in a good mood when I catch up with you, either. Guaran-damn-teed. Thus far, you've seen only my good side. You do not want to get on my bad side."

"Dear God, I was right. I *have* married a domineering martinet," she complained.

"Too late now." He wheeled around and strode across the room in quick economical strides that reminded her of a panther's gait. She figured he could pounce like one, too, if need be. Then he paused at the door to smile devilishly at her. "I forgot to ask if you changed your mind and decided to spend the night with me. It *is* our wedding night."

"Thank you, but no." She faked a smile. "You have done enough already."

His expression sobered in the blink of an eye. "I meant what I said, *Anna Jones.* Do not leave without me."

She blew out her breath in exasperation. "All right. We will ride out after we check on Bart and have breakfast."

She wasn't sure he believed her, but he left nonetheless.

✝ ✝ ✝

Van paced restlessly in Bart's suite, unsure he trusted Natalie to stay put. He checked the hallway at regular intervals, expecting to see her exit quietly from her room.

"You plan on doing this all night?" Bart asked as he dipped the cloth in the basin of cold water Natalie left on the end table, then applied the compress to his puffy eye. "You're making me dizzy with your pacing and I have enough problems as it is."

Van jerked to a halt, unaware that he'd been wearing a rut in the carpet. "I expect her to leave, clinging to the ridiculous notion that *I'll* come to harm if I go with her. If, indeed, that's the real reason my secretive wife wants to skip town without me. Damn it, why won't she confide in us? It makes me suspicious as hell."

"Me, too," Bart remarked, then gestured toward his injured arm. "Are you going to replace the bandage? Or am I supposed to do it while you pace and fret like a mother hen?"

Van glared at him. "I'm not fretting. I never fret."

"Seems to me that it would require less energy to bunk down inside her door. You are married to the woman, after all. Propriety is hardly in question here."

Van lurched around to place a fresh bandage on Bart's upper arm. "For all I know, she fed me a crock of lies and there is no greedy stepfather or ex-fiancé trying to find her. Maybe she shot someone or swindled somebody out of the money she stashed in her clothing. The fact that she counted out large denomination bank notes to pay me arouses more doubt and suspicions."

Bart's brows shot up in surprise and Van nodded. "She has money up her sleeves and in the hem of her gowns. She is also very aware of where her satchels are at all times.

It has to mean something. Plus, she won't let me see the license after she signed her name."

"She is as tight-lipped as a clam," Bart agreed, then winced when Van touched a tender section of the wound unintentionally. "I tried to cajole her into confiding in me, but she refused, claiming it was for your own good and mine."

"I tried to intimidate her into confiding in me, too, but she sassed me," Van grumbled. "Damn woman. She's as stubborn as she is independent." He suddenly bounded to his feet and lurched toward the sitting room. "I'm going to check on her. I think I'll take your advice and camp out at her door. Maybe I can get some sleep."

"You do that. Meanwhile, I'll be here nursing a wounded arm, black eye and split lip. As for you, you married an elusive woman harboring only God knows how many dangerous secrets that might recoil and bite us in the ass. Oh, and congratulations to you for marrying trouble, Van. It keeps life interesting, to say the least."

Van poked his head around the bedroom door, glared at Bart and said, "You are not as funny as you think you are. And, thus far, I see nothing to recommend married life."

Bart snickered as he settled himself comfortably in bed. "You should have married a pushover. If you'd have had a traditional wedding night, you'd be in better spirits."

Van walked away, scowling.

Exotic fantasies tormented him while he tried to sleep outside her door—his pistol at the ready, in case trouble showed up. Luckily, no one wandered by to wonder if he had been kicked out on his wedding night.

Even though Van didn't trust his mysterious, secretive wife, he wanted her. Only her. That bothered him. He'd never been particular when it came to scratching an itch and easing male needs. He told himself that he was partial to Natalie—or whoever she was—because she was his lawfully wedded wife. But he was afraid his feelings went deeper. She teased him, she amused him. She frustrated him and intrigued him. She aroused him with the slightest kiss and the lightest touch of her body brushing against his.

Van was suffering from a severe case of lust and it was wearing his disposition thin. Plus, his inner battle between doubt and desire was maddening.

He blew out an agitated breath when her door opened silently and her shadowed form—with a suitcase clutched in each hand—hovered above him.

"Going somewhere again, sunshine? Over my dead body."

She glared at him and said, "Don't tempt me." Then she slammed the door.

Chapter Six

Natalie swore under her breath when Crow opened the door she had slammed in his face. "I thought I made it clear that just because you're my husband doesn't mean you are entitled to boss me around."

"I must have forgotten." He tossed her a sarcastic smile. "Sort of like you did when I told you to stand guard by Bart's door and you barged in while I confronted the three hooligans who planned to finish off Bart tonight."

He had her there, she admitted. She had thumbed her nose at his commands, determined to aid Bart and Crow if they encountered trouble. Which they certainly had.

Her thoughts went up in smoke when Crow dragged his pillow and pallet into her room to place it in front of her door. She glowered at him for blocking her escape route again.

"Are you inviting me to your bed instead?" he challenged.

She considered it for a half second then said, "Yes."

That must have surprised him for his thick brows nearly shot off his forehead. "So what's the catch, sunshine?"

She wasn't about to tell him that she thought she might stand a better chance of escaping if he fell asleep in her bed rather than having to step over him while he was sprawled in front of her door. And curse it, she should have gone out the window earlier. Unfortunately, the route was precarious and she hadn't wanted to break an arm or leg because she had a long ride ahead of her.

"There is no catch. I was just thinking of your comfort."

"Your concern is touching," he scoffed, and locked her door.

When he shed his dark shirt, exposing the washboard muscles of his belly and his powerful shoulders, Natalie lost her train of thought. Confound it, she was far too aware of the brawny warrior who was now her husband. Counting the battle scars on his arms, ribs and shoulders wasn't helping to ease her attraction to him. Instead, she felt compelled to kiss away any remembered pain he'd suffered.

Then she wanted to make a deliberate study of the rest of him… *Never mind what else you're tempted to do with him,* she scolded herself harshly. Her problem was that she'd become caught up in the fact that Crow was her husband and she was entitled to certain wifely rights to appease her feminine curiosity.

"Sunshine, are you coming to bed?"

She snapped to attention when she noticed that he'd sprawled on the bedspread and cushioned his head on his linked fingers. He was a fine male specimen. She couldn't take her eyes off those rippling muscles and corded tendons on his chest and abdomen.

Without removing her clothing, Natalie stretched out beside him. After all, she still planned to sneak out the instant he dozed off. To her frustration, he rolled to his side and draped his arm over her waist, then angled his bent leg over her knees, effectively pinning in her place without applying pressure.

Her irritation with him fizzled out when he pressed the most incredibly tender kiss to her lips. Sensual awareness sizzled through her when his hand drifted dangerously close to the underside of her breast, then settled on her belly. Her body burned with unappeased need when he nudged his chin against the curve of her neck, then relaxed beside her.

Three hours later, she awoke to make her escape, only to find the sneaky rascal had tied her ankle to his.

"Making sure my captives don't escape me is one of the things I do best," he whispered in her ear.

Goose bumps pebbled her skin, despite her irritation with the clever rascal. "I'm really beginning to hate you, Crow."

"I'm starting to hate you, too, wife," he said in a husky voice that sent another pleasurable sensation curling through her body. "Get some sleep. We have a long ride ahead of us tomorrow."

Avery Marsh swore vehemently as he searched the mansion for the dozenth time, looking for the Robedeaux-Blair jewels and the stash of money his deceased wife tried to hide from him. No doubt, that sassy little bitch he'd tried to marry off to Kimball, in exchange for a cut of the fortune, had taken the money and valuables when she skipped town.

His angry thoughts trailed off when Thurston Kimball III strutted into the parlor, puffing on his pipe. "The two mercenaries we hired to run Natalie to ground haven't been successful." He blew a lopsided smoke ring around his blond head, then struck a haughty pose.

In Avery's opinion, Kimball had little practical use,

except that he was desperate for money to pay his gambling debts, so he readily agreed to Avery's scheme to marry Natalie in exchange for money.

"I received a message after you placed that cleverly worded article in the newspaper and mentioned the supposed maid you invented for us to throw suspicion on." Kimball puffed on his pipe. "Several witnesses remembered seeing a woman enter the train depot, wearing widow's garb. She was the only passenger traveling alone to Fort Worth. It must have been Natalie." Kimball frowned in distaste. "Good God, why would she flit off to an outpost on the very edge of civilization and leave New Orleans behind?" He shuddered at the thought.

"Because she thinks it's the last place we might look for her," Avery predicted. "That chit has always been too smart for her own good, too defiant. No matter how I played up to her, I swear she could see through me."

"I doubt she saw through my pretend interest in her," Kimball commented. "I've fooled countless women in my time."

Avery doubted *that,* but he needed this swaggering cock's help if he was going to lay claim to the Blair fortune.

"We are leaving for Fort Worth on the next train," Avery declared.

Kimball gaped at him in astonishment. "You are joking."

Avery bore down on him. "I'm dead serious and you might find yourself left for dead—or worse—if you don't come along. We made a deal, and the sooner we overtake my belligerent stepdaughter and get the two of you married the sooner we can dispose of her." He smiled nastily. "Since I led the press to believe she has been abducted by a money-hungry maid there is no reason to let that wily little snip live to tell her side of the story."

Mumbling and grumbling, Kimball pivoted on his well-shod heels to gather his luggage for the unwanted trip. "We damn well better find her fast. This is the height of the social season in New Orleans. I do not intend to miss it. There are too many innocent maids ripe for the plucking."

Avery headed upstairs to pack his luggage. He intended to be on the next train headed to Texas. He made a mental note to insist his henchmen, Jenson and Green, accompany him. He had contracted both men specifically because they were short on scruples.

Whatever Natalie was up to, Avery and his hired gunmen would hunt her down. He had spent more than three years slowly but surely poisoning his wife so no one would suspect his involvement in her long-term illness before he took control of the fortune.

"I should have poisoned Natalie instead," he groused as he grabbed a suitcase to fill with clothing. "She is more trouble than her mother ever was."

Two days after Van and Natalie left Wolf Ridge, headed for Nine Mile Station and then to Taloga Springs, Bart lounged on the settee, sipping coffee and recuperating from his injuries. Opal Higgins, the middle-aged female attendant whom Van had hired to run errands for Bart, rapped at the door.

"I brought your newspapers and the mail arrived."

Bart clutched the pistol resting beside his hip. After the goons had attacked him, he had vowed to be more cautious. No telling who might have coerced Opal. Bart wasn't about to let his guard down and be pounced upon again.

"Come in."

Bart relaxed when Opal, the large-boned, square-faced farmer's wife who had been eager to take the temporary job to earn extra money, waddled inside. She set the stack of newspapers and correspondence on the coffee table.

"Will that be all, Mr. Collier?"

The poor woman had the personality of a potted plant, Bart noted. She was the exact opposite of Natalie, who was bewitching, mysterious, intelligent and amazingly difficult for even Van to handle. That amused and disturbed Bart simultaneously. He liked seeing his friend challenged in ways that didn't involve cross-country chases and deadly gunfights. But Natalie's secrecy still bothered him.

"Thank you, Opal. That will be all for today."

Without another word she trooped off, taking his empty breakfast tray with her. Bart checked the mail for possible assignments for Van. Not that Van would accept any for more than a week, since he'd decided to escort his new wife to Taloga Springs and teach her to become self-reliant in the process.

He muttered under his breath when he received a second letter from the Harper Brothers that said, We're coming for you, half-breed. Your days are numbered. It was signed The Harper Brothers.

Grumbling, Bart set aside the intimidating note then picked up the Kansas City newspaper, then one from Houston. He was thumbing through the *Louisiana Gazette* when one particular article leaped out at him.

"Oh damn!" he muttered as his gaze zeroed on the first name that demanded his attention.

Natalie Robedeaux-Blair, heiress to the Blair shipping fortune in New Orleans, has been abducted. Her personal maid is missing and wanted for questioning. Her family is offering a reward for infor-

mation leading to the arrest of the abductors. Miss
Blair's fiance, Thurston Kimball III, has postponed
the wedding scheduled in two weeks. He is desperate
to locate his bride-to-be and pay whatever ransom
necessary to ensure her safe return.

Cursing, Bart half-collapsed against the back of the
couch. "Shipping heiress Natalie *Blair?*" he croaked.

The irony of Donovan Crow married to the heiress who
had more money than God left Bart stunned to the bone.
It took a full minute to wrap his mind around the prospect. Then an uneasy sensation trickled down his spine
and knotted in his belly. What if the supposed Natalie
Blair wasn't the real Natalie Blair at all! Damn it, what
if she had concocted her sad tale of being victimized by
her stepfather and fiancé to gain Van's assistance? What
if she was the *maid* who had stolen the money, disposed
of the heiress and had assumed her identity? What if she
had married Van under false pretenses? What if...?

All sorts of unpleasant scenarios bounced around Bart's
brain. He tried to tell himself that he was leaping to wild
conclusions because he was fiercely protective of Van.
It outraged him to think Natalie—or whoever she really
was—had duped him and Van and had played them both
for gullible fools.

"She damned well better be who she says she is," he
muttered as he shot to his feet. "If not, Van married a
cunning criminal who disposed of a wealthy heiress, stole
her identity and her money and conned *him.*"

With his injured arm cradled in a sling, Bart stalked off
to gather his belongings. He was bound for the stage depot
at Nine Mile Station and on to Taloga Springs, hoping to
intercept Van and warn him to beware.

He wasn't sure how fast Van was traveling by horseback

but if Bart sent a telegram ahead to the city marshal, Van would receive it, he predicted confidently.

Suitcase in hand, Bart took the steps two at a time to reach the lobby. He sent a telegram warning Van of the deceit and informing him of Bart's pending arrival. A half hour later, the morning stagecoach left town—and Bart was on it.

"It's time for our nightly lessons," Van announced after he and Natalie had made camp in an isolated area away from the stage road. "The attack is coming from behind you this time. Use what I showed you last night."

He pounced on her and hooked his arm around her neck. He was pleased to note she was becoming less mechanical in her techniques of blocking him with one hip while doubling over to toss him off balance.

"Again," he insisted. "And don't take it easy on me this time. Pretend this is an honest-to-goodness attack that threatens your life."

"I don't intend to injure my mentor," she said, glancing over her shoulder at him. "What use would you be in your line of work if I broke your arm?"

"What use will you be if you don't survive an attack?" he countered. "Now pretend I'm one of the bastards you despise for manipulating your life."

Van watched with satisfaction when the usual twinkle in her dark onyx eyes became a hard glint. "That's better."

He attacked her without giving her the chance to brace herself. Yet she exploded into action and thrust her hip into him—a little too close to his crotch. His breath came out in a grunt when she lowered her shoulder and toppled him forward. Van hit the ground with a jolting thud that knocked the air out of him.

As he had instructed—repeatedly, each night after they

made camp and practiced self-defense techniques—she snatched his pistol from his holster and held the shiny gun barrel right between his eyes to make certain she had his undivided attention.

When she smiled triumphantly, he knocked aside the pistol, grabbed her by the hair of her head and yanked her down on top of him. He crushed his mouth against hers in a rough assault as he rolled her to her back and sprawled atop her. She squawked beneath his devouring kiss.

"Now what are you going to do, sunshine?" he growled threateningly after finishing the kiss. "You became too cocky after you got the drop on me. Now look where you are. What did I tell you about playing your ace in the hole by hitting a man where he can be hurt the worst? You waited too long to react."

She raised her head and stared up at him with a strange expression on her face.

"Next time don't hesitate," he snapped gruffly.

He was annoyed with her for not reacting effectively, annoyed with himself for being aroused by the feel of her lush body pressed suggestively to his.

"You won't get a second chance if a man decides to molest you. Always expect the worst," he lectured, "and you'll never be caught with your guard down…"

His voice trailed off when she bypassed the chance to deliver a debilitating blow and knock him off her. Instead, she arched up to kiss him tenderly, as if she had the rest of the evening to feast on him—and intended to do just that.

Van cursed himself for responding so fiercely, so instantly to her kiss. Wasn't it enough that these nightly self-defense lessons were murder on him? Did he have to fight nearly overwhelming temptation every blessed night?

"What the hell are you doing?" he demanded when she finally allowed him to come up for air.

Her dark-eyed gaze searched his for a long moment before she said, "I'm not sure."

"Well, you better figure it out. If you think distracting your attackers with kisses will bring them to their knees, think again. They will take you up on an invitation like that so you better prepared to give a man exactly what he wants," he muttered harshly.

"And what do you want, Crow?" she questioned, holding his steady gaze. "Would you pass up the opportunity?"

"What I want is to know why you insist on keeping your identity from me, *Natalie,*" he said unexpectedly. "Or is that another alias?"

Her dark eyes nearly popped from their sockets and her jaw scraped her chest. "How—?"

"You let it slip when I encouraged you to drink that first night. You also mentioned Avery and Thurston. Who are they to you? I've given you a dozen opportunities to tell me the truth but you have refused. Which makes me wonder what you are hiding and why" When she clamped her lips shut and glared at him, Van gestured west. "Go bathe in the creek while I hunt for supper."

She stared at him for another annoyed moment. "You got me inebriated on purpose," she hissed angrily.

"You've lied to me and withheld information so that makes us even," he countered in a sharp tone.

Muttering, she rolled to her feet. She walked away without another word, without a backward glance.

Van blew out a frustrated breath. Well, at least he'd put a stop to her seduction before he caved in. What the devil had gotten into her anyway? he wondered. Was she purposely tormenting him? Well…it had worked. His unruly body was chastising him for rejecting the temptation to turn his fantasies into reality.

And damn it, the more time he spent with her, the more he wanted her—and he hadn't thought it possible to want her more than he had the first night he put her to bed—without taking his own pleasure.

Hell, when had he turned out to be so blasted noble?

Scowling at himself, he strode off. "You are going no farther than Taloga Springs," he told himself as he retrieved his rifle from the scabbard on Durango's saddle. Otherwise, Van was fairly certain his male body was going to burst into flames if he spent too many days with Natalie. Or whoever the hell she was.

He scoffed at the irony of this misadventure. He had gone into the wilderness and he had been tested and tempted to the extreme. *She* was the one who was supposed to be tested. Everything was working exactly backward and he was earning every damned penny she paid him for the use of his name and these maddening survival lessons.

Van blew out an exasperated breath. They had only been on the trail four days and he was so aware of her that he could barely think straight. Even worse, he had insisted they sleep side by side in case trouble came calling. Unfortunately, feeling her warm presence beside him and inhaling her enticing scent the whole livelong night was a dozen kinds of hell. No amount of money was worth depriving himself of what he suddenly wanted more than he wanted his next breath.

Damn it to hell! He wished Durango could sprout wings and fly her to Taloga Springs so he could shoo her on her merry way. Then he could return to his normal life and forget he ever married his secretive—and all too alluring—wife.

* * *

Troubled by the fact that she had unknowingly revealed her first name, as well as Avery and Thurston's, to Crow, Natalie paddled around the stream. Despite her annoyance with him, bathing relieved the aches and pains caused by so many continuous hours in the saddle. Had she known Crow knew her first name, she would have taken the stagecoach and bypassed the survival lessons—and his suspicious questions.

Not to mention her fumbling attempt to seduce him. She rolled her eyes in dismay. What had she been thinking?

Natalie reluctantly admitted that she secretly wanted to experiment with passion since she'd developed this fierce attraction to Crow. She wanted him—and him alone—to teach her about desire. That had not been part of her original plan, but how could she have known she'd find the man so utterly fascinating and wildly irresistible... at least until she learned how he had deviously obtained secret information from her.

No doubt, she was nothing more than another assignment to Crow. He didn't want her the way she had come to want him. It was rather embarrassing to realize she didn't possess enough alluring charm to tempt a man. Not any man, she amended. Just Donovan Crow, damn him!

Natalie groaned quietly. How was she going to face him after that embarrassing little episode...?

Her attention shifted to the movement she noticed in the shadows of the trees. Alarm zinged through her and she tried desperately to remember what Crow had taught her.

Unfortunately, paralyzing fear sent every practical thought flying out of her head when two brawny Indian braves stepped into the clearing. They pointed their rifles directly at her.

Natalie covered herself as best she could—considering she was naked and standing shoulder-deep in the stream. Her clothes and her pistol were draped over the bushes and they might as well have been a hundred miles away for all the good they were doing her now.

Another wave of panic buffeted her as the warriors approached the creek bank. Dear God, what if they had overtaken Crow and he was lying somewhere in a pool of his own blood? What if she was their next victim?

Natalie couldn't restrain herself when one of the men, dressed in buckskins, came toward her, as if he meant to walk into the water and grab her. She screamed bloody murder, yelling, *"Crow!"* at the top of her lungs.

Her life was about to be over before her long awaited adventure began!

"Crow! Help!" she screeched—and quickly forgave him for using underhanded means to ferret out the information he'd wanted from her.

Chapter Seven

Natalie's terrified voice blared into Van's wandering thoughts, sending him racing to the creek with his rifle at the ready. He skidded to a halt and ducked in the bushes when he saw two Comanche braves looming on the stream bank. Although the spring-fed water wasn't completely transparent, it didn't matter. A man's vivid imagination could easily fill in all the enticing details of Natalie's lush feminine body.

Hell! Van thought. His eyes were popping and his tongue was hanging out, so why should he be surprised the warriors were hypnotized by the arousing sight?

Determined to get control of himself, Van rose to his feet. "Stop gaping at my wife," he shouted in the fluent Comanche dialect that he had learned growing up.

The warriors lurched toward him and Van relaxed when he recognized Chulosa and Teskee. He had known them both since childhood and he visited them periodically at the reservation. He wondered if they had permission to leave Indian Territory. If not, they would be in serious trouble with the Indian agent, the military and the Texas Rangers.

"You married a white woman?" Chulosa hooted as he lowered his rifle barrel to the ground.

"Why would you do that?" Teskee wanted to know.

"Long story," Van replied as he approached. "The more important question is why are you two here?"

"I would appreciate it if you could hold this powwow somewhere else so I can bathe and dress," Natalie requested. Her irritated gaze landed squarely on Van. "What are you saying to them?"

Van glanced sideways, wishing he couldn't see her body quite so well in the rippling water. The sight, he was certain, would be burned into his eyeballs for all eternity. Calling upon his willpower, he led the braves uphill to the campsite.

"Why did the woman agree to marry you?" Teskee asked as he sank down cross-legged on Van's pallet.

"She said I was perfect for her," he replied wryly.

Both men glanced, befuddled, at each other then stared pensively at Van.

He flicked his wrist, dismissing the topic of conversation. "Why did you leave the reservation? You know the consequences of being truant."

"We will risk the consequences to find decent food for our people," Chulosa explained. "The meat supplies you sent are gone. The rancid beef the army provides and expects us to eat is unfit for coyotes. Too many people are becoming sick."

"We have come to hunt deer, rabbit and whatever we can find so our people won't go hungry or die," Teskee insisted.

"I sent food and supplies last month," Van reminded them. "How can they be depleted so soon?"

"Some of the soldiers are selling the goods for their own profit," Teskee replied. "They even have scouts keeping watch to alert them when you enter camp so they can be prepared."

Van scowled at the news. "As soon as I escort my wife to Taloga Springs, I'll head to the reservation," he promised.

"We will go with you," Chulosa volunteered. "You will need protection and extra weapons this time. The new lieutenant named Suggs keeps telling his superiors that you should not be allowed to come and go as you please because you are half Kiowa. To an Indian-hater like him, that is the same as a full-blood that should be imprisoned on the reservation."

Damnation, thought Van. Wasn't it enough that the Harper Gang was out for his blood? Now the corrupt military officer wanted him unarmed and confined so he wouldn't pose any threats. Oh, and he couldn't forget the two bastards and their henchmen who might be hunting for Natalie. They wouldn't be pleased to discover she had married Van, who now stood in the way of the men anxious to steal her inheritance—or so Natalie claimed.

Van wondered what else could go wrong with his so-called wedding trip, but he was afraid to ask.

Dressed in her breeches, shirt, vest and boots, Natalie jogged uphill to camp. She'd nearly suffered heart seizure earlier when she'd glanced up to see the Indian warriors looming on the creek bank. She shook her head in self-disgust, for she had forgotten everything Crow taught her. She had yelled his name and screamed bloody murder.

She *should have* taken action.

How did she expect to survive in the wilderness when Crow sent her off on her own?

Her shoulders slumped in frustration when her thoughts circled back to the self-defense lessons from earlier this evening. She hadn't been repulsed when Van kissed her a little too roughly. Sweet mercy, she had been aroused!

What was the matter with her? She should have defended herself, not invited him to continue.

Maybe it was because her attraction to him kept getting the best of her after days of his constant companionship. She had wanted to know what it would be like to share his embrace rather than have him pounce on her so she could practice self-defense techniques.

The fact that she spent every night sleeping next to his muscled body, feeling his reassuring presence, made it seem natural to touch him familiarly. In addition, he was the last person she saw before she fell asleep and the first person she saw each morning. She was too comfortable around him, too satisfied with his appealing presence.

Next thing she knew, she would be incapable of beginning a new day without gazing into those silver-blue eyes and viewing his lopsided smile that did funny things to her pulse and touched her reckless heart.

"You'll be headed for heartache if you don't watch out," she lectured herself sternly as she approached the campsite. "Plus, you can never trust him if he finds out who you are."

Her thoughts flitted away when she heard the murmur of voices, then saw Crow and the two braves sitting cross-legged by the campfire. They were passing around the bottle of whiskey Crow kept in his saddlebags.

Even though she moved quietly toward them, all three men glanced up. She wondered if she would ever learn to be so attentive and aware of her surroundings. *You had darn well better be, Nat,* she told herself. *Otherwise,*

you're liable to wake up dead and ruin your great adven-
ture in the wilderness.

"Sunshine, these Comanche warriors are my friends,"
Crow said in English. "This is Chulosa and Teskee."

Natalie smiled cordially at the two men dressed from
head to toe in buckskin decorated with long fringe. Their
skin was darker than Crow's and their eyes were coal
black. They weren't as tall as Crow, but they were as lean,
muscular and in prime physical condition like Crow.

She walked over to shake their hands but they stared
curiously at her fingertips. Despite their obvious reluc-
tance, she clutched each man's hand and shook it firmly.

"Any friend of Crow's is a friend of mine," she insisted.

The one called Chulosa stared at her with a bemused
frown. "Why did you marry Crow?" he asked in stilted
English. "Could you not find a white man who would have
you?"

She shot Crow a sideways glance, noting that he was
doing his damnedest—and failing miserably—to bite back
a grin.

"No, I couldn't find a white man to suit. I have been
told that I am very difficult. But Crow is perfect for me
in every way. It's a good match."

"Told you," Crow said to his Comanche friends. Then
he glanced at Natalie. "We will hunt supper while you
gather more wood for the fire." He handed her one of his
six-shooters. "We'll signal you by whistling before we
return to camp so don't shoot us by mistake."

When the three men ambled away, Natalie crammed
the pistol into the waistband of her breeches, then headed
back to the tree-choked creek to gather firewood. She
wasn't surprised that she hadn't heard gunfire—that might
draw unwanted guests—before the men returned to camp
carrying two rabbits and a squirrel. She, however, hadn't

mastered the art of pitching stones to bring down potential food for meals. If she didn't stock up on dried beef and canned goods before she forged off alone, she'd starve in a couple of weeks.

While the Comanche warriors skinned the meat, Crow strode off to bathe. Natalie unpacked the tin plates and cups, then made coffee while he was gone.

"Do you have permission to leave the reservation?" she asked Chulosa and Teskee.

The braves shook their heads, sending their dark braids rippling on their shoulders. "Our people need decent food because the soldiers take what is ours," Chulosa said angrily.

"We risked arrest because our families and our clan need untainted food," Teskee added grimly. "Your white soldiers do not care if our tribe dies off. They have poisoned us in the past to reduce our population. They often single out a warrior, who is too vocal about our mistreatment, and claim the reason they gunned him down was because he resisted arrest. No one believes us when we protest the abuse and killings. There is only the white version of the stories."

Natalie detested the thought of anyone being persecuted, tormented and confined. She knew all too well how it felt to be controlled and denied freedom. She couldn't begin to imagine how the Indian tribes felt when white settlers overran their land, poisoned their food and water supplies, slaughtered their livestock and herded them like cattle to reservations to suffer even more atrocity.

Her angry thoughts scattered when the warriors glanced up a moment before she heard Crow's approach. He looked refreshed after his bath and he had chosen to dress exactly like his friends. He glanced at her, as if unsure whether she approved of his fringed buckskins, bone necklace and beaded headband.

The thought that her opinion mattered to him touched her. Impulsively, she walked over to kiss him right smack-dab on the lips. His friends snickered in amusement as they glanced back and forth from her to Crow.

For the life of her, she didn't know why these displays of affection came so easily while she was with Crow. Previously, she spent her time discouraging and thwarting male advances that were designed to court her inheritance, not her personally. Somehow she had managed to convince herself that being *married* to Crow granted her the right to touch him and kiss him anytime she wanted.

It wasn't that she was putting on an act to convince everyone she had feelings for Crow. She *did* have tender feelings for him. She had seen him at his best and worst and she had witnessed his every mood. She swore that, after only a week, she knew him better than she knew her male acquaintances in New Orleans after a year.

"We will leave you alone after the meal so you can join with your husband," Chulosa said as he reached for a slice of the juicy meat.

Natalie's face flushed with heat but she told herself it was her own fault after kissing Crow in front of his friends. Not that she hadn't entertained a dozen thoughts of doing more than sleeping beside Crow. She certainly had. Not to mention that consummating their marriage might make it more difficult for Marsh and Kimball—wherever those two bastards were—to dissolve this union.

However, she had made advances toward Van before the Comanche braves arrived and he had held her at bay and questioned her motives. Her pride was still smarting about that. She never dreamed men turned down sexual gratification, even if they weren't wildly attracted to a woman.

An hour later, the braves made themselves scarce and Crow folded his hand around hers to lead her toward the supplies stacked beside the tethered horses.

"We're going to erect a tent for privacy," he announced. "You need to know how, in case you're in the wilds and a thunderstorm blows in."

Natalie followed his instructions while he showed her how to drape the oversize tarp over a tree limb and then stake down the corners to shield her from the rain.

"It's better than packing a tent that has braces and stakes that you have to repack when you break camp," Crow assured her. "It's important to make use of what is available and travel light so you can break camp and move quickly."

"I'll keep that in mind," she murmured before she used the blunt side of his ax to drive in makeshift stakes.

When Van strode off to fetch their pallet, Natalie glanced up at the dome of stars forming overhead. She wondered how she had survived so long in a crowded city. She might still be a greenhorn with a lot to learn but she had a great appreciation for the outdoors. She wasn't sure she could tolerate confinement again.

The thought made her wince, knowing how daunting it must be for Indian tribes, who had lost their freedom and had been forced to give up sacred ground and their customs to live in the white man's world. Slavery of any kind tormented the soul.

When Crow rejoined her inside the improvised tent, nervousness flittered through her body. They hadn't been alone since she had tried to turn their survival lesson into a seduction—which assured her that she also had a lot to learn in that department, too.

She watched Crow perform his nightly ritual of removing his boot pistol, the derringer inside the waistband of his breeches, a six-shooter and the bowie knife strapped to his ankle. Amusement overrode her unease.

"I swear you carry more hardware than a traveling salesman," she teased, hoping to break the tension.

"We are going to equip you the same way when we reach Taloga Springs," he insisted. "My motto is to be heavily armed and prepared for everything."

"Can't wait," she enthused. "I—"

Without warning, Crow clamped his hand over her mouth. She could feel the tautness in his body. Now what? she thought.

"Stay out of sight," he whispered while he reclaimed all his weapons—including the pistol he'd given to her earlier.

She blinked in surprise when he slithered beneath the back edge of the tarp that was butted up against the tree trunk. Her attention shifted to the sound of galloping horses and the shouted command for the two Comanche warriors to throw down their rifles.

Despite Crow's order to stay inside, Natalie tucked her two-shot derringer in the band of her breeches and crawled outside, bounding to her feet. Campfire light reflected off the three rifle barrels that swerved toward her while she surveyed the ragtag riders. They were dressed in the same fashion as cowboys—or outlaws, it was hard to say which. Sombreros covered their heads and bristly whiskers lined their jaws.

She assumed Crow had crept off, hoping to circle behind the intruders. It seemed sensible for her to provide necessary distraction for him. "You are welcome to share our leftovers from supper," she said cordially. "You can water your horses at the stream while I reheat food."

The dark-haired, hazel-eyed intruder, who looked about Crow's age, stared at her consideringly. Then he glanced at the Comanche warriors who kept their arms over their heads. "Did these truant renegades take you captive, ma'am? If they did, you don't have to fear for your life if you tell me the truth." He inclined his shaggy head toward Teskee and Chulosa. "They crossed the Red River without permission. We received orders to return them to the reservation."

"No, they didn't harm me. They graciously consented to escort me across this rugged country to reach Taloga Springs…. And you are?" she asked, still unsure of their identity.

"Texas Rangers," the second rider, with frizzy red hair and green eyes, spoke up. "We patrol this section of the state."

"Then I should like to see your badges," she insisted.

Reluctantly, they displayed the badges they kept in their vest pockets.

"Why are you riding to Taloga Springs?" the third rider, who had blue eyes, straight blond hair and a thick neck and chest, inquired. "It's a rough place, even for the toughest of men."

"I have my husband for protection," she explained.

The Texas Rangers glanced skeptically at the Comanche braves. Then the dark-haired Ranger asked, "Where is this supposed husband of yours?"

"Right behind you," Van growled ominously as he stepped into view. He held both six-shooters at the ready. "Throw down your weapons and make it snappy. I'm in a lousy mood because you are interrupting my honeymoon."

The startled Texas Rangers tossed aside their rifles and pistols. With hands held high, they twisted in the saddle to face Van, who continued to hold them at gunpoint to protect his Comanche friends from harm.

"Crow?"

"Montgomery," Van acknowledged with a clipped nod to the hazel-eyed, dark-haired Ranger. "Haven't seen you for a while. Didn't miss you much."

Van was acquainted with the three Rangers through several assignments that brought him in contact with their battalion. But he refused to classify them as friends. Although these men weren't directly responsible for the deaths of his clan members, he would never forget the heartache of his tribe, as well as the Comanche, suffered at the hands of the Rangers and the army. These men were aware of the reasons for his cautiousness and standoffish attitude toward them.

"You're married?" the second Ranger—Bristow was his name—hooted incredulously. "To *her?* You are kidding."

"No, he isn't kidding," Natalie said firmly. "Crow is perfect for me. Furthermore, I don't appreciate people doubting my good judgment."

It amused and flattered him that she was his staunch supporter. "Sunshine, I thought I told you to stay in the tent," he reminded her with a pointed glance.

"Did you? I guess I wasn't listening, dear."

She batted her big black eyes and smiled so innocently that it was hard to be aggravated at her for disobeying his direct order. Thus far, she had obeyed his commands to stay put *zero percent* of the time. But to be fair, she had provided the distraction needed for him to get the drop on the intruders who turned out to be Rangers. Like all other men, they became sidetracked by her intelligence and beauty.

Worked every time.

"Now that we are all acquainted," said Phelps, the

blond haired, blue-eyed Ranger who was the oldest of the threesome, "we'd like to climb down and parley with the Comanche."

"Soon as you unload all your hardware, including the concealed weapons," Van insisted, and then rattled off an order in Comanche. "My friends are under my protection until we sort this out."

The warriors strode over to check the Rangers' boots and sleeves to make sure they were unarmed. After confiscating three bowie knives and three derringers similar to Natalie's, the warriors motioned for the Rangers to dismount.

"I'll heat the coffee for our powwow," Natalie volunteered. "I'm sure our guests would like to relax until the food is ready."

"There are problems at the reservation again." Van sat down by the fire to join the Rangers. Teskee and Chulosa completed the circle. "My friends came to hunt meat for their starving families. They also told me about the theft of the food and supplies by soldiers at the fort. Food and supplies that *I* personally provided," he added gruffly. "A Lieutenant Suggs seems to be in charge of the latest theft ring."

He stared stonily at the Rangers. "I don't appreciate thieving soldiers depriving my family and friends of decent food and replacing it with contaminated beef."

"How do you plan to stop the theft ring?" Montgomery questioned, nodding his thanks when Natalie handed him a cup of coffee.

"I'll be paying Suggs a visit after I accompany my wife to Taloga Springs."

Bristow frowned pensively. "That still doesn't excuse your Comanche friends from taking an unannounced leave from the reservation."

Van expelled a caustic snort. "I've heard it said that Rangers make up their rules as they go along. Why can't the Indians who are being starved and mistreated make up a few rules to fit their desperate situation?"

"You have a point." Phelps smiled wryly, then sipped his coffee. "Since you follow the same policy you should join our ranks."

"I've heard rumors that you were being recruited," Bristow commented.

"I've declined," Van announced. "I prefer to pick and chose my assignments."

"For a high price, I hear," Montgomery mumbled enviously. "Maybe I should change my line of work."

"You do that. In the meantime, someone with authority and gumption needs to escort Chulosa and Teskee to the reservation and see that they arrive unharmed...and they stay that way." Van stared pointedly at the Rangers. "Army corruption needs to be reported and stopped. You have the authority to make it happen."

The Rangers nodded in agreement.

"Have to tell you that I've never been thrilled with the army, either," Phelps confided. "We've locked horns with them on policy several times."

"Then it's settled," Van declared. "None of us like the army and its officers, who can't handle their positions of authority without resorting to corruption."

The group was silent for a few minutes while Natalie passed out the reheated meat and stew from supper.

"What's your name, ma'am?" Bristow asked, and then grinned broadly. "I'm guessing it's not really Sunshine."

"No, it's Natalie." She glanced at Van then sat down beside him. "Natalie Jones...Crow."

"Natalie..." Montgomery repeated thoughtfully.

"Didn't our captain mention something about a Natalie Something-Or-Other being abducted?"

Van studied his wife discreetly. He noted the hint of tension in her smile and saw the damnable shadow of secrets in her eyes. He wondered if her stepfather and ex-fiancé were circulating the information in hopes of tracking her down quickly. He also wondered—again—if she had told him the truth.

Another cloud of doubt about her identity filled his mind. He cast it aside, preferring to discuss the matter with Natalie in private. Before the Rangers asked questions he didn't want to answer, Van switched the topic of conversation quickly. "I want to know your specific plans for escorting Chulosa and Teskee across the Red River."

"If you gentlemen will excuse me, I'll retire for the evening." Natalie rose gracefully to her feet. "I'll prepare breakfast before everyone leaves camp in the morning."

Van watched her walk away—and realized the other men were hypnotized by the feminine sway of her hips. Fierce possessiveness assailed him but he told himself that he would have to get used to that. Natalie commanded masculine attention, whether she invited it or not.

"If not for having my wife on this trip, I would detour to the reservation," Van insisted. But he refused to send her to Taloga Springs alone. She wasn't ready to solo in the wilderness. He wasn't ready to turn her loose.

She is still my wife, he reminded himself. *Even if in name only.* The thought prompted the memory of how she had tempted him to the crumbling edge of resistance earlier this evening and how he'd come to crave what he had told himself, repeatedly, he shouldn't have...

"Is that agreeable, Crow?"

Van scowled. "Repeat that, please. I was thinking about something else."

All five men grinned as they glanced directly at the tent and then back at Van.

Montgomery said, "Gee, can't imagine what that something else might be. By the way, your wife is one of the most attractive women I've had the good fortune to meet."

The other men nodded in agreement. Van sighed inwardly. Marrying a gorgeous woman with secrets in her past and adventure in her soul was more than a man could handle. Yet, Van liked having her underfoot…but not as much as he'd like to have her all to himself in bed…

The wayward thought made him squirm as desire channeled through his body. He tried to pay attention to the plan the Rangers mapped out for the trip to the reservation. But it took some doing.

Chapter Eight

Natalie managed to get only a smidgeon of sleep that night. But having Crow's inviting warmth beside her and fretting about the circulating report of her so-called abduction made her anxious. There was no telling what scheme Marsh had hatched in his attempt to track her down.

Obviously, her stepfather had left no stone unturned and spared no expense. The far-reaching report would make it difficult to travel any direction without concern for her safety. She presumed Marsh had offered a reward for information.

Money he planned to pay from my inheritance if he manages to get his greedy hands on it, she thought bitterly.

The next morning, preoccupied with thoughts of Marsh and Kimball, Natalie nodded a greeting to the Rangers, who had bedded down at the camp site. She scurried around, building a campfire according to Crow's specifications and preparing breakfast—also as Crow had taught her. At least she had mastered a few skills, she congratulated herself. Now, if she could cease depending on Crow in times of danger she might make real headway.

"Where did you say you called home?" Montgomery, the hazel-eyed, dark-haired Ranger, asked when she approached him.

Natalie thought fast. "Natchez, Mississippi." It was where Marsh had sent her to a private college and where she had taught school for a time. "I came west to visit my aunt in San Antonio, then I met Crow," she lied convincingly. "It was love at first sight."

Montgomery arched a thick brow, then shrugged. "Whatever you say, ma'am. With Crow's legendary reputation, you shouldn't have to fret about your safety. Not too many people dare to cross him."

Those were her thoughts exactly.

Bristow, the Ranger with curly red hair, green eyes and an engaging smile said, "When Rangers descend on outlaws, we bring hell with us. Crows brings his own special brand of hell, I'm told. Which is why the soldiers who are cheating the Comanche and Kiowa have reason to fear him."

"Crow cares very deeply about his clan and the tribes who raised him." She glanced into the distance to see Crow diligently brushing down Durango before tossing a saddle on his back. "This Suggs character will answer for his corruption. Indeed, I will do all within my power to see him court-martialed and tossed in jail."

And she would, too. There were advantages to being a Robedeaux and Blair. She would pull a few political strings to stop the fraud and abuse against the Indians who raised Crow.

Montgomery chuckled. "Did you become an advocate for Indians after you married Crow?"

"No, I strongly support any group of people subjected to domination and abuse," she clarified. "Women also fall into that category, Mr. Montgomery. I don't want to see anyone restrained or cheated."

The Rangers lifted their cups for refills. Natalie poured coffee then stared questioningly at them. "Have any of you heard news about the Harper Gang that escaped jail recently?

Phelps shrugged a thick shoulder. "Nothing conclusive. I assume you're asking because they swore vengeance against Crow."

"I care a great deal about my husband," she assured them. "I intend to protect him from harm by all means necessary."

The Rangers stared skeptically at her. They didn't seem to think that, being a woman, she could protect anyone from anything. But they also didn't consider a man in Crow's line of work valued marriage material. Well, they were wrong. She meant it when she said Crow was perfect for her.

An hour later, the Comanche braves and the Rangers rode north. Natalie hurried off to dismantle the improvised tent and gather her belongings. Crow smiled approvingly when she strapped the supplies and luggage behind her saddle.

"Very efficient, sunshine. You receive high marks for preparing breakfast and packing up to move out."

She smiled in response to his praise—which he offered sparingly. "I had an excellent instructor." She swung into the saddle to head toward Nine Mile Station and on to Taloga Springs. "As much as I relish living as one with nature, I'll admit I'm yearning for the comfort of a soft bed and relaxing in a real bathtub that isn't filled with fish and the occasional snake."

She glanced over to see those silver-blue eyes fixed on her. The intensity of his gaze startled her.

"I appreciate your kind words about me to Monty and the other Rangers and your support for my people. And your intent to protect me from harm. Bart is the only one who thinks I'm worth the effort."

"I *know* you're worth the effort," she said before she trotted through the trees.

"Wrong way, sunshine," he called to her, grinning. "Remind me to purchase a compass the first chance I get. You've picked up several survival skills very quickly. But you have no sense of direction whatsoever."

Apparently not, she thought to herself. She was headed in the direction of heartache because Crow's presence in her life and his endearing grin were getting to her in more ways than she could count.

Avery Marsh, followed by Kimball and the two hired henchmen, stepped down from the train in Wolf Ridge. He was tired, irritable and annoyed that Natalie, dressed in her widow's digs, had reportedly took the train west from Fort Worth to this godforsaken outpost where the railroad tracks finally ran out.

Kimball surveyed the community with distaste. "They call this a town? What do people do with themselves here?"

"Raise cattle, plow the ground and run shops," Fred Jenson, the tall, lean henchman, replied. "For entertainment they play billiards and cards in the saloons."

Kimball perked up. "Maybe this whistle stop has possibilities after all." He glanced back at Avery. "While you check on Natalie I'll wet my whistle at a saloon and see if I can make extra traveling money."

Avery glared at Kimball's departing back. The man was self-absorbed and as useless as an extra toe. However, having him out from underfoot for an hour had its rewards.

The cocky dandy bragged about his sexual exploits constantly and droned incessantly about how clever and intelligent he was. There had been times during the journey that Avery contemplated *losing* Kimball permanently—after he'd served his purpose, of course.

Glancing this way and that, Avery determined which hotel accommodations would suffice then hiked down the street to the Simon House. While Jenson and Green posed questions at the restaurants, in hopes of locating Natalie, Avery approached the hotel clerk.

"I was hoping to meet my daughter here," Avery said pleasantly. "She dressed as a young widow for her protection but she has dark eyes and auburn hair."

The clerk nodded enthusiastically. "You are talking about Anna Jones, aren't you? So you must be Mr. Jones."

"I must be," Avery said, flashing his most charming smile. "Can you tell me which room she's in?"

The clerk looked at him oddly. "She didn't inform you that she left town after she married Donovan Crow?

Married? To Donovan Crow? *The* Donovan Crow? Hell's bells! Avery had not seen that coming. Now he would have to alter his well-laid plans. Damn that wily little bitch. He'd make her sorry she'd pitted herself against him. Avery had spent a lifetime planning golden opportunities for himself and he was damn good at it. Natalie would not outsmart him.

"I thought she was going to wait for me to show up," Avery said, masking his irritation behind a troubled frown. "I was hopelessly delayed and she is hopelessly impetuous. Now I'll have to trail after her."

The blond-haired, round-faced clerk swiveled the hotel registry toward Avery. "You'll need a room because I heard they are headed to Taloga Springs and the next stage doesn't leave until tomorrow morning."

* * *

Two days after the Rangers and Comanches headed north, Van saw Natalie gathering inedible vegetation on the riverbank. "Don't touch that!" Van snapped abruptly.

She snatched her hand away from the green plant as if she'd been snakebit. When she flashed him an injured look, he regretted his sharp tone.

"I only wanted to gather wild carrots for supper," she explained as she rose from a crouch, then sidestepped from the marshy area near the water.

"Those aren't wild carrots." Van examined the handful of herbs she had picked. He tossed out two other plants. "The plants you nearly pulled from the marsh were poison hemlock."

Wide-eyed, she gaped at him. "They looked like carrots."

He nodded. "Yes, they do. Which is why people unfamiliar with these plants suffer accidental poisoning."

"What are the other plants I thought were herbs?"

"Nightshade," he informed her. "The hemlock is worse. Make sure your horse doesn't ingest that stuff, because it can be fatal to him as well as to you. As children in the village, one of our duties was to herd our horses away from the marshy creek banks to avoid poisonous plants."

Natalie's shoulders slumped dejectedly and she blew out her breath. "I'll never figure all this out," she mumbled. "I wanted to prepare a special meal because you said we'll reach Taloga Springs tomorrow and we'll part company."

The thought didn't set well with him. He could escort Natalie only as far as Taloga Springs. Then he needed to follow up at the reservation and investigate the army officer accused of stealing food and supplies from his people. He was torn between his hungry desire for Natalie and his loyalty to the tribe that raised him.

"Here," he said, refusing to dwell on the moment when they went their separate ways. "These wild carrots and mushrooms are edible."

"Thank you," she murmured. "I didn't intend to repay you for all your trouble by poisoning you." She glanced up quickly and frowned. "What are the symptoms of poisoning? I suppose I should know, in case I accidentally pick the wrong plants in the future."

"Nervousness, trembling, convulsions, dilated eyes," he told her. "It's best to empty the stomach as quickly as possible. Otherwise…" His voice trailed off, allowing her to draw her own grim conclusions. "Other poisons have different symptoms such as muscle weakness, dizziness, severe headache and confusion."

He noticed the ponderous frown that claimed her lovely features. "Something wrong, sunshine?"

"Dear God!" she erupted abruptly. "I never gave that a thought!"

"Never gave what a thought?"

"That bastard!" Muttering and scowling, she stamped back and forth on the sandy ridge above the river. "Why didn't I suspect that? I should have."

"Would you mind telling me what you're talking about?"

"That's how he did it."

"*Who* did *what?*" Van demanded impatiently.

She wheeled around, her dark eyes burning with fury. "My stepfather. I swear he slowly but surely poisoned my mother. She began complaining of headaches and weariness a year after their marriage. I was too young and ignorant to question Mama's failing health. I thought she'd become unhappy and lost the will to live when she realized Marsh was a poor substitute for my father, even if theirs hadn't been a love match."

Natalie lurched around to pace in the opposite direction. "Hell and damnation, I should have questioned her illness instead of accepting it as easily as she did. My stepfather claimed he had consulted several doctors in town, but I'm willing to bet he didn't. In addition, he bustled me off to boarding school, claiming my mother wouldn't take time to rest if she thought I needed her attention."

"I'm sorry, Nat," he commiserated. "If you want me to investigate I will…. Where do you call home?"

She shook her head vehemently then wiped the tears dribbling down her cheeks with the back of her had. "No. It's too late for Mama. I just want to put the past to rest."

Van was suspicious of her refusal to tell him she hailed from New Orleans like she did the night she was drunk. He didn't understand why she wouldn't want him to investigate if she suspected foul play. There was far more to her story than she let on and he was beginning to wonder how much was truth and how much was fiction she invented to protect her mysterious identity and her past.

Natalie drew herself up and inhaled a deep breath. "I'll start a fire and clean the wild vegetables that aren't poisonous," she insisted before she hiked uphill.

Van watched her walk away, curious whether the report of abduction related to her, wondering what it would take to gain her confidence. He asked himself what his life would be like when she rode away, now that he'd become accustomed to having her with him constantly. By tomorrow, she would exit his life as quickly as she had arrived.

Emotions he didn't want to confront kept playing tug-of-war inside him. Not to mention the unappeased desire he'd kept on a short leash. Sleeping beside Natalie night after tormenting night, without yielding to nearly overwhelming temptation, was wearing him out.

Frustrated, Van stamped off to find wild game for

supper. And afterward, he considered resorting to peyote to numb his senses and put himself into a deep sleep without those arousing fantasies hounding him. However, that would leave Natalie vulnerable if trouble came calling—as it had a nasty habit of doing in the badlands of Texas.

"Why did I agree to this marriage?" he asked himself. "Oh yeah, now I remember. This was supposed to be the easiest money I ever made. Now there's a laugh."

Van didn't see a damn thing easy about wanting Natalie Whoever-She-Was with a burning need that refused to go away, even while he was taking nightly cold baths in the creeks and streams. His willpower was fading and it was difficult to keep his distance from her. Worse yet, the biggest threat he had to face was protecting her against *himself.*

"*Easy* money?" he grumbled. "Like hell it is!"

The disturbing suspicion that Avery Marsh might have poisoned her mother tormented Natalie to no end. Preparing the campfire and the evening meal wasn't enough to take her mind off the infuriating thought. She'd told Crow that she didn't want him to investigate—because she didn't want him to know who she really was. However, she intended to find out if her suspicions were true. Avery Marsh was not getting away with murder! She'd like to poison *him* and see how he liked it.

Emotions roiled inside her as she ate her evening meal, then walked down to the river to clean the dishes. It was bad enough that she was upset over Marsh's possible cruelty. That, combined with the tormenting thought of bidding farewell to Crow the following day, tortured her beyond measure.

She glanced downstream where Crow bathed. The impulsive urge to join him and end the suspense of wondering what it would be like to share his passion overwhelmed her.

Natalie turned away, but the tantalizing prospect of seeing Crow naked and touching him intimately leaped to mind once more. "Well, he *is* your husband," she muttered at herself. "You are entitled to other benefits besides seeing his name on the marriage license."

Her thoughts circled back to Marsh's betrayal and roiling anger assailed her again. Her mother had wasted away, thanks to Marsh's cruelty. Her father had died in an accident at the wharf at a young age. It seemed that living in the moment was the best policy because who knew what tomorrow held?

And what *she* wanted at the moment was to be with Crow in ways she had never experienced.

She lurched around to make a beeline for the river. She lost her nerve momentarily when she saw Crow standing hip-deep in the river, staring directly at her. His raven hair dripped water and his bare chest sparkled with droplets that reflected the colorful rays of sunset. He reminded her of a mythical god, luring her ever closer to impossible temptation.

When she began unbuttoning her shirt, his hand—clamped around a bar of soap—stalled in midair. "What are you doing?"

"Undressing to bathe. I've reached a decision."

"That's nice. Let's discuss it in camp in about fifteen minutes. Now go find your own place to bathe."

She removed her cap and shook out her hair. With her shirt hanging open, she heel-and-toed out of her boots. Then she unfastened her breeches.

Crow thrust up his hand to forestall her. "This is not a good idea, sunshine."

"Yes, it is," she retorted. "I hired you to teach me to

survive in the wilds. Now I want to hire you to teach me about passion."

Crow's striking silver-blue eyes bugged out and his clean-shaven jaw scraped his chest. She hadn't seen him that shocked since she breezed into the Road To Ruin Saloon to announce she was his fiancée.

Natalie was in no mood to be rejected again. It would be the crowning blow to a lousy evening. Already, her emotions were churning like a cyclone. Although she wasn't sure how to entice a man past his ability to resist, she intended to try because Crow was the only man she had ever desired.

"You better rethink this reckless decision," he told her gruffly. "I'm—"

His voice halted when her breeches pooled around her feet. Her boyish shirt barely covered her upper thighs and she was pleased to note that he was all eyes. *Well, at least I have his undivided attention,* she thought. *That's a start.*

"I might not be your first choice, but I have certain wifely rights, you know, Crow."

"Wh—" He tried to speak but no words came out.

Natalie gathered her nerve and did something she had never done in front of a man. She peeled off her shirt and walked naked into the water. Although she felt extremely self-conscious and her face pulsed with heat, she vowed Crow wouldn't dismiss her easily.

She wanted him and she meant to have him—just this once before he rode out of her life for good.

And who knew? Her first and only night with Crow might turn out to be the greatest adventure of all. He was not going to distract her or talk her out of it, either. Anyway, this was no different from a man visiting a brothel to appease his needs. Why would Crow turn down free sex with a wife he wouldn't have to bother with after tomorrow?

"You are absolutely certain this is what you want?" Crow chirped as she walked boldly toward him.

"I'm certain or I wouldn't be here," she said, amazed that she could still speak.

She was pleased when his unique-colored gaze roamed hungrily over her. She decided he liked what he saw well enough. His rapt attention bolstered her confidence and she even managed to toss him a flirtatious smile.

"I suppose I should negotiate with you first. Just how much extra is this lesson in love going to cost?" she asked.

She nearly melted into a puddle of mush when Crow flashed a rakish grin that encompassed every bronzed feature of his face.

"A thousand is my going rate."

"A thousand?" she smirked, delighting in the playful side of his nature—one he didn't expose very often. "How many women have hired you for lessons in passion?"

"Counting you?"

She nodded as she drew close enough to glide her hands over his broad shoulder and link her fingers behind his neck. "Yes, counting me."

He hooked his arm around her waist and drew her intimately against him. She knew without a doubt that she had aroused him. The intimate knowledge filled her with even more self-confidence. It emboldened and empowered her.

"Just you, sunshine," he growled huskily as his head came steadily toward hers. "Only you…"

His mouth came down on hers in a devouring kiss. Natalie gave herself up to the ravenous need sizzling through her body and whispering in her soul. She had made the right choice when she selected Donovan Crow

as her lawfully wedded husband. Furthermore, she wanted
to go on kissing him until the end of time because he had
the power to scatter every thought from her mind. That's
what she wanted right now. Not to think at all. To explore
the fierce sensations she'd discovered when she was with
the one man who tempted her beyond bearing.

Van knew he shouldn't succumb to the mercy of his ravenous desire for Natalie. Unfortunately, she had stunned
him to the bone and destroyed his thought processes when
she undressed and walked naked into the water to join
him.

His imagination hadn't done her justice because she
was flawless perfection. He wanted to make a feast of her,
but he wasn't sure how long he would be satisfied tasting
the honeyed nectar of her dewy-soft lips and gliding his
hands over the lush curves and swells of her body.

"So this is what desire feels like," she rasped as he
lifted his head to drag in much-needed air.

His restless hands continued to caress her. He only
hoped he could arouse her to the same fervent degree that
she had aroused him. "How far do you want this to go,
sunshine?" he asked, his voice rough with unappeased
need.

Curly lashes swept up and she smiled impishly at him.
The intriguing sparkle in her eyes caused a chunk of his
heart to break loose and tumble down his rib cage.

"How much passion will a thousand dollars buy me?"

He smiled roguishly. "All you want and then some."

He scooped her into his arms so that her body bobbed
on the water's surface, glowing like gold in the shimmering light of sunset.

"And then some is what I want with you, Crow."

Her smile faded as she stared intently at him. Her hand

lifted to trace the line of his jaw, and then his lips. Van felt a jolt of pleasure rivet his body. He brought his head to hers for a tender kiss. He wanted to make this experience with Natalie a moment to remember because he knew it would be his first and last. She would be gone tomorrow. He would have served his purpose for her and she would no longer need him for whatever her secretive venture required.

He also knew the suspicion of losing her mother to deliberate poisoning had upset her and had sent her running to him for comfort and compassion. He shouldn't take advantage of her vulnerability, but when he touched her his noble intentions went up in smoke.

"I'll ask once more. Are you sure this is what you want?" he repeated huskily, knowing he'd burn into a pile of molten coals if she changed her mind.

"It's exactly what I desire." She traced the bridge of his nose and his high cheekbones. "And keep in mind that I do nothing halfway or halfheartedly, Crow."

He grinned. He adored that about her, especially right now. She had made up her mind she wanted him and he couldn't talk her out of it, even if he wanted to, which he didn't.

For his part, Van wanted her in a way that he'd never realized it was possible to want anyone or anything in his life. She mattered to him. He desired her past the point of his resistance. Come hell or high water—or both—he was going to discover what paradise on Earth felt like. And she was it.

If Natalie asked for the moon and a few stars, he'd find a way to fetch them for her. He was that far gone. He was at the complete mercy of his throbbing desire to claim her as his own for this one magical night before she followed her dreams and schemes and walked out of his life forever.

Van vowed to make their passionate tryst an adventure unto itself. No matter how much it cost him in self-restraint, he would find a way to pleasure and satisfy her.

To that dedicated end, Van skimmed his lips over the tips of her breasts while she floated in his arms. Her soft moan of pleasure encouraged him to draw more satisfied sounds from her lips. He devoted several languid moments to flicking his tongue against her pebbled nipples, then cupped one full breast in his hand. When he suckled her gently, she arched toward him. Another breathless sigh tumbled from her lips—with his name attached to it.

He adored the raspy sound of her voice. He delighted in knowing he aroused her. He smiled against her nipple when she squirmed restlessly against him. Her hand drifted across his chest but he grabbed her fingertips and redirected them to her breast. Then he nibbled at them before he suckled her again.

"Don't distract me. I've been harboring this fantasy of discovering the taste and feel of every inch of your gorgeous body since the night I put you in my bed after you passed out. That evening didn't turn out the way I wanted."

Her thick lashes fluttered up and she stared straight at him. "You find me desirable?"

He chuckled at the absurd question. "One look in the mirror should answer the question about how lovely you are."

"But there have been times when I've wondered if I appeal to men or if…"

Her voice trailed off and he wondered if she was about to mention instances with other men. The image of her with anyone but him tormented him, though he kept telling himself he had no right to be possessive or jealous of her past affairs. After all, he had been intimate with other women. Of course, no one had intrigued him as she had, but still…

"You have no idea how much it has cost me in self-control to sleep beside you every night and restrain myself," he admitted. "Which is why I couldn't turn you down tonight. I have no willpower left when it comes to you."

"None whatsoever?" She grinned so provocatively that another corner of his heart caved in. "Are you just saying that because I'm paying you?"

"Sure, sunshine. I want you to get your money's worth," he whispered as his hand drifted down her ribs to encircle her navel.

Her playful amusement turned to a quiet moan when his hand drifted lower to trace the curve of her inner thigh. Fire blazed through Van's bloodstream when he skimmed his hand over the tender flesh between her legs and felt the heat of her desire burning for him.

He bent his head to glide his tongue between her lips at the same moment that he dipped his finger into her heated core. A tidal wave of need crashed over him as he stroked her gently—and simultaneously aroused himself to aching extremes. He vowed to leave Natalie as hot and hungry for him as he was for her…but at what cost to his ravenous body!

Van had never dedicated so much time to pleasuring a woman. He'd never wanted to because the women who came and went from his bed in the past only satisfied a physical craving. But this mystical moment with Natalie, while the blazing sunset turned the world to flames, was nothing like his previous encounters. He couldn't take his pleasure with her unless she wanted him beyond bearing.

The thought challenged him to be more creative, to be gentler and more patient in his seduction than he'd ever been. He was rewarded with the sound of her breathless moans drifting across the rippling water.

"Come here," she panted while he stroked her with thumb and fingertip.

"I told you not to rush me," he murmured against the swell of her breast. "I'm living a fantasy."

"You're driving me crazy is what you're doing," she whimpered as her body involuntarily arched toward his gliding fingertips and lips.

"Really? Then let's see how you react to this…." He lifted her hips to him, flicked at her with his tongue, then kissed her intimately.

She came apart in his arms, trembled beneath his lips and fingertips. She cried out his name as her body shuddered around his hands and mouth. Gasping for breath, she twisted to hook her legs around his hips.

Van was smiling at her in supreme satisfaction, for he knew he had pleasured her immensely. But when she curled her hand around his aroused flesh and guided him to her, he forgot to breathe—and couldn't remember why he needed to.

He arched instinctively toward her as his hands settled on her hips. He drove into her without restraint and watched her eyes fly wide open. He stilled when he breached the fragile barrier that assured him that he was her first experiment with intimate passion. For certain, Natalie was his first time with a woman's first time.

The knowledge brought him to his senses long enough to call upon his nearly depleted reservoir of restraint. Despite the ardent need that demanded that he drive relentlessly into her until he found wild release, he withdrew—and it nearly killed him.

"Crow…" she murmured as she held his gaze and

hooked her hands behind his head. "Don't stop doing what you're doing."

"Don't really want to, sunshine," he replied, barely recognizing his voice, for it was hoarse with need. "Just trying to give you time to adjust to…well…to me."

She nuzzled her forehead against his, then brushed his lips lightly with hers. "You're sweet, but—"

Her voice dried up when he drove himself to the hilt, then retreated to plunge into her silken body again and again. He wanted to tell her that he wasn't the least bit sweet and there was nothing gentle about the ardent needs pounding through him in that desperate moment. His body had taken command and he was hopelessly out of control.

With each frantic thrust, he felt passion's flames scorching him inside and out. Then the fires of overwhelming desire consumed him. He clutched her so tightly in his arms that he feared he'd suffocate her when he shuddered in all-consuming release.

Sweet mercy! Van thought as he gasped for breath— and found none forthcoming. But then, if he stopped breathing altogether and died in the circle of Natalie's arms while he was buried deep inside her, he couldn't think of a better way to go.

The realization that nothing in his vast experiences in life remotely compared to sharing Natalie's innocent passion nearly brought him to his knees. It was unsettling, considering this was the last night they would be together. He could never recapture the incredible sensations and the previously untapped emotions she had unleashed inside him.

He'd found the passion of a lifetime, even if it could only last one night. He smiled ruefully as he rubbed his chin against the elegant curve of her neck. He remembered how Bart had questioned his rash decision to marry

Natalie when he knew so little about her and hadn't had time to confirm her story. But being this close to her, holding her possessively in his arms and knowing that nothing else compared to this moment with her seemed worth whatever repercussions he might face.

"Crow?" she murmured against his chest.

"Yes, sunshine?"

"How much will it cost me to do this again tonight?"

He chuckled as he brushed a feathery kiss against her satiny cheek. "As it happens, I'm running a two-for-the-price-of-one special this evening."

"Well, in that case…"

When she reached down to cup him in her hand and stroke him intimately, desire exploded inside him in the blink of an eye. Van scanned the area near the riverbank to make sure they were still alone then he forgot everything he ever knew because she led him ashore to make a thorough study of him. She was careful to veer away from the marshy area where hemlock grew before she urged him onto a makeshift pallet of her discarded clothing.

It didn't take her long to discover that every experimental touch of her hands and lips drove him one step closer to crazy. His last thought, as he drew her down on top of him then buried himself deeply in her honeyed warmth, was that his bewitching wife might still be a novice at surviving in the wilds but she excelled in passion.

And there, beneath a canopy of twinkling stars and the whisper of the breeze rustling in the leaves of overhanging trees, Donovan Crow discovered defeat for the first time in years. He had surrendered to Natalie Whoever-She-Was without putting up a fight…and he loved every erotic moment of it.

Chapter Nine

Natalie awoke the next morning with a satisfied smile on her face, though she felt a mite tender in a few unfamiliar places. Not that she was complaining. The previous evening spent in the river, on the riverbank and in the shelter of their improvised tent—where she devised a few more techniques to pleasure Crow—had been incredible. Plus, *he* had taught *her* things about her body—and herself— that she hadn't known.

She wouldn't have waited a single day to consummate their marriage if she had known Crow was so tender and skilled at teaching her about passion. She would like to rewind time so she could spend every night sampling the erotic delights Crow had unveiled to her.

He had restrained her from completely discovering every corded tendon, muscled plane and masculine contour of his magnificent body. Now she would never have the chance to pleasure him as much as he had pleased her.

Stretching leisurely, she glanced sideways to note that Crow had left their pallet. Today was no different from any other day, she reminded herself. He was always the first to rise. He reconnoitered the area, tended the horses and built the campfire.

Natalie drew in a deep breath, enjoying the smell of smoke that drifted from the fire. She had also come to appreciate sitting by the fire, watching the hypnotic flames dance in the darkness. She had never experienced anything like it at home in New Orleans. She had been deprived of so many simple pleasures of being one with nature—and with the magnificent silver-blue-eyed warrior she had married.

Reluctant to leave the warm pallet, Natalie sat upright to rake her hands through the tangled auburn strands that tumbled over her shoulders. She grabbed the neatly folded garments Crow thoughtfully left for her and got dressed. When she stepped outside, Crow was hunkered beside the campfire, turning the prairie chicken that roasted over the flames.

When he glanced sideways, awkwardness bombarded her. There were no secrets between them now...well, except for that gigantic secret—about being the heiress to a shipping fortune—that she'd purposely kept from him.

His gaze roamed possessively over her and she blushed. He knew how she looked naked and how easily he could arouse her to the heights of breathless passion. He knew how wildly she responded to his tender kisses and intimate caresses.

Despite the beet-red blush staining her cheeks, she strived to appear nonchalant. She knew she hadn't pulled it off because a knowing smile quirked his lips.

"Feeling okay, sunshine?"

She forced a dazzling smile and shifted nervously from one booted foot to the other. "Sure, and you?"

"No complaints."

Well, this was uncomfortable. But she would never regret the night she had spent with Crow and she refused to let self-conscious feelings spoil her last day with him.

"I have no regrets whatsoever," she blurted out as she walked over to pour herself a cup of coffee.

He stared at her for a long, silent moment. "You sure about that?"

"Positively certain. Which reminds me…how much do I owe you? Another thousand?" She set aside her coffee cup, then reversed direction to reenter the tent and retrieve her money.

When she walked back to him, she playfully grabbed his hand and laid the money in his palm. "Paid in full, Crow. A pleasure doing business with you," she said in a playful tone.

He frowned as he stared at the bank note, then handed it back to her. "That won't be necessary. The pleasure was all mine. But mind telling me how you came to have these large-denomination bills?"

She inwardly winced, then mustered an impish grin. "Robbed a bank."

"Interesting. Come to think of it, you paid for my name on the marriage license with large denominations, too. And you do seem to have an endless supply of funds with you." His wary gaze zeroed in on her. "I heard a thief struck the railroad near Fort Worth recently. That wasn't you, was it, sunshine?"

She batted her eyes at him and drawled. "Of course not, dear. I've been saving up for this trip west for a long time."

Despite her playful tone, he continued to stare skeptically at her with those penetrating silver-blue eyes. Then he refocused on the large bank note. Curse it, she should have asked the banker for smaller bills when she made the withdrawal from her account. She had been careless and Crow was nothing if not a well-trained detective who asked all sorts of probing questions when his curiosity was aroused—as it was now.

She dropped a kiss on his lips, hoping to distract him. It must have worked because he said, "We are three or four hours from Taloga Springs." He put meat and bread on her tin plate, then handed it to her. "It's a tough place because it sits near the cattle trail to Dodge City. Cowboys ride into town to blow off steam at night. Gamblers and grifters hover around to prey on the drovers. Most of the women in town are paid by the hour. Cattlemen in the area are constantly feuding with each other over free range, water rights and missing calves. Fights break out on a regular basis so pay attention to what's going on around you."

"I'm not planning to remain in town but one night," she assured him between bites. "I'll catch the stagecoach to Dodge City to see what a real cow town is like before I head to Colorado to view the mountains. I plan to make use of my widow's digs, just as I did during my trip to Wolf Ridge."

"Just don't expect to be spared from robbery if your coach is stopped," he warned as he eyed her somberly. "I don't know how much money you still have stashed in your clothing but if you are too protective of your satchels, thieves will become suspicious and turn your luggage inside out."

Natalie inwardly cringed at the prospect of losing the Robedeaux-Blair jewels, some of which had been trans-ported from France with the original family when heads rolled during the revolution.

"I assume from the look on your face there is more money tucked away. Otherwise, you couldn't afford this cross-country adventure. Am I right?" he questioned intently.

"I do have a stash to support myself until I decide where to settle down and find a job," she hedged, hoping to dissolve his suspicions. "But it is true that my business dealings with you have diminished my funds."

"Sorry, but I don't—"

"Work cheap," she finished for him. "I know." She couldn't quite meet his gaze when she added, "You were worth the price, Crow."

"Glad to be of help. Client satisfaction is important." He rose to his feet to pour leftover coffee on the fire. "Time to pull up stakes and pack our belongings. The road near Taloga Springs can be dangerous for travelers so we will parallel the path as much as possible. The town isn't called Hell's Fringe for nothing."

Natalie swallowed the last bite of her breakfast, then spread out the glowing coals so they would burn out quickly. She gathered the dishes and headed to the river to wash them while Crow packed away the makeshift tent.

Although he was friendly enough this morning, he had distanced himself from her. She wondered if that was how men dealt with women after a casual evening tryst. Well, he needn't try to discourage her from hanging all over him, she mused irritably. After all, she did not intend to demand more of him than she had asked last night.

"What did you expect, fool?" she chastised herself as she practically scrubbed the finish off the coffee pot and tin plates. "That Crow would fall at your feet and declare undying love for you after your tryst?"

It would have been nice, she thought. At least then, she would have known there was something interesting and attractive about her that appealed to him besides the fact that she was female and she had made herself available to him. At least she hadn't had to wonder if he was attracted to her fortune. That was a first for her.

"You're a fine one to talk about caring for a man, just for himself, after the bargain you struck with Crow," she grumbled at herself. "You made the mistake of liking him a little too much—"

"Talking to yourself, are you, sunshine?"

Natalie was so startled by the sound of his voice that she pitched toward the river—and would have taken a swan dive into the water if Crow hadn't grabbed the nape of her shirt to steady her.

"Do not sneak up on me, damn you," she snapped as she struggled to bring her racing heartbeat under control—and prayed he hadn't heard what she had said about him.

"Sorry. Sneaking up on people is part of my job." He hoisted her to her feet and helped her scoop up the dishes. "I'm told that I excel in sneaking."

There was something about the way he stared at her that caused alarm bells to clang in her mind. The look in his eyes was even more remote and distant than it had been at breakfast. Arousing Crow's suspicion was dangerous business. She'd give anything to know what he was thinking.

She pasted on a casual smile, hoping to mask her growing concern. "Something wrong, Crow?"

"You tell me, sunshine."

"Not a thing I can think of," she said breezily. "Let's mount up and ride. I'm anxious to see what the fringes of hell look like."

She didn't glance back at him, just strode uphill. But she could feel the icy weight of his gaze on her. He had been acting strangely since she'd teasingly handed him the money this morning and he'd returned it. As much as she yearned to have Crow with her indefinitely, she knew it was time to part company. He was posing questions about her past—and her endless money supply—that she was afraid to answer.

Although she was falling in love with him, he was a man, and men always had their own agendas. Therefore, she couldn't trust him completely. Love him? Yes. Trust him not to betray her for her fortune? No. Definitely not.

If Van hadn't spent years perfecting and maintaining a carefully controlled neutral expression he would have been spewing curses that would turn the air purple. It was bad enough that he was leading the way through canyon country—and had to deal with the bittersweet memories of his childhood home. Those haunting visions from his past never failed to sour his disposition. All he had to do was close his eyes and the sights and sounds of those hellish days when the Rangers attacked and the army brutally slaughtered their livestock and *accidentally* killed a few men, women and children caused tormenting resentments to bubble to the surface.

To make matters worse, Natalie's mysterious riches sent up warning flags in his mind. He recalled the large bills she had paid him earlier for signing the marriage license. At the time, he had been too distracted by the attack on Bart and a possible attempt on Natalie's life to give it much thought.

Yet he had given it very serious consideration this morning because he sensed she was purposely withholding vital information from him.

So, naturally, he investigated by searching her belongings while she washed dishes at the river. Lo and behold, he'd discovered the hidden compartment in the bottom of her tattered carpetbag. He had dipped in his hand and strands of diamonds, rubies, emeralds and sapphires dripped between his fingers. He had stared in disbelief at the fortune in jewelry.

Hell's bells, the precious stones, set in gold and silver, were large enough to choke his horse! Not to mention that he'd found more money than he had in his bank account in Wolf Ridge.

Van contemplated Natalie's unswerving refusal to divulge her last name and confide her past. Suspicion loomed large in his mind. He hadn't wanted to be mistrustful of her, but he suspected last night's intimate encounter was part of her cunning scheme to gain his allegiance and his protection. Just in case her secretive past caught up with her and she needed reinforcements.

Why had she found it necessary to pose as a widow? Was it to conceal her identity from lawmen? Was it because she had stolen a fortune in jewelry and money recently? Had she conned him into marrying her by feeding him lies and paying for his services as a gunfighter until she was miles away from the scene of whatever crime she had committed?

He knew he'd served several purposes for her—a name on the marriage license, a skilled shooter and protector. Everything she told him was a crock of lies designed to gain his trust, he mused resentfully.

A wicked stepfather and unfaithful fiancé? Ha! He suspected she had concocted that whole story. And it was a nice touch the way she tossed in suspicions about her mother being poisoned after he had pointed out the hemlock in the marsh. He cursed himself for being tripped up by her exceptional beauty, by her sad tale and by his uncontrollable desire for her. He had been a gullible fool and his pride was smarting until hell wouldn't have it.

The thought of how she had him twisting in the wind made him furious. He had spent the previous night enjoying a man's wildest fantasy, only to plunge headlong into the black hole of doubt and suspicion. Van had been used plenty of times and for various reasons by his clients. He had been well paid every blasted time. But Natalie had touched off emotions and filled him with sensations that he wasn't prepared to deal with—and wasn't sure how to fight.

Feelings of betrayal coiled inside him. All the money she had paid him for the use of his name and for survival training couldn't appease the anger burning through him. He had told himself at the onset of their business dealings to remain professionally detached, but had he listened to himself? Hell no, he had blundered blindly ahead, flattered that a stunningly lovely woman would want to marry *him,* a man most decent women cautiously avoided.

That should have tipped him off immediately. Decent? Natalie? Ha! What kind of woman proposed to a man she had never met and wouldn't give her real name? The *deceptive kind!* he thought bitterly.

Like an imbecile, he had been delighted when she proclaimed to everyone who would listen that he was perfect for her in every way. He just hadn't realized what *every way* meant to a cunning witch like her. When she had seduced him into teaching her the meaning of passion, he had succumbed to his secret desires for her. Deep down, he'd known she was too good to be true and he had *allowed* himself to be deceived because he was so intrigued and wildly attracted to her.

Van cursed himself up one side and down the other for failing so miserably in this assignment. For all he knew, he was aiding and abetting a wily criminal who had stolen jewels and money and was using him to make her getaway on horseback—away from trains and stagecoaches that lawmen might check.

Damnation, how could I have been so naive and stupid? he railed at himself harshly. He should have questioned her motives a week ago. Now he was certain every clever remark, every practiced smile had been designed to lure him under her spell and make him a willing pawn.

Hell, he would have trusted her more if she *couldn't* come up with the money to pay his fee and had offered a lame excuse about making monthly installments after she settled into a community and took a paying job. But his doubts had been festering since the beginning and increased when the Rangers mentioned the story of a woman named Natalie who had been abducted.

Now, his escalating suspicions and his overwhelming sense of betrayal hounded him to no end as he trekked toward Taloga Springs. If he had a brain in his head—and he liked to think he did, at least until he ran headlong into this witty, conniving female—he would go directly to Indian Territory to deal with the corrupt lieutenant. In his present state of mind, he might tear that cheating bastard apart, limb from limb.

His thoughts scattered like buckshot when he noticed the approaching stagecoach kicking up dust as it moved rapidly over the caprock that skirted the deep ravines and colorful canyons. Van snapped to attention when he saw two masked riders scrabble up the slope ahead of him. They tried to halt the stagecoach by firing their pistols in the air.

Just what I need to vent my frustration, he thought eagerly as he gouged Durango in the flanks.

"Stay here," he called over his shoulder to Natalie before he raced off like a bat out of hell.

Natalie watched Crow thunder through the dry arroyo, then scrabble uphill in pursuit of the bandits that halted the stagecoach. Despite Crow's sharp command to stay put, she pulled her cap down on her forehead to conceal her identity and then took off after him. She might not be the best reinforcement for him, but she was available and willing and she could flash her pistol and look threatening.

However, if she had any sense she probably should ride to Taloga Springs alone and leave him to handle the situation by himself. For sure, Crow hadn't been stimulating company the past few hours. Heavens, he couldn't have been more standoffish if he had been in a different state! Natalie didn't know what she had done to find herself on the icy side of his frosty disposition. She suspected that he regretted their intimacy and was trying to make a clean break.

Damn it, hadn't he been listening to her? She had assured him that she expected nothing more than one night of passion. If consequences arose, she would deal with them. He would never know or feel obligated. She had his name on the legal document. That's all she had ever asked of him.

Natalie nudged the strawberry roan up the steep embankment. Her horse stumbled in the loose gravel, then bolted sideways when more gunshots resounded around the canyon. Her concern for Crow overwhelmed her. She was afraid he had suffered injury and she needed to be there to help him—

She swallowed a yelp when her mount dropped to its knees in an effort to maintain its balance on the narrow ridge. Unprepared, Natalie went flying from the saddle. She groaned in pain when she slammed her shoulder into a slab of rock. She tumbled helter-skelter down the embankment, skinning both knees and her chin before bouncing to a stop.

When her horse bolted to its feet and shook himself,

Natalie reached out with her good arm to grab the trailing reins. Every muscle screamed in protest as she came to her knees, only to be dragged downhill when the strawberry roan evidently decided there had to be an easier way to reach the elevated caprock and the road upon it.

"Stop…whoa, damn it," she hissed. She yanked hard on the reins but the horse dragged her another ten yards before coming to a reluctant halt.

"Maybe you aren't cut out for the Wild West, after all," she muttered at herself as she wobbled unsteadily to her feet.

In fact, maybe she should return to New Orleans to confront her treacherous stepfather with her new suspicions. If he deliberately poisoned her mother, she vowed to see him hang for his crime. Or stand him in front of a firing squad.

Fool that she had been, she had accepted his explanation of her mother's lingering illness and his claims that her doctors had tried to treat her without success.

Natalie vowed she was never going to take anyone's word for anything without checking facts first. On that determined thought, she tugged on the horse's reins, forcing him to follow her up the steep incline.

Van couldn't see who had fired a shot from inside the coach to fight off the masked men, but the bullet plugged one outlaw in the arm. The second highwayman caught sight of Durango scrabbling uphill and twisted in the saddle to fire off a shot, but Van fired first. The bullet struck the man's gun hand and the weapon flipped end over end then plunked onto the road. When both men tried to turn tail and ride off, Van held them at gunpoint with both six-shooters drawn and aimed directly at their chests.

"Get off your horses. Now!" Van barked ominously.

"Van?"

He glanced at the coach, surprised to see Bart Collier poke his head out the window. Well, that explained whose excellent marksmanship helped to thwart the holdup.

"What the blazes are you doing here?" Van asked as he retrieved two strands of rope from his saddlebag to restrain his prisoners.

"Donovan *Crow?*" one of the masked men croaked. "Well, damn the luck!"

"We heard you got married and retired," the other outlaw grumbled.

"Married? Yes. Retired? Not hardly. I live to arrest bandits like you." Van secured the prisoners then quick-marched them to the stagecoach to check for available seating. There was no space for his prisoners.

"I guess you boys will have to ride horseback to town." Van reversed direction to shovel them back to their horses.

"You shot us," the first outlaw complained as Van jerked off the concealing mask. "We need medical attention, not a jarring ride to the calaboose."

"The city marshal will see that you receive all the attention you have coming to you when you're in jail," Van said unsympathetically. "Until then you'll hold."

As was his custom with his prisoners, Van secured them in the saddle—backward—then tied their feet to the stirrups. He'd found the technique effective in discouraging escape attempts.

"You ain't gonna last long," the second brigand muttered at him. "I heard the Harper brothers are gunning for you. They claim they're gonna dance on your grave, *if* they decide to go to the effort to dig one."

The attempt to frighten and intimidate Van was a waste of breath. He'd heard it all before—most of it more degrading and insulting than this. "Thanks for the tip, I'll be on the lookout." Van led the bandits to the rear of the stagecoach, then secured the reins. "I'm sure you boys prefer to see where you've been, because I guarantee you won't like where you're going."

The thieves proceeded to tell Van where *he* could go and what *he* could do with himself when he got there, but Van had heard that before, too, so he ignored the bandits.

He halted Durango beside the window. He noted the film of dust on Bart's bowler hat and the lack of a sling on his arm. Then he surveyed Bart's fellow passengers—a man and two brazenly dressed females. They looked the type who displayed their wares in brothels—of which there were a half dozen in the raucous town beside two converging cattle trails.

"You didn't say why you're here, Bart," he prompted.

Bart glanced this way and that. "It's a private matter that can wait until we reach town."

"What about those three bullies jailed in Wolf Ridge?" Van asked.

Bart pushed his drooping glasses up to the bridge of his nose. "They'll hold... Where is your wife?"

He hitched his thumb toward the labyrinth of rugged canyons that dropped off the caprock. "I left her down below."

He didn't mention that he was royally irritated with her for not telling him who and what she was. He spitefully considered letting her make her own way to Taloga Springs. She thought she could fend for herself in the wilderness, did she? Then let her try. What did he care? He'd been paid in full and she had lied to him repeatedly—about everything!

He glanced over his shoulder at the rugged canyon and wondered if he could live with himself if she came to harm before he delivered her safely to town. He blew out his breath, then reined Durango in the direction he had come. "Rent us rooms at the Wildhorse Hotel, will you, Bart? It has the best accommodations in town, though that isn't saying much. We'll talk later."

"Count on it," Bart said grimly as he settled against the back of the coach seat.

"Mr. Crow! Wait up! I have a proposition for you."

Van glanced back at the bulky, well-dressed man who sat across from Bart in the stagecoach. The older man wore thick spectacles and boasted a full head of gray hair.

"Sorry, I'm in the middle of an assignment at the moment." He inclined his head toward Bart. "This is my business agent. You can take up the matter with him."

Van trotted Durango to the edge of the caprock then looked down to locate Natalie. Despite feeling betrayed and irritated, he frowned in concern when he saw her horse grazing at the base of a ravine, but he couldn't see her. Damn it, hadn't he told her to stay put? When had she ever?

Since her clothing blended in with the tan and brown layers of rock near the base of the cliff, it took Van a moment to spot her. She was climbing to her feet and dusting herself off. Apparently, she had taken a spill.

Van eased Durango down the steep incline, letting the sure-footed gelding pick the best route. When he reached Natalie, he noticed her skinned knees and skinned chin. A layer of dust coated her clothing.

"Which excuse are you going with this time?" He settled his stony gaze on her. "You didn't *hear* me? You *forgot* what I said? Or you just weren't *listening?*"

She slanted him an annoyed glance—which didn't faze him in the least because he was aggravated with her for a dozen good reasons. For starters, she had lied to him about why she wanted to marry him. Secondly, she had ulterior motives for wanting to learn to fend for herself so she could lay low—in case bounty hunters chased her when her name appeared on Wanted posters for abduction, theft and who knew what other crimes.

"I guess I must have been thinking about something else," she said smartly. "Like trying to provide you with backup, in case those bandits blasted away at you."

"You were going to cover *me?*" Crow crowed incredulously.

She tilted her skinned chin upward. "Yes, I was. But as mean and nasty as you are sometimes, I don't know why I bothered."

She limped toward her horse, then gingerly pulled herself into the saddle. Van suspected she had more bruises and scrapes from her tumble downhill than were visible.

Not that I care, he thought resentfully. She had bruised his pride and betrayed his trust. She didn't deserve his sympathy. What she was about to receive from him— when they reached town—was a relentless grilling. He wasn't going to let up on her until she had spilled the truth. The whole truth and nothing but!

"Hurry up," he snapped as he reined Durango toward the ridge. "Bart is in the stagecoach and I have two prisoners I need to stuff in the calaboose for safekeeping."

"Bart is here? Why?"

"He says we'll discuss the reason in private, not with a stagecoach filled with strangers."

Van nudged Durango uphill, leaving Natalie to follow in his wake. He kicked himself all the way to town for misjudging the spirited chit he had married. He had half a mind to ask Bart to begin divorce proceedings immediately. He shouldn't let her cower behind his professional reputation. She could find some other gullible fool to marry the second time. He wanted to be done with her once and for all.

Damn it, how was it possible for their incredibly intimate tryst in the dark of night to turn so sour in the light of day? And so much for his unerring ability to judge a person's character. Apparently, he was blind and stupid when it came to women.

Blind and stupid when it came to his *wife,* he amended as he trotted off without looking back.

Chapter Ten

"How much farther to this godforsaken town?" Thurston Kimball grumbled as he shifted uncomfortably on the hard stagecoach seat. A cloud of dust swirled through the windows, coating his expensive jacket. He rolled his eyes in disgust as he batted away the dirt with his monogrammed kerchief.

"We should be in Taloga Springs by nightfall," Avery Marsh replied. He sneezed when the breeze delivered a snout full of dust. He definitely wasn't cut out for the climate in Panhandle Texas, he decided. Moreover, he'd see that troublesome witch pay for his inconvenience when he finally caught up with her. And it damned well better be soon!

Avery glanced at the two burly henchmen enclosed within the coach. Jenson and Green would deal severely with Natalie, he'd make certain of it. It didn't matter that she had tried to outsmart him by marrying the legendary gunfighter. That half-breed would be no match for Avery's henchmen. Crow would never see the bullet coming. His widow would marry Kimball—and live just long enough to transfer her fortune to her husband and stepfather.

Avery covered the lower portion of his face with his own monogrammed kerchief, then settled himself against the uncomfortable seat. All that kept him from complaining to the same extremes as Kimball was focusing on delivering revenge on Natalie. Then he would have complete control of the Robedeaux-Blair fortune once and for all.

On that satisfying thought, Avery closed his eyes and tried to catch a nap. It was impossible. The rough road left him bouncing around so he anchored his hands on the window frame and reminded himself this miserable trip was Natalie's fault. And oh how he was going to make her regret it!

"Damn it to hell!" Van growled when Bart placed the New Orleans newspaper on the table in his suite and tapped his forefinger on the front-page article. Van read the story in its entirety and spewed pithy curses. "Modest inheritance, my ass! She's a *Blair?* The Blair *heiress?*"

"I'm not certain about that yet," Bart said. "We don't have a physical description of Natalie Blair. The Natalie we know might have disposed of the real heiress and assumed her identity. She might be the paid companion named Anna Jones. Or she could be a con artist who stole all the money and fled. Then there is the possibility she was in cahoots with the supposedly wicked stepfather and fiancé, then double-crossed them and took off with everyone's share of the fortune."

Van's mind whirled like a carousel. Once again, he recalled the conversation with the Rangers about a woman named Natalie being abducted. At the time, Van had chosen to think the best of the woman who insisted on marrying him.

He thought the absolute worst about her now.

"So the money she paid me in large denominations for this assignment, and the fortune in jewelry I found in the secret compartment of her ragged carpetbag, were stolen. She conspired with this Avery Marsh character, double-crossed him and took off with his cut of the fortune. And that's why she believes he might be hot on her trail."

"Back up a minute," Bart said, frowning curiously. "You found jewelry? That added motive raises more suspicion. I've seen cases like this before, especially back East where vast fortunes are involved. You've worked cases with elaborate schemes in your day, too, Van."

"Yes, and I could be the victim of this one." Van's fingers curled, wishing he could strangle Natalie for deceiving him, for using him and preying on his emotions. "I want a divorce."

"Divorce is frowned upon, you know—"

Van flapped his arm dismissively. "I don't give a damn. Just take care of the paperwork as soon as possible, Bart."

He nodded somberly. "This sounds bad, but you need to ask for your wife's version of this story before you act," he advised—sounding like a damn lawyer instead of a trusted friend. "You've never been one to jump to conclusions. No sense starting now. Besides, I'd like to see if Nat can talk her way out of this entanglement."

"Then *you* go listen to her poison lies," Van muttered as he paced the confines of the suite. "I'm not interested."

Bart appraised him all too carefully. "You're taking this rather personally. Mind telling me why? This assignment was supposed to be a clear-cut business arrangement."

"I'm taking it personally because I despise being played for a fool. Let's leave it at that."

Bart crossed his arms over his chest while Van wore a rut in the rug. "You care for her, don't you?"

He rounded on his friend. "I care that she betrayed my trust and lied to me. I hate being wrong."

"Who doesn't?" Bart inserted.

"I should turn her over to the city marshal and let her rot in jail with those two stagecoach bandits we brought in with us."

"You aren't being completely honest with yourself," Bart challenged. "I understand that your pride is smarting, but you wouldn't be this upset if you didn't care about Nat to some degree, at least."

Van halted in midstep, then blew out his breath. He didn't want to admit to Bart or himself that he'd broken his hard-and-fast rule and had developed a sentimental attachment for that infuriating wife of his. He had felt responsible for her and had allowed the arrangement to become personal when she seduced him…

Had she planned that, too, to gain his loyalty?

More angry thoughts and conflicting emotions swirled inside him like a churning tornado. He needed answers. He wanted the truth but he wasn't sure he could get a straight answer from that quick-witted, dark-eyed beauty who had cast a wicked spell over him.

Bart grabbed the newspaper from the table and headed for the door. "Let's see what Nat has to say for herself. Might as well get this over with so you won't be so upset."

"I'm not upset," he all but yelled at Bart.

"Right. What was I thinking?"

While Crow had stuffed the outlaws in jail, Natalie had purchased more clothing for her journey to Dodge City. Then she hurried back to her room to soak in the brass tub. After washing off the trail dust, she applied poultice to the scrapes she had sustained during her wild tumble down the side of the canyon.

Considering the cold-shoulder treatment Crow had given her since early this morning, she was surprised he had handed over the healing salve when they rented their rooms. The fact that he had placed her in a private room indicated he had used her body to appease his needs, had quickly tired of her and was ready to move on.

No doubt, her inexperience showed and Crow preferred women who could please a man a dozen different ways.

Damn him, he hadn't meant a single word he'd said last night. His empty words were meant to flatter and manipulate. She should have recognized the technique because the strutting dandies in New Orleans had spouted meaningless flattery at her for years.

If she hadn't been so upset by the possibility of her mother being deliberately poisoned, she wouldn't have run to Crow for comfort. Not to mention feeling sentimental about parting company with Crow and falling victim to her reckless desire for him.

It was glaringly apparent that his interest in her was purely physical. His male needs appeased, he was anxious to walk away without a backward glance. Sweet mercy, what a fool she had been!

"You have what you wanted," she lectured her reflection in the mirror, then dabbed poultice on her skinned chin. She had a husband with a legendary reputation and a no-strings-attached marriage that allowed her to outrun Marsh and Kimball. She had her long-awaited freedom and her inheritance. Very soon, Marsh would have to take up a new residence in New Orleans thanks to her—

Her thoughts scattered when someone rapped on the door with enough force to rattle the hinges. "Who is it?"

"Van."

Didn't he sound pleasant? She expected him to bite her head off when she opened the door. Surprisingly, he had his mouth clamped shut and a muscle ticked in his rigid jaw. He flashed her The Stare he was famous for. Then he stalked over to slam down the newspaper on the small table in the corner.

"Explain this and make it fast, sunshine," he snarled.

With a nagging sense of dread, she met Crow's glittering silver-blue glower that practically burned a hole in her chest. She glanced back to see Bart enter the room. He sent her a clipped nod of greeting, then went to stand beside Crow.

Natalie's stomach dropped to her ankles when she read the newspaper article detailing the alleged abduction of Natalie Blair and the theft of the jewels and money.

"Damn that man," she muttered angrily.

"I assume you're referring to Avery Marsh?" Crow hurled harshly. "So who is he really, sunshine? Your partner in crime? The one you double-crossed? Are you the personal maid impersonating the heiress? And what did you do to her?"

She sucked in her breath at his angry tone and the realization that he had searched her private belongings. "Which will offend you more, Crow? Discovering that I'm filthy rich and failed to mention it to you? Or that I conspired with Avery Marsh to dispose of the poor, defenseless heiress, then gathered all the money and jewelry I could carry without looking like a Wells Fargo railroad car?"

He practically stood on top of her and growled, "Don't sass me, damn it. I want the truth and I want it now!"

As intimidation went, Donovan Crow was a master. Nevertheless, Natalie quickly conjured up the memory of him tossing back his raven head and bursting out in laughter. Not that she would ever witness his amusement again. Fortunately, the vision did help her hold her ground when the fire-breathing dragon loomed over her.

Natalie had vowed never to cower and never to be at the mercy of any man ever again. That included her formidable husband. He had been an incredibly tender lover the previous night, but what a difference a day made! Now he was spitting flames. This was why he had been so distant all day, she realized. He'd immediately presumed the worst and convinced himself that she'd stolen jewelry and the cash she'd paid him.

That was the rub—she didn't trust him and Crow sure as the devil didn't trust her. He'd found her guilty without hearing her side of the story. And Bart, damn him, was Crow's true-blue friend. He had come running with newspaper in hand to protect Crow and accuse her of crimes she hadn't committed.

She thought dejectedly about how no one cared what happened to her and she had no family left to verify who she was. No one would protect her from Marsh's manipulative lies and insinuations. She was on her own.

"Well?" Crow snapped impatiently. "Are you planning to concoct a few more lies to explain the abduction and theft? I have places to go, sunshine. I've wasted too much time on this assignment already. But I'll be *damned* if I'm going to be charged with abetting a wily criminal posing as an heiress!"

His booming voice ricocheted off the walls and came at her from all directions at once. Natalie squared her shoulders and mustered her composure. "You want the truth? Will you even believe the truth if I give it to you?"

"Let's hear it," he barked sharply. "Start talking before I'm tempted to shake it out of you. And by the way, I want a divorce. Bart will draw up the document and you will sign it, just as readily as I scratched my name on the marriage license. Where is the damn thing? I want to see it."

Tears threatened to cloud her eyes while Crow glared at her like the Most Wanted Criminal in the West. Bart watched her every move—as if he intended to turn each gesture and comment against her in a court of law.

"Don't waste your time trying to milk my sympathy with those crocodile tears. I don't have any," Crow growled. "Let's hear your version of the story."

His condemning tone fueled her temper and slashed her pride. Natalie elevated her skinned chin to a defiant angle and faced down both doubting Thomases.

Whirling around, she fished the marriage license that was rolled in her unmentionables at the bottom of her satchel. Then she waved it under Crow's nose.

"My real name is Natalie Francoise Robedeaux-Blair," she informed them. "I was named after my maternal great grandmother. Francoise's family sailed from France when the king's and queen's heads rolled during the revolution."

She struck a sophisticated pose that would have done her noble family proud. "The family lost their vast land holdings but they relocated their lucrative shipping business to New Orleans."

She couldn't tell if either man believed her. Their expressions never changed. Especially Crow's. His facial features looked as if they were chiseled in granite.

"My family prospered but my mother was the only surviving child to live to adolescence. Her parents, entrenched in European tradition, arranged her marriage to Edwin Blair, whose titled English family became involved in banking. It wasn't a love match, but my parents honored their obligations to merge two wealthy families. Things were fine until my father died in an accident on the wharf."

"So you claim *you* are the abducted heiress mentioned

in the newspaper article?" Crow interjected in a skeptical tone. "*Not* the conniving servant who disposed of the real Natalie Blair so you could steal her identity, jewelry and money?"

His cynical tone made her want to go for his throat. And she would have—if she thought she could get away with it. Instead, she nodded her curly wet head and stuck her nose in the air. "I haven't had a maid since I was sixteen and I have a pedigree longer than my arm. And yes, I enjoyed a pampered lifestyle. My mother lived alone for several years, filling her days and nights by attending charity events and soirees. Then Marsh convinced her that he had his own fortune and was hopelessly enamored with her," she added resentfully.

"You considered him a shyster from the onset of the courtship?" Bart asked.

"I didn't know him well enough at the time but I never liked him. He seemed too pretentious to me, but he complained to Mother that I was jealous of her affection for him and I didn't give him a chance.

"When Mother became ill, he was the picture of devotion." She glanced bleakly at Crow. "Marsh sent me off to boarding school in Natchez where I later became a teacher. He claimed he was sparing me the anguish of watching Mother wither away from a mysterious disease that even the best doctors in the city couldn't name or treat."

"And it didn't occur to you until yesterday when I warned you against gathering poisonous plants that your mother might have been poisoned and left to die from one dose after another?" Crow questioned intently.

"No," she murmured, swallowing hard. "I was young, naive and too far from home to realize what might have happened. I was wrapped up in my own grief about being alone in the world if my mother didn't survive. By the time

I returned home six months ago my mother was...," She inhaled a steadying breath and continued, "practically skin and bone."

"You didn't become suspicious of your stepfather's intent until he arranged your betrothal to your unwanted fiancé?" Bart asked.

"Yes, he was *too* insistent in making the arrangements quickly, while I was upset about losing my mother. I overheard a few conversations that sounded like whispered conspiracies to contract my family's fortune." She looked directly at Crow and said, "You have no idea how difficult it is to tell if someone actually cares about the person you are on the inside when so much wealth is at stake. Some people will do and say anything to attach themselves to fortunes. Which is why I have so little faith in men and why I withheld my name from you."

"So you made arrangements to leave New Orleans without Marsh knowing your intent," Bart presumed.

Natalie nodded. "I have no doubt that I would have died shortly after my forced wedding to Kimball. It would have been too easy for Marsh to claim that I suffered from the same mysterious disease that befell my mother."

She walked over to replace the marriage license in her satchel. If Crow pushed through the divorce, the document would do her no good whatsoever as protection against Avery Marsh.

"Before I left town, I contacted my own lawyer and paid him generously to remain loyal to my interests. I instructed him to serve an eviction notice to my treacherous stepfather two weeks after I left town. Also, I asked him to buy up Kimball's gambling debts from his creditors and demand that he pay the IOUs immediately."

"If what you're telling us is true, I recommend that you

send a telegram to your lawyer so he won't believe this newspaper article," Bart counseled.

"I intend to. In addition, I will alert him that, in the event of my premature death, Marsh and Kimball should be considered primary suspects."

Natalie stared determinedly at Bart. "After you draw up the divorce papers Crow requested, I would like to hire you to bring formal charges against Marsh for the deliberate poisoning of my mother. Also, I would like you to conduct an audit of the shipping company's accounts to see how much money that swindling bastard has embezzled the past four years."

Bart didn't reply immediately, but eventually he nodded.

Crow glared at him. "*Now* you believe her?" he muttered. "You're the one who buzzed up here by stagecoach to wave that newspaper article in my face."

Bart studied Natalie critically for a long moment. She lifted her skinned chin and met his gaze squarely. She refused to beg or plead to be believed. If Bart turned against her, too, then she would sneak off in the middle of the night and take her chances with marauding outlaws. She wasn't waiting around for Crow to accuse her of theft so Bart could file formal charges. Crow was now a closed chapter of her life.

"I'll check into the suspicions of murder," Bart agreed. When Crow snorted in annoyance, he tossed him a somber glance. "I think she really is Natalie Blair, heiress to the New Orleans shipping fortune. I will, however, make a few contacts to verify her claim."

Natalie's shoulders sagged in relief. "Thank you."

"I'm not completely convinced," Crow said, and scowled. "I want more proof—"

His voice evaporated when the windowpane shattered and a rock bounced across the floor.

"Ooofff!" Natalie's breath came out in a pained whoosh when Crow shoved her down to the carpet and sprawled on top of her. She hadn't noticed that he'd drawn his pistol until she raised her head to see the barrel aimed at the broken window.

"It's only a rock," she panted as she squirmed beneath his heavy weight. "You should have let it hit me in the head. I'm sure that would have pleased you to no end."

"Maybe not as much as you might think," he muttered, still focused intently on the window.

"If it had killed me you would have the Robedeaux-Blair fortune all to yourself," she reminded him.

"I don't want your money." He crawled onto his hands and knees, then inched cautiously toward the window.

"Why not? Everyone else does. They're willing to *kill* to get it."

He swiveled his head around to stare at her with those unnerving silver-blue eyes that once burned with passion and now sizzled with distaste. "All I want is a divorce because you lied to me."

"So you only want half of what I own, do you?" she smarted off. "Fine, you can have it then I will sic Marsh and Kimball on you. But I don't advise you to eat or drink anything my stepfather serves because I'm convinced the main ingredient will be poison."

"Children, please," Bart mocked while he crouched on the opposite side of the window, his pistol at the ready. "We'll haggle over the devil's details later. First, let's figure out who pitched the rock. Anyone going to volunteer to stand up, look outside and take the sniper's first bullet?"

"I nominate Crow," Natalie said with a smirk. "Stubborn as he is, the bullets will bounce right off him."

The comment earned her Crow's frosty glare. Not to be outdone, she flashed him a smile that dripped icicles.

Chapter Eleven

"Well, that didn't work." Marsh sent the henchman named Fred Jenson a disapproving glower. "I found out what room Natalie was in but your bright idea of luring her husband to the broken window was a disaster. Now they will be suspicious and on guard for a possible attack. Might as well have sent them an engraved invitation!"

"Crow is smarter than I thought," Fred Jenson said, then spit a wad of tobacco into the dirt.

Marsh made a mental note not to step in it. Scowling, he veered toward the back of the livery stable to reach the spot where his second hired gun, Taylor Green, waited.

"I'm hungry," Green complained. "We haven't eaten since this morning. I work better on a full stomach."

Marsh stared pointedly at Green's protruding belly that spilled over his belt buckle. He was sure the gunman took outside jobs, just to satisfy his gluttony. The man had talked about the best places to eat in Louisiana most of the trip.

Damn it, Marsh just couldn't hire good help when he

wanted someone murdered—and not be blackmailed for
it when the deed was done.

"Might as well feed your face." Marsh veered toward
Turner Hotel, where he and his cohorts rented rooms.
"We'll launch another attack tonight."

He strode off with Green lumbering behind him and
Jenson bringing up the rear. Now he had to round up Kimball. The prancing dandy had gone to a saloon to clean
out the pockets of hapless cowboys at the poker table.

Not for the first time, Marsh wished he'd had the good
sense to poison Natalie instead of her mother. The cunning
female was leading him on a frustrating chase.

Van inched his head up high enough to peer down on
the street below. He was sure the flying rock had come
from the corner of the livery stable—and no one had better
bother Durango, or Van would lift scalps. That horse was
reliable, loyal and dependable. Unlike some people he
knew. Van glared pointedly at Natalie, who had pushed
into a sitting position to grab the rock that had sailed
through the window.

"No note attached," she said. "A shame the person
didn't identify himself so Crow would know who to
shoot."

"Cut the sarcasm, Marquise. Or whatever you call
French royalty," he added snidely.

She rolled her eyes at him, then rose agilely to her
feet. "I'll prowl the streets, dressed as a boy to see what I
can find out. You are too high-profile and a much larger
target."

Van stared her down, for all the good it did. And *she*
called *him* stubborn and bullheaded? Ha! "You aren't
going anywhere, Your Highest of Highnesses."

She elevated her skinned chin. "You can't tell me what

to do." She shrugged on an oversize vest that concealed her feminine curves and swells. "I *paid* you for your completed assignment. We are officially separated—at *your* insistence. Bart can draw up separation papers before the divorce settlement."

She crammed her hair beneath her cap and yanked it down until her ears stuck out from the side of her head. Then she smeared soot from the lantern on her face.

With one final burn-in-hell's-biggest-bonfire glare, she swept from the room. A moment later, she returned to retrieve her piddly two-shot derringer, then tucked it into her waistband and left again.

"A week of married life and look what a disaster it's become," Bart remarked. Then grinned.

"As I mentioned earlier, you're the one who showed up here, waving the newspaper, insisting my wife is a charlatan and criminal," Van remarked as he bolted to his feet, careful not to stand in front of the window.

"You are my friend," Bart defended, rising to his feet as he shoved his drooping spectacles back in place. "Naturally I wanted to verify Natalie's story. If there is as much money at stake as she insists, then she could be in grave danger. This Marsh character sounds ruthless. He might kill anyone standing in the way of the Blair fortune. You first, I suspect."

Van scowled as he raked the broken glass into a pile using the side of his foot. "The only reason you believe her now is because she offered you a job investigating and trying a case of possible murder."

"No, I plan to hire *you* to investigate the allegations of murder," he commented.

"Ha! *No*," Van declined adamantly. "I'm not going anywhere near New Orleans."

"You should." A wry grin twitched Bart's lips. "You'll own half of Blair Shipping after the divorce settlement."

"I don't want her money, if in fact she actually has any beside what she stashed in her clothes and satchels."

"May I ask you something?" Bart said while using the newspaper to scoop glass into the trashcan.

"No."

He went on as if Van hadn't spoken. "What put you and Natalie at each other's throats? As I recall, you seemed agitated with her before I showed the article to you."

"I told you, I found the jewelry and excess money," Van prompted.

"What else?"

He knew Bart, being a lawyer, would keep firing questions until he was satisfied with the answers. He was as relentless in a courtroom as Van was trailing criminals. "I don't want to talk about this right now," Van said with finality. "I intend to find out who pitched the rock and why."

"Could be the Harper brothers," Bart speculated. "I received another message from them before I boarded the stagecoach to find you. They said your days were numbered."

"Pffttt!"

"Maybe Marsh and Kimball are here," Bart suggested. "They could have tracked Natalie, just as she feared they would."

"I hope it is. They can verify who Natalie is."

"You would take the word of possible liars, swindlers and murderers over her?" Bart challenged. "I contend Marsh and Kimball will lie through their teeth if they think it will help them get their greedy hands on the Robedeaux-Blair fortune…. Where are you going?"

"Hunting." Van breezed across the room. "It might take all night but I'll find the rock thrower. Count on it."

With that, he shut the door behind him, leaving Bart to deal with the rest of the shards of glass that littered the floor in Natalie's room.

Natalie skulked down the fire escape of the Wildhorse Hotel, then clung to the shadows as she scurried silently through the alley to find the culprit. She wished she hadn't been so irritated with Crow, for she might have remembered to ask him for a physical description of the Harper brothers who were out for his blood. They would have to get in line, she mused sourly.

It wouldn't take the gang long to find out if a high-profile gunfighter like Crow was in town. It made sense the Harpers would attack immediately.

"What was I thinking?" she muttered under her breath as she crept along the side of the livery stable. She should have married a nobody and slipped into anonymity right alongside him. But no, she thought she needed someone capable of defending her in case of trouble.

Her reasoning had been skewed since the beginning, she realized. Worse, she was attracted to the wrong kind of man. Donovan Crow was the biggest mistake she'd ever made. He was also a walking contradiction. One minute he was kind and considerate, and the next minute he was harsh and insulting.

Although granting Crow the divorce he demanded would complicate her situation with Marsh and Kimball, she wouldn't fight it. She could only hope Bart and her attorney in New Orleans could gather evidence to ensure those two conniving devils paid their dues.

Another solution occurred to her as she tiptoed around the side of the general store to reach the boardwalk. To escape Marsh and Kimball, she might stage her own death and take Natalie Blair completely off the front page— and out of the picture—for good. She could become Anna Jones or anyone else of her choosing. She could leave instructions to place her fortune into a trust that she could use to cover her living expenses while she moved from one locale to another, seeing the sights she had only read about in books.

In time, she hoped to see Marsh and Kimball locked in the penitentiary. Then she would have nothing to fear from them.

Pain stabbed at her heart again. Crow hadn't wanted her for who she was on the inside. She'd been the time he was killing. The thought prompted feelings of anger and rejection. She thought she had selected the perfect husband, but she was no more than a temporary release for him, a completed assignment with fringe benefits.

Damn him! Besides all that, he refused to believe the truth about her identity. He had hurt her and mistrusted her. Which only proved what she had learned the past few years. Men were a lot more trouble than they were worth—

Natalie snapped to attention when she heard a familiar voice wafting from Rattlesnake Saloon. To her frustration, she saw Thurston Kimball III ensconced at the corner table, engaged in a poker game with three scruffy-looking men wearing ragtag clothing and sombreros. They had tied red bandanas around their thick necks. Since they had their backs to her, she couldn't identify them. If they were Marsh's henchmen, she wouldn't be able to recognize them on sight.

She sucked in her breath and ducked her head when she saw Avery Marsh on the street. With his storklike legs and a goatee that made him look like a billy goat, he was easy to spot. Marsh moved quickly down the boardwalk toward her. He seemed intent on poking his head in the door of each of the three saloons he passed. When he spotted Kimball, he veered inside without giving Natalie more than a passing glance. Thank goodness!

Natalie lingered by the swinging doors to watch Marsh walk up beside Kimball. She was tempted to grab her derringer and blast away at the bastards. Unfortunately, she hadn't perfected her shooting skills and one of the henchmen might blast her back.

Biding her time, Natalie crammed her hands in the pockets of her breeches and clomped down the boardwalk, calling as little attention to herself as possible. Two men lumbered from the café and collided with her. Natalie reeled sideways but she couldn't regain her balance. She stumbled off the boardwalk and slammed into the horse tethered at the hitching post. The horse threw its head and leaped sideways when she sprawled facedown in the dirt.

"Serves you right, brat," said one of the men, smirking.

Natalie kept her mouth shut and glared at the bully. He was tall and lean with baby-fine dark hair, a hawklike nose and dark eyes spaced too close together. He wasn't dressed like a cowboy. Nor was he wearing the fancy trappings Marsh and Kimball favored. Just worn breeches and a dingy white shirt with an open collar.

"Yeah, stay out of our way, kid," the second man sneered as he looked down his long nose at her.

She spared the man with the oversize belly, round face and full jowls a quick glance. His gray eyes were dull and flat—to match his intelligence, she suspected.

Tiring of their intimidating game, the twosome swaggered down the boardwalk, then entered Rattlesnake Saloon. Before Natalie could climb to her feet, a firm hand clamped around her forearm, hoisting her upright. She muttered under her breath when she realized Crow had come to her assistance and that he had witnessed the incident.

"I thought you said you could take care of yourself," he mocked as he ambled along beside her.

"I just did." She dusted off her clothing and checked to make sure her cap still covered the hair pilled atop her head. Thankfully, it did.

"You have a funny way of showing it," he replied.

She squared her shoulders and tilted her skinned chin to a proud angle. "I'm in one piece and those bullies didn't realize I was a woman, so I consider it a smashing success."

"Come on, *kid,* let's get you off the street before some other bully decides to rough you up for sport."

"What do you care if he does?"

"Didn't say I did."

Crow directed her to remain within the shadows of the boardwalk, then nudged her into the alley to use the metal fire escape for the hotel. Natalie decided, there and then, she was leaving town immediately. Darkness had settled over the countryside so she could flit off without being noticed. Plus, being with Crow after he'd hurt her feelings a dozen different ways was too painful. She was entirely too sensitive and vulnerable around him.

In addition, she didn't need Marsh, Kimball and the three henchmen taking shots at Crow. Aggravated though she was with him for thinking the worst about her, she didn't want him injured—or worse.

She decided to lead Marsh and Kimball out of town— away from Crow and Bart so they wouldn't be in danger. This was her battle now, and she was on her own.

"Did you figure out who threw the stone through the window?" Crow asked as he escorted her to her room.

"No," she lied, but she suspected Marsh, Kimball and

the three scraggly looking hombres at the poker table in the saloon were responsible. No doubt, Marsh had hired the men to dispose of Crow so he could focus on finding her and stealing her fortune.

Crow stopped short when he stared at the broken window in her room. "Since the owner hasn't repaired the pane you'll have to spend the night with me."

"No, I won't. I love fresh air," she said breezily.

Crow walked over to scoop up her satchel and carpetbag, then clutched her arm. Natalie set her feet—and cursed him soundly when he uprooted her from the spot and quick-marched her down the hall to his suite.

"Fine, I'll stay with Bart," she insisted. "He believes I am who I say I am."

"No, he doesn't. He's just being nice. Now me? I believe every word you say," he replied sarcastically.

Natalie glared daggers at him when he shoveled her into his suite—always the best accommodations available while Crow was in town. Maybe he was more like Marsh and Kimball than she realized, she thought bitterly.

Shaking loose from his grasp, she walked through the sitting room to the bedroom. She peered out the window at the street below, while Crow lit a lantern. She could see Rattlesnake Saloon and she tensed when Marsh, Kimball and five men exited together. Sweet mercy! Marsh had assembled an army of assassins. She couldn't expect Crow to take on *five* mercenaries and survive. Granted, Bart was an expert marksman, too, but his arm was still on the mend and he would be useless if it came to hand-to-hand combat.

Natalie quickly closed the curtains when Crow approached. She wheeled around to distract him until the seven men bedded down for the night. She hoped and prayed they hadn't rented rooms in *this* hotel. That had disaster written all over it.

"I'm leaving first thing in the morning," she blurted out. "If you want me to sign papers for legal separation and divorce, then fetch Bart."

"He hasn't had time to draw up the documents."

She flicked her wrist dismissively. "I'll sign a blank paper. I expect Bart to be fair."

He gave her The Stare but she looked the other way. "You are not leaving here alone, Nat, and that is that."

She crossed her arms over her chest, raised an eyebrow, and then met his hard look. "This is not your decision."

"It is if I decide to take you back to Fort Worth for questioning about a jewel theft in New Orleans."

Natalie's temper hit a rolling boil in the blink of an eyelash. She was leaving. Now. Tonight. Scowling, she tried to veer around the solid, immovable object that was Donovan-hardheaded-Crow. He snaked out an arm to latch on to her, causing her to stumble sideways.

"You are staying here, sunshine. Like it or not."

"Which I don't."

"Doesn't matter. Hell's Fringe is full of demons lurking in the darkness. You aren't setting foot on the street again."

Van stared into her upturned face, watching the sparks fly from her obsidian eyes. His gaze dropped to her lush lips and he felt the fierce, ill-fated attraction bombard him. He'd been fighting one conflicting emotion after another the whole livelong day. He wanted this firebrand but he didn't trust her. He desired her but he couldn't forget that she had lied to him—and probably still was.

When she shoved the heels of her hands against his chest to knock him off balance so she could dart off, Van grabbed her with both hands. She raised her knee to gouge him in the groin—exactly as he'd taught her to do, though he hadn't planned to be the recipient of one of those disabling blows.

He spun sideways so that her knee connected with his hip. She swore at him, then tried to stamp on his foot, but he shifted again to counter every move he'd taught her.

"You won't win," he assured her gruffly.

She went perfectly still in his encircling arms. Then she tilted her face to his and stared at him with those black-magic eyes rimmed with long curly lashes. *Famous last words,* he thought when he felt her body melt provocatively against him. She was forcing him to battle his worst enemy—himself. Van knew before his lips involuntarily slanted over hers that he was about to taste sweet defeat. As angry as he was with her, his uncontrollable desire for her ultimately won out.

Her arms slid over his shoulders and she arched into him. Then she opened her lips to invite him deeper. He closed his eyes, groaned in surrender and plunged his tongue into her mouth to share her breath and savor the pleasure of her kiss. His hands moved with a will of their own as he mapped her luscious curves. He resented the clothing that deprived him of seeing her satiny flesh.

When he felt her fingers working the buttons of his shirt, he shrugged off the garment. "Turnabout is fair play, sunshine," he said roughly. "Shirt for shirt. Breeches for breeches."

She smiled impishly and he reacted as he always did— he nearly melted in a fiery pool of desire. She unfastened his breeches, eased them down his hips an inch at a time and then left them in a crumpled heap on the floor. He returned the favor, then savored her curvaceous body with hungry eyes.

"I have a fantasy of my own that I want to play out,"

she insisted as she walked him across the room until the back of his knees collided with the edge of the bed.

When she urged him to sit, he sat. Then she knelt between his legs and erotic desire hammered at him. She pressed her lips to his chest as her hand closed around his throbbing erection—and he struggled to draw breath.

"What fantasy do you want to fulfill, sunshine?" he wheezed with what little air was left in his lungs.

She slanted him a sly glance then bit him lightly on the belly. "You're about to find out...."

Then she kissed and nibbled her way down his abdomen to take him into her mouth. Van groaned in sweet torment when she nipped at him with her teeth, then flicked at him with her tongue. He had never granted a woman intimate privileges with his body, but he granted Natalie her fantasy because he was helpless to stop her when the pleasure she gave him rippled through him in constant waves.

She stroked his aching length with her fingertips while she suckled him lightly. Van swore the top of his head was about to blow off when she kissed and caressed him again and again. Fire blazed across his flesh and sizzled though his bloodstream. He could feel himself drawing ever nearer to the crumbling edge of self-control. When he reached for her, she whispered the same words he had said to her the previous night.

"Don't distract me."

He swore he was going to pass out when her fingertips trailed down the inside of his legs, then moved up again to cup him in her hand. Her thumb stroked leisurely from base to tip while she drew him into her mouth and traced his throbbing length with her tongue and teeth.

"Have mercy..." he choked out when wild need blazed through him, burning him alive.

"Give no quarter, show no mercy," she murmured

against his rigid flesh. "We may be celebrating our pending divorce, but I vow you will never forget your first wife. I'm saying my own version of fare-thee-well to my one and only husband."

Van moaned in sweet torment while she worked her erotic magic on his ultra-sensitive body. She left him blind with need and he swore he was going to die from unappeased desire any minute. Then she straddled his legs. When she settled exactly upon him, he became the flame pulsing inside her.

"You should be against the law," he growled as he arched helplessly against her.

"You already think I am," she whispered as she linked her fingers behind his neck and moved in perfect rhythm with him. "I see no crime in enjoying you one last time before we part company. Do you?"

Her voice faded when he twisted sideways, taking her to her back in one swift, fluid motion. She peered into his bronzed face, watching the golden flames from the lantern cast light and shadows on his angular features.

Natalie asked herself why she was so bold and brazen with him. How could she yearn for him beyond reason when she itched to pound him over the head for fueling her temper with his cynicism? She couldn't explain her fierce, uncontrollable desire for Crow any more easily than she could fly to the moon. Despite his dark suspicions about her, she still wanted him once more before she walked out of his life and lured her enemies away to protect him from harm.

She didn't know if she would survive Marsh and Kimball's attempt to dispose of her. But they would *not* harm Donovan Crow, she promised herself fiercely. He had burrowed into her heart and breathed life into her soul.

Her thoughts sailed away like a ship skimming the

sea in a brisk wind. She stared into Crow's fascinating silver-blue eyes and knew without question that she was experiencing her greatest adventure. The feel of his muscular body moving intimately against her, burning like a living flame inside her, took her higher and higher still.

Sensation after indescribable sensation swamped and buffeted her. She swore she was soaring in motionless flight, flying past the stars to grasp that one spectacular feeling she had discovered only when she was one with this raven-haired warrior she had married.

Her breath lodged in her throat when infinitesimal pleasure exploded around her. She dug her nails into his forearms and held on for dear life as she spiraled out of control. Her body sizzled like a meteor blazing across the heavens to its own fiery destruction as rapture consumed her.

"Damn you, sunshine," she heard Crow growl against the side of her neck. His muscular body shuddered and vibrated against her while he held her as tightly as she clung to him.

"Damn you, too, Crow," she whispered back and then she smiled in satisfaction as ecstasy streamed through her.

Impulsively, she pressed a feathery kiss to his shoulder, his high cheekbone. Then she ran her hand down his spine to map his muscular hip. A few moments later, he eased down beside her. Ten minutes later, the sound of his methodic breathing assured her that he had dozed off.

Natalie knew she had a small window of opportunity to escape before Crow woke up. That was all the head start she would need.

Chapter Twelve

Without daring to breathe, for fear she would wake Crow, Natalie inched off the bed. She rummaged through his saddlebags for the strands of rope he carried to secure prisoners. Working quietly but carefully, she tied one wrist then the other to the bedposts while he lay facedown in the tangle of sheets.

She stopped dead still when he shifted slightly. He didn't wake—Thank God!—so she staked him out. She didn't want to be on hand when Crow awoke to discover she had left without his permission and left him a prisoner in his own room.

I don't need his permission, she reminded herself as she dressed quickly, then borrowed his boot pistol and bowie knife—that lay scattered on the floor like casualties of war. *Besides, what I need from him, he can't give.*

After she extinguished the lantern, she plucked up her satchel and carpetbag. On second thought… She quickly switched a few articles of clothing from the carpetbag to the satchel and grabbed traveling money to tide her over. She purposely left behind the tattered bag filled with priceless jewels and most of the bank notes. In case her attempt to lead Marsh, Kimball and the small army of assassins away from Crow ended badly for her, the Robedeaux-Blair jewels would be safe in his hands.

Silently, Natalie exited the bedroom and scurried across the sitting room. She stepped into the hall, then dashed toward the metal fire escape. She wasn't sure where to find the bastards who were hot on her trail, but she presumed Kimball's compulsive gambling habit would lure him back to one of the saloons before the night was out. Once Kimball recognized her, he would alert Marsh and she would ride north, drawing the men behind her.

Natalie's well-laid plans blew up in her face when she stepped onto the elevated outdoor landing of the fire escape to see Marsh and the two men who had knocked her off the boardwalk ascending the metal steps. Exploding into action, she lowered herself like a battering ram and barreled into them.

The tall henchman with a pointed beak and close-set eyes doubled over and cursed when she slammed her satchel into his gun, knocking it loose. Fingers interlocked, she lifted her clasped hands to deliver a teeth-jarring blow to the underside of his chin. When his head snapped backward and he bit his tongue, Natalie shoved him with her shoulder on her way past him. He slammed into the railing and flipped over. He hung on for dear life and tried to anchor his legs to the banister before he finally took the short way down to the ground.

Natalie relied on every tactic Crow had taught her and devised a few of her own to fight her way past the second hired assassin who blocked her path. When he made a grab for her, she bit a chunk out of his hand, then kicked at his pistol with the toe of her boot. She landed a blow to his groin. He covered himself as he went down hard on the

step and curled into a tight ball. Natalie used his back as
a springboard to launch herself at the stork-legged Marsh,
who brought up the rear. It was where he belonged—the
ass.

Marsh yelped when she slammed her satchel into his
billy goat goatee, sending him stumbling down a step.
When they were face-to-face, his soulless gray eyes narrowed on her, then widened in recognition. Swearing
foully, he tried to clamp both hands around her throat
and choke the life out of her. Natalie hooked her boot heel
around his leg and jerked hard. Marsh squawked as he
toppled sideways and latched on to the railing to steady
himself.

Natalie leaped past him, dodging his outstretched hand
when he tried to lunge at her. She flew down the remainder
of the steps and raced away from Wildhorse Hotel as fast
as her churning legs could carry her. She headed directly
for the livery stable and burst inside to toss a bridle on the
strawberry roan. She was tempted to "borrow" Durango,
but she figured Crow was going to be furious enough with
her, without taking his beloved horse—one he loved far
more than he would ever love her.

Natalie scooped up the saddle draped over the top rail
of the stall and tossed it on her horse. She hurried around
the corner to the alley, then fastened the girth. Casting
apprehensive glances over her shoulder at irregular intervals, she tied her satchel in place, then mounted the gelding. She skirted through the alley behind the livery stable
and Turner Hotel, then veered back to Main Street.

Hunkering over the horse's neck, she peered through
the doorway of one saloon then the next until she spotted Kimball playing poker and puffing on his pipe in the
Lookout Saloon.

Thurston, are you looking for me?" she called out loudly, then removed her cap so he would recognize her.

His blond head snapped up and he bolted to his feet, jarring the table and spilling drinks on the cards. The men at the table cursed him, but he was too intent on glaring at her to pay them any mind.

Natalie bowed mockingly from the saddle and shouted, "Catch me if you can!"

She swatted the strawberry roan on the rump with her hat. The horse raced off as Kimball darted around the tables to burst outside. Natalie made tracks from town, following the road north to Dodge City—wherever that was. She had no idea how far she would have to ride to find shelter, but she had been taught to cover her trail so she veered off the trodden path toward the creek. She reined her horse into the water to make the tracks difficult to follow. Guided only by the light of the moon, she walked the horse upstream until the water became deep. Then she went ashore to weave her way through a thick grove of willow trees.

If she could locate one of the stagecoach stations used to exchange horses she might be able to hitch a ride through no-man's-land—the strip of land beside the Indian Territory and between Texas and Kansas. Crow had mentioned that the place was jumping alive with outlaws. She could only hope the stagecoach had hired several heavily armed guards to fend off attacks.

Natalie allowed herself a few moments to bid a final fare-thee-well to her husband and sent a prayer winging heavenward that her plan to lure Marsh and company away would protect Crow from harm. If she had to sacrifice herself to ensure he survived this disastrous assignment, then so be it. She loved him, after all....

"Oh, dear God!" she choked out when the realization hit

her like a hard slap in the face. "Well, so much for avoiding sentimental attachments during this misadventure."

Natalie was thankful she hadn't made that exasperating epiphany while she lay in Crow's powerful arms. If she had blurted out the confession he didn't want to hear she would have embarrassed and humiliated herself beyond words. She predicted Crow would have recoiled...and run for his life.

Ah well, she told herself optimistically as she skirted the creek that glowed like a ribbon of silver in the moonlight. She couldn't complain that she hadn't had one great adventure already, short-lived though it might be. She had ventured into the wilderness. She had been tested thoroughly. She had faced overwhelming temptation with Crow and she had fallen in love for the first and only time in her life. In addition, she had done more living in the two weeks since she had left New Orleans than she had in twenty-two years.

Natalie drew in a deep breath and expelled it slowly as she zigzagged through another copse of trees. She knew she would never live to see twenty-three, not if Marsh had anything to say about it. Her only hope was that Bart would pursue her suspicions about Marsh poisoning her mother. That bastard should pay dearly for his crime. If she died at his hands, she didn't want it to be in vain.

Avery Marsh swore viciously as he scraped himself off the metal step at Wildhorse Hotel, then checked himself for serious injury. He put weight on his left leg and rubbed his throbbing ankle.

He glanced up to see Fred Jenson struggling to pull himself back to the landing—and failing. The henchman cursed the air blue when his leg slipped, his arms gave out and he dropped like a rock to the ground. Avery peered over the rail to see Jenson rolling in the dirt, holding his left knee.

Taylor Green climbed onto all fours, still gasping for breath. The blow Natalie had delivered to his groin had made it impossible for him to stagger to his feet. He, too, was swearing colorfully.

"Now you've met Natalie Blair," Avery muttered as he used the railing to steady himself while he hopped down the steps on one foot.

Jenson lifted his head to stare at Avery in astonishment. "That was the heiress? That's the same brat we plowed into on the boardwalk earlier this evening."

"You did?" Avery croaked.

"Yeah, but we didn't know the kid was a female in disguise."

The walking wounded hobbled down the alley to reach the street. Avery cursed sourly when he saw Kimball sauntering down the boardwalk, puffing on his pipe. The man didn't have a scratch on him.

Kimball waved his arms in expansive gestures when he noticed Avery and the henchmen hobbling toward him. "You won't believe who I saw."

"Natalie in another disguise," Avery said, scowling.

Kimball looked them up and down. "What the blazes happened to you?"

"*Natalie* happened to us," Jenson growled. "She fights dirty."

Kimball's eyes popped. "She did this much damage before she galloped out of town, headed north?"

That was not the news Avery wanted to hear. He was tired from the long journey from New Orleans. His ankle pulsed in rhythm with his heartbeat. The last thing he wanted was to climb aboard a horse and chase off into the darkness to locate that cunning troublemaker. However, a lot of money was at stake. He couldn't afford to wait until dawn to hunt her down.

"Go rent four horses from the livery," he demanded.

"Me?" Kimball crowed. "I'm not a lackey, I'm—"

"The only one who can walk without limping," Avery snapped in interruption. "Get at it, Kimball. But fetch us a few bottles of whiskey to ease our pain first."

Annoyed at being bossed around, Kimball put his nose in the air then spun on his well-shod heels. "I should never have agreed to this scheme," he grumbled. "There are easier ways to marry a fortune in New Orleans, without chasing all over creation for a woman I never wanted in the first place."

Avery glared at Kimball's departing back. The man was worthless. Kimball didn't know it yet, but he would never return to his precious New Orleans to enjoy the social season. He had already outlived his usefulness.

In fact, after Kimball retrieved the whiskey and horses, he wouldn't be necessary at all.

He fished into his pocket, then handed Jenson several bank notes, compliments of the Blair fortune. "We'll only need three horses…and just as many riders," he said with a meaningful glance.

Jenson nodded grimly, then hobbled across the street to wait for Kimball at the livery stable.

Van was spitting mad when he awoke to find his wrists anchored to the bedposts. He was facedown—and naked. "Damn it to hell!" he growled into his pillow. He jerked against the restraints—and received nothing for his efforts.

He managed to turn over onto his back, but his wrists were crisscrossed and he had no leverage whatso-ever. He lay there until he exhausted every curse in his repertoire—all of them directed at Natalie. Since she had closed the thick curtains and doused the lantern, he couldn't see anything—except red.

She had used him again. She had made him a slave to his irrational desire for her, then tethered him like a horse and slipped away to only the devil himself knew where.

Van swore a few more times, not that it helped. He tried to contort his body a dozen different ways but it was a waste of time. He'd save all his energy for the time he got his hands on that sly vixen, he promised himself.

He lay there for what seemed hours, though it was likely only thirty minutes before he heard Bart's trademark rap at the door of the sitting room.

"You'll have to kick open the door!" he called out.

"Why?" Bart said from the hallway.

"Just do it!" he barked impatiently.

It took two hard thrusts from Bart's boot heel for him to gain entrance to the suite. "Where the devil are you?"

In hell. "In bed." Damn Natalie for leaving him in this embarrassing predicament.

He heard Bart stumbling around in the dark and barely made out his lean form when he reached the doorway.

"Are you feeling all right, Van?" he asked in concern.

"Hell, no! Light the lantern on the table to your left."

That done, Bart pivoted toward the bed—and burst out laughing when he realized Van was wrapped in the sheet with his arms crossed over his head.

Van swore again.

"Don't tell me. Let me guess. This is Natalie's doing, right?"

"Just untie me," Van demanded sharply.

"Sure. Would you like me to hand over your breeches, too? Oh, here they are on the floor. Hmm, wonder how that happened."

"You are not funny," Van grumbled. "When I find her... and I *will* find her...I'm going to kill her with my bare hands."

"Better not. I'd have to testify against you in court. Plus, you'll lose all the fortune in her dowry, if she does turn out to be the real Robedeaux-Blair heiress."

Van had never been so humiliated in his life. That minx had picked a fine way to celebrate their pending divorce, hadn't she?

He blew out a relieved breath when Bart had finally had his laugh and untied him. "Get those divorce papers ready and make it snappy," he demanded curtly as he swung his legs over the side of the bed. "I want—"

He forgot what he intended to say when he noticed that Natalie's satchel and *his* bowie knife and boot pistol were missing. The tattered carpetbag lay at the foot of the bed. Clamping the sheet around himself, Van walked over to root around in the bag.

"Holy hell!" Bart croaked when Van lifted a necklace that dripped oversize diamonds and rubies and a fistful of large denomination bank notes.

"Why would she leave this behind?" Van asked Bart.

Bart shrugged uncertainly. "Maybe she left it with you for safekeeping."

"Or to make sure the legal owners couldn't take it away from her when they catch up with her.... Oh, hell!"

"Oh, hell *what?*"

Swearing profusely, Van snatched up his breeches and stepped into them while Bart politely glanced the other way. "Maybe the men who are after Nat arrived in town. Perhaps they hurled the rock through the window. She might have spotted them on the street while she was checking around, dressed in her wayward waif disguise."

Bart frowned, bemused. "Then why didn't she say so?"

Van stared somberly at his friend. "Maybe she didn't want us to know because she was afraid we would confront them and discover her version of the story is a manipulative lie."

Bart winced. "Which suggests she left you behind while she made tracks out of town. Maybe she plans to circle back to retrieve the money and the jewels when the coast is clear."

"Still think she's innocent of wrongdoing?" Van asked as he crammed the carpetbag containing money and jewels inside his saddlebag for safekeeping.

Bart opened his mouth, closed it, then huffed out a breath. "I don't know what to think."

Van thought Natalie was a scheming fraud who had used her keen intelligence and her luscious body to lead him—by a certain part of his anatomy located below his belt buckle—exactly where she wanted him to go. Damn it, she had turned him into a dozen kinds of fool and he kept allowing it because he had fallen under her seductive spell.

Outraged with her and himself, Van grabbed his shirt and fastened himself into it. "I'm going to track her down, no matter how long it takes."

"I better go with you," Bart insisted. "You are not in a good frame of mind to confront your runaway wife."

"*Ex*-wife," Van corrected as he plopped down on the edge of the bed to pull on his boots.

"Technically she's still—"

When Bart noticed Van's venomous glower, he shut up. After a moment he said, "I'll change clothes and meet you at the livery stable in a few minutes."

Still smoldering with scorched pride and flaming temper, Van grabbed the weapons—the few his soon-to-be ex-wife had left behind—and scooped up his saddlebags.

He strode through the suite and down the hall, taking the steps two at a time to reach the small, unadorned lobby and the boardwalk beyond.

The sound of tinny piano music and drunken guffaws wafted from Rattlesnake Saloon into the street, along with a cloud of cigar and cigarette smoke. Van made a beeline for the livery, wondering if Natalie had stolen Durango for her fast getaway.

That would be the crowning blow to his frustration, he decided. A woman could make a fool of a man ten times over, but she had damn well better not steal his prize horse!

Guided by moonlight and the lantern hanging just inside the entrance, Van entered the stables. He breathed a sigh of relief when he saw his shiny black gelding in his stall. However, the strawberry roan was gone. Natalie had skipped town, as he expected. He wondered if she expected *him* to deal with the supposed stepfather and ex-fiancé while she flitted…

Van's thoughts evaporated instantly when he walked up beside Durango—then noticed the man sprawled face-down in the empty stall where Natalie's horse should have been. Sickening dread skittered through him. The cut of the man's clothing was too stylish for a cowboy fresh from a trail drive. The stovepipe hat was another telltale sign the man was out of his element and that he was accustomed to wearing expensive, tailor-made garments.

When Van heard muffled footsteps, he glanced over his shoulder to see Bart, dressed in a buckskin shirt, dark breeches and riding boots. Bart slowed his step when he noticed the grim expression on Van's face.

"What's wrong?"

"Dead body."

"Uh-oh…"

Van opened the stall gate while Bart grabbed the lantern to get a better look. Blood oozed from the wound in the middle of the man's back. A stab wound. But there was no dagger in sight. Van had taught Natalie well, hadn't he? He was surprised she hadn't left his bowie knife at the scene of the murder to throw suspicion on *him*.

"Good God," Bart muttered when Van rolled the dandy onto his back to get a better look at his expensive jacket, cravat and fashionable breeches. The corpse's light blond hair was filled with straw. His skin was pale, as if he rarely ventured into the sunlight. His hands didn't have a callus anywhere to be found and his green eyes stared sightlessly into the darkness.

"He looks like the tenderfoot I used to be when I first arrived in Texas from Boston," Bart remarked.

"You never looked this prissy," Van insisted.

"Thanks. I'd like to think not. Still, this man doesn't fit into this rowdy town at all."

"He won't have to fret about looking out of place anymore," Van murmured after he checked for a pulse in the man's neck—and found none. "This tailored suit will be fine where he's going."

"Is he carrying identification?" Bart asked.

Van dug into his pants pockets to find them empty. "He's been robbed." He fished into the pocket of the brocade vest to retrieve an engraved pocket watch. "Well, hell. It's Thurston Kimball III. He's in no condition to give us a physical description of the real Natalie Blair. How inconvenient."

Did Natalie think he wouldn't incarcerate his own wife for theft and murder? Had she played him for a fool from the very beginning? He swore every action and every comment had been designed specifically to lend credence to her convincing performance.

"I know what you're thinking," Bart said. "But you could be wrong. This could have been self-defense—"

"A stab in the back with my missing knife?" Van scoffed.

"Someone other than Nat might be involved," Bart went on quickly. "Maybe robbery was the sole intent and Kimball fought back then turned to run."

"And maybe pigs fly in Boston, Bartholomew, but they sure as hell don't in Texas," Van muttered sarcastically. "Go fetch the city marshal, will you? Jed Dawson has sleeping quarters in the back of his office."

Bart lurched around and jogged off. Van rose from a crouch to stare at the sophisticated and stylishly dressed Thurston Kimball III. He doubted the man had known what hit him until it was too late. Kimball probably wished he had never become entangled with the dark-eyed beauty that had flitted off into the night.

"You should be thankful I married her before you did," he told Kimball, though the man was long past listening. "Avoiding wedlock didn't save you, though, did it? Wonder what wedlock has in store for me?"

Grimly, Van strode off to fetch the livery owner from his quarters to rent a horse for Bart to ride. By the time Bart and Marshal Dawson arrived, Van had saddled Durango and the rented sorrel.

"Any idea who did this?" Dawson hiked up his sagging breeches while he stood over the body. "Wonder if the two men who robbed the stagecoach in no-man's-land last week hit town to prey on a few more victims."

"I don't have a clue," Van lied so Bart didn't have to. "Bart and I have an errand to run at a nearby ranch." That sounded plausible, didn't it? "We'll be back tomorrow."

Dawson arched his thick brows. "You taking a job with one of the ranchers hereabout? They are having fits with trail herders who help themselves to a few calves to take along to sell for extra profit to the meat buyers in Dodge City. Not to mention the report of a few horses being stolen lately."

"I'm thinking of looking into the situation," Van mumbled evasively. "Can't say if I'll be interested in taking the assignment or not."

"I sent word to the Rangers about those two stagecoach robbers. But if you come across those bandits, bring them in. The stage line is offering a reward. It's all yours if you capture them, Crow."

Van had no interest in doing the Rangers a favor, or capturing the thieves or collecting the reward. All he wanted was to track down Natalie—pronto.

Dawson stared at the sprawled body, heaved a sigh, then pivoted on his heels. "I'll fetch someone to help me haul this departed soul to the undertaker."

When the marshal exited, Van and Bart led the horses outside to mount up.

Bart settled himself in the saddle then glanced curiously at Van. "Do you have any idea which way Nat might have gone?"

"My best guess is north because traveling through canyon country at night is too risky."

"Then let's go with your best guess." Bart reined down the street.

Van followed behind him. He wondered how he could restrain from choking the life out of that cunning wife of his when he caught up with her.

That's why Bart is here, Van reminded himself as he urged Durango into a trot and then a gallop.

Chapter Thirteen

Natalie had never spent a more miserable night in her life. She was on the run and she didn't have the luxury of Crow's pallet to bed down on the ground. Not that she could sleep, of course. Having Marsh, Kimball and five hired mercenaries after her kept her nerves on edge. However, she had managed to catch two short naps while the strawberry roan rested and drank from the stream she crisscrossed.

Tired and achy, Natalie worked the kinks from her back, then mounted her horse. The sun made its first appearance on the horizon, splattering molten-gold rays over the hillside and turning the stream to rippling flames.

Natalie grimaced as she headed north on the road that would take her across no-man's-land to reach the infamous cow town known as Dodge City. There were very few trees to break the terrain, which meant she would be exposed and vulnerable to attack. Crow had cautioned her to remain on high alert when there was no place to hide. She reassured herself that if outlaws—and Marsh's death brigade—could see her then surely she could see them, too.

Her hopeful thoughts scattered like a covey of quail when she saw three riders trotting down the road. A shout went up behind her and she recognized Marsh's voice. She glanced every which way, trying to decide on the best course of action. She dug her heels into the horse's flanks and reversed direction.

Curse it! She had no choice but to race back to the wooded area near the stream to play hide-and-seek as long as necessary. *Do you really think Marsh and his goons will give up and go home with so much money at stake?* she asked herself as she ducked away from the bullet that whizzed past her shoulder and plugged into the tree she passed.

A horrifying thought exploded in her mind when she realized Kimball and the three straggly haired goons from Rattlesnake Saloon weren't with Marsh's brigade. Sweet mercy! Had they split up so the other four men could attack Crow?

Natalie felt sick, knowing she had tied up Crow to facilitate her escape. She had left him vulnerable and defenseless. If he came to harm, she would never forgive herself.

Fear sizzled through her as she flattened herself against the saddle and pressed her cheek against her horse's neck. Another gunshot sailed past her, missing her horse by inches. She could hear Marsh cursing the air blue, but she didn't look back, just zigzagged through the saplings that cluttered the steep incline near the creek bank.

When she finally braved a glance over her shoulder, she realized Marsh and his two goons were closing in faster than she'd hoped. She recognized the tall, slim gunman with the hawkish nose and close-set eyes that she had encountered on the fire escape the previous night. He aimed his pistol and took her measure while he raced toward her.

Frantic, Natalie jerked on the reins to veer left at the last possible moment after the gunman fired. Then she veered left again when he fired a second time.

"I gave orders to shoot to kill!" Marsh bellowed at her. "If you don't stop I'll turn my men loose on you for target practice."

Natalie thought fast. "If you kill me you'll never find the money and jewels I buried last night!"

She heard Marsh swear as she skidded her horse down to the creek, then splattered through the shallow water. She also heard the thunder of hoofbeats racing after her at high speed before another shot crackled in the morning air. Her horse screamed in pain and Natalie cursed when the strawberry roan stumbled, then went down on its front knees.

"I'm so sorry," she wailed when she realized the shooters had aimed for her horse. They had decided to keep her alive—for a short while, at least—until they tortured information about buried treasure out of her.

Before the horse tipped sideways, Natalie jerked her foot from the stirrup so her leg wouldn't be pinned down and crushed. She bounded off like a jackrabbit, estimating how long she could play cat-and-mouse with these three ruthless bastards before they caught up with her. She didn't hold much hope of lasting very long and she sorely wished she could have trained with Crow for a few months instead of a week. Then perhaps she might have stood a fighting chance of escaping.

Again, she wondered what kind of chance Crow stood if the mercenaries had indeed divided forces to bear down on him while this vicious threesome attacked her.

"Shoot her legs out from under her!" Marsh boomed.

Natalie dived sideways to avoid being shot, rolled over and bolted to her feet to take cover behind a tree thick enough to withstand flying bullets. Unfortunately, it was useless. All three men on horseback surrounded her, pointing their pistols directly at her chest.

"Jenson, tie her up," Marsh barked.

"You are a helluva lot of trouble, bitch," Jenson, the hawk-nosed hombre, grumbled as he dismounted.

"I hear that a lot," she said, then caught him off guard by plowing into him, knocking him sideways.

She ducked under his horse's belly and grasped the reins, using the animal as protection against oncoming bullets. She somehow managed—she figured fear provided the strength needed—to bound into the saddle and race away.

"Don't shoot my damn horse!" Jenson roared at his pot-bellied cohort. "I'm not walking back to Taloga Springs."

Natalie wondered if Crow would be pleased with her attempts to escape disaster by using the skills he taught her, combined with her own wits. But she suspected he had cursed her to hell and back when he awoke to find himself tied to the bedposts. She inwardly grimaced, picturing him at the mercy of Kimball and the three burly goons. He might have been attacked, just as the bullies had set upon Bart while he was sleeping off the sedative.

Dear Lord! she thought. *I'm the curse of both men's lives and I've placed them in grave danger.*

Riding hell-for-leather, praying Crow and Bart had survived, she thundered along the creek bank, dodging trees and underbrush as best she could. Then it occurred to her that she should *attack,* not retreat, for she had nothing left to lose. She wanted vengeance on Marsh for targeting her family to appease his insatiable greed. By damn, she would have revenge—or die trying.

Natalie grabbed the two-shot derringer tucked in the waistband of her breeches, but kept it out of sight as she reined back in the direction she had come.

Napoleon and Custer had their last stands...and so would she. She would put up a fight out here in the middle of nowhere. She was going to confront, head-on, the merciless bastard who deliberately murdered her mother. Marsh might kill her—and there was a very good chance of it—but she would draw his blood before she flew off to the pearly gates.

On the wings of that valiant thought, she jabbed her heels into the horse's flanks and charged full steam ahead. When she was within firing range she raised her pistol and blasted Marsh.

He yelped in horror when her bullet plugged his shoulder.

She was slightly off the mark. She could have put him out of her misery if she had aimed six inches to the right— and struck his cold, black heart.

A bullet screamed past her thigh and Natalie glared at the round-bellied gunman on horseback who'd shot at her. She fired off her second and last bullet, but she missed the snarling henchman by several inches. He aimed to fire at her before she could retrieve the boot pistol she had borrowed from Crow. She sagged in relief when the gunman's trigger clicked against the empty chamber. He had expended the bullets in his pistol and quickly reloaded.

Determined to battle to the bitter end, she rammed the barrel-bellied henchman broadside with her horse. Then she took a roundhouse swing at him with her arm, catching him upside the head with her derringer. He squealed in pain and somersaulted backward from his horse. His frizzy brown head slammed into a fallen limb, stunning him momentarily. Natalie was all set to smile in triumph… until Jenson stepped from behind a tree to pounce on her.

Natalie screeched in surprise when he grabbed a fistful of her shirt, then yanked her so hard that she cartwheeled from the saddle. She struggled to gain her feet and make another run for it. But to her dismay, Jenson lowered his shoulder and knocked her forward. She stumbled and skidded across the ground, re-skinning her chin. Before she could draw her legs beneath her, he threw himself down on top of her, knocking the air from her lungs in a pained whoosh.

"Gotcha," Jenson sneered at the back of her head. "When Marsh finishes with you, it'll be *my* turn. I'll hear you beg for mercy, hellion. Count on it!"

Natalie wanted to sass him, but she couldn't catch her breath. Plus, she couldn't reach the knife or boot pistol to launch another attack. She decided to bide her time until she could breathe again and come up with another plan. She only hoped her captors didn't check her for concealed weapons. Otherwise, she didn't have a chance in hell of escaping. For certain, her captors wouldn't underestimate her again.

"Lord have mercy," Bart hooted, owl-eyed, while he and Van halted on the rise of ground above the creek to watch Natalie take on the three men. "Did I just see what I thought I saw? What daring! Whoever she is, she is magnificent."

"She is amazingly adroit, damn the little daredevil," Van muttered. "She could have gotten herself killed!" Though why he should care he couldn't say. Or rather, he was in no mood to delve into the reasons why he had been holding his breath while he witnessed his crazed wife mount a brazen charge against the men who attacked her.

Van had been beside himself with fear and concern since gunshots had shattered the peaceful silence of dawn. He had pushed Durango to his limits and raced up the road, hoping beyond hope that he wouldn't find Natalie lying in a pool of her own blood. Furious though he was with her, he didn't want anyone else to lay a hand on her.

He reserved that privilege for himself.

He intended to shake her until her pearly white teeth rattled and her eyes rolled back in her head, first chance he got. It was what she deserved for tying him up and leaving him in an embarrassing predicament...before she killed the dandy Van found lying motionless in the livery. Now she was taking on three armed men, as if she were bulletproof.

The woman was insane. There was no other explanation.

Van snatched his rifle from the scabbard on the saddle to take aim at the men who shot at Natalie. But she had engaged in hand-to-hand combat and he couldn't risk hitting her by mistake. When the gunmen knocked her to the ground and held her in place, Van raised his rifle to stare down the sight.

He swore under his breath when Natalie's captor bolted to his feet and yanked her up in front of him. He hooked his arm around her neck, making her choke to catch a breath.

Scowling, Van shoved the rifle into its scabbard then dismounted. Bart followed suit.

"Do we have a plan of action?" Bart whispered.

"Yes, sneak up and eavesdrop on the conversation to learn the extent of Sunshine's involvement with these cutthroats."

Tethering the horses in the trees, Van led the way through the underbrush while he listened to the fancy dressed gent with the muddy-blond hair, mustache and goatee who cursed Natalie for shooting him. Van wondered if this was the man named Marsh and if he deserved a good shooting. He wanted to believe Natalie's version of the story, but he vowed to reserve judgment until he gathered more facts.

The stork-legged gent, who had ripped off the hem of his shirt to stem his bleeding wound, stormed up to Natalie and backhanded her while the man called Jenson held her in place.

Van gnashed his teeth and told himself to hold position.

"What did you do with the money and jewels, bitch?" Marsh demanded hatefully.

Despite her bloody lip, she tilted her skinned chin upward and said, "I already told you I buried it for safe-keeping, Marsh."

Which Van knew was a lie—and he wondered how much of what she had told him was a lie, too.

"Buried it where?" Marsh snarled at her while Jenson lashed her to a tree to make sure she didn't elude them again.

"It's downstream a mile...or three," she replied flippantly. "I forget. Confusion and severe headaches apparently run in my family. No doubt, I'm suffering from the same terminal malady that killed my mother."

Van saw how Natalie was baiting Marsh with her suspicions about poisoning her mother. Which led Van to believe that she *had* told him the truth—part of it, anyway. Her comment lifted the heavy weight bearing down on his chest and reassured him that he wasn't such a bad judge of his wife's character after all.

Thus far, Marsh hadn't accused her of double-crossing

him by running off with the jewels and money. However, that still didn't excuse her for tethering Van like a horse, leaving him naked and maybe even stabbing Kimball with *his* bowie knife! Perhaps it had been self-defense, if Kimball had seen her making her escape from town, Van mused. Hopefully, eavesdropping on the conversation by the creek would answer his troubling questions.

"I knew I should have disposed of you first, you sassy little firebrand," Marsh spat at her. "But you won't be around to point an accusing finger after you sign over the Blair fortune to me."

"You've wasted your time and effort tracking me down," she told her scowling stepfather. "My new husband is entitled to half the Blair fortune. If you dispose of me, he will inherit all of it. Hell will freeze over long before he signs it over to you. He knows exactly who and what you are."

Bart and Van stared somberly at each other. He was tremendously relieved to know his wife wasn't the practiced liar, cheater and thief he was afraid she might be. But the jury was still out about her involvement in Kimball's death.

"We'll see about that," Marsh growled. "I have him slated for execution. I might even use you for bargaining power to demand his cooperation."

Van noticed Natalie didn't blink an eyelash while she stared Marsh down. "You are sorely mistaken if you think there is any love lost between us. Donovan Crow has no sentimental attachment whatsoever for me. I made a business arrangement with him and that is as far as his feelings go."

Bart glanced speculatively at Van, who refused to react to her comments. He was in the middle of the most crucial assignment in his life and he was determined to remain professional and detached. Natalie's life depended on it.

Besides, how could he jump down her throat for embarrassing him beyond words for that tied-to-the-bed stunt if she were dead? He had to rescue her—*somehow*.

"We'll see what Crow has to say after he bears witness to the results of your torture," Marsh sneered then massaged his injured arm. "A few brands burned on your legs and arms should convince him that I mean business. Start a fire, Green," he ordered the barrel-bellied goon who had regained consciousness after Natalie had knocked him senseless earlier.

"My pleasure," Green said, and smiled vindictively.

Bart surveyed the scene unfolding before them for another anxious moment then he cast Van a how-much-longer-are-we-going-to-let-this-go-on stare.

Van decided he had all the information he needed. He picked up a fallen limb and hurled it sideways to bounce off a tree trunk. All three men jumped back a step, then wheeled around to point their weapons toward the unidentified sound.

"What the hell was that?" Marsh grumbled. "Jenson, go find out."

Jenson didn't look thrilled with his orders but he skulked off in the direction of the noise.

Van pitched another limb in the opposite direction and Green lurched toward the new sound.

"Maybe it's the renegade Indians I managed to avoid last night," Natalie supplied helpfully. "My husband told me a war party of Indians escaped the reservation to raid and plunder. Crow even admitted that he had lifted a few scalps in his time. I hope we don't lose our scalps because I still have use for mine. *Yours,* I could care less about, however."

Van managed a faint grin, as did Bart. The three greenhorns from Louisiana looked concerned when Natalie laid it on thick. She used every possible weapon in her arsenal. My, but the little minx was imaginative, Van mused.

His thoughts stopped dead in their tracks when Marsh knocked the cap off her head. He grabbed a fistful of her long auburn hair and yanked hard, forcing her head to an awkward angle that made her yelp in discomfort.

"You listen to me, you smart-mouthed bitch," he jeered viciously. "No matter what else happens, you are going to die for the trouble you've caused—"

His voice transformed into a pained howl when Natalie raised her knee and drove it into his groin. Marsh involuntarily released his fierce grip on her hair to cover his crotch. He choked for breath as he dropped to his knees, gasping and groaning.

While Natalie struck out to clip Marsh in the head and jaw with two well-aimed blows from the toe of her boot, Van sprang into action. He went in low and fast, signaling Bart to stay put for necessary backup. By the time the three captors realized he was charging at them, Van had already fired off shots with the six-shooters clutched in each fist.

Jenson went down with a yelp of pain and grabbed his wounded thigh. Green screeched when Van's bullet plowed into his gun hand. Marsh tried to bolt to his feet to use Natalie as his protective shield but she kicked him in the chest with both feet before he could put his pistol to her head.

Van headed straight for Marsh when Bart stood up, pointed both peacemakers at the downed men and yelled, "Stop where you are or you'll be as dead as a man can get!"

* * *

Natalie stared in disbelief when Crow swooped down on Marsh like an avenging angel of doom. He lifted Marsh off the ground by the nape of his shirt and shook him until his head whiplashed twice. She was enormously relieved to know that Crow and Bart had survived whatever attack Kimball and his three mercenaries might have launched on them. At least she wasn't responsible for their deaths.

She wasn't sure she could have lived with that.

If Crow hadn't showed up when he did, she would have been disfigured with burns. She had exhausted every attempt to counter Marsh and his vicious henchmen and she had been operating on nothing but resentment, sarcasm and bluff for the past half hour.

Her thoughts trailed off when Crow stuck his snarling face in Marsh's and said, "You'll pay dearly for hitting my wife. You'll lose the hand you used to strike her."

Natalie lifted her left knee and gestured her disheveled head toward her boot. "Want to use the knife I borrowed?"

"Have you used it already, sunshine?"

She gave him a bemused look. "No, I was saving it as my last resort."

She didn't know why he looked so relieved, but she didn't question him while he loomed over Marsh's five-foot-ten-inch frame like a spitting cobra. Crow grabbed Marsh's right wrist and drew blood with one swipe of the sharp blade.

Marsh screamed like a stuck pig. "Stop! I'll give you half the Blair fortune if you let me go," Marsh bartered frantically. "The jewels, the money, the shipping business. You'll be wealthy and never have to work again."

Crow smiled nastily, much to Natalie's delight. The expression caused Marsh to quake in his boots, especially when Crow grabbed a handful of his dingy-blond hair and laid the blade of the bowie knife against his scalp.

"No!" Marsh screeched, his tombstone-gray eyes as wide as dinner plates.

"Why did you kill your wife?" Crow demanded as he yanked Marsh's head back at an unnatural angle. When Marsh didn't reply, Crow drew beads of blood along his hairline. "Answer me or I'll lift your scalp."

When Crow leveled his trademark stare on Marsh, he practically swallowed his Adam's apple. "I wanted control of the Blair fortune," he chirped. His face turned a lighter shade of pale while blood dribbled across his forehead, then ran down the length of his nose.

"Which one of you stabbed Kimball and left him in the livery stable?" Crow growled, turning to stare at Natalie.

She blinked in surprise at this news. Then she puffed up with offended dignity. How could he think she was responsible? Would he ever take her at her word or would he always insist on hearing the truth from someone else first?

"Jenson did it," Marsh blurted out.

"Under Marsh's orders," Jenson insisted as he pressed leaves over his wound to stem the flow of blood.

"You are both under arrest for murder and conspiracy to commit murder." Crow stared directly at Jenson. "You stabbed Kimball in the back and didn't give him a fighting chance."

Natalie regretted Kimball's senseless death at Marsh's orders. He had been a philanderer, a lush and compulsive gambler, but he hadn't been as bloodthirsty as Marsh.

"I suppose Kimball served his purpose in your scheme of fraud, murder and greed," Natalie hissed at Marsh. "Just as you used Mother for your purposes, then disposed of her."

Sweet mercy, the urge to wrest loose from the ropes that held her to the tree so she could choke the life out of this selfish, ruthless bastard nearly overwhelmed her. "Cut me loose, Crow," she growled. "Marsh is mine. You had your turn with him already."

Crow smiled faintly, then shook his raven head. "He's all mine, sunshine. I'll have a complete, detailed account of his crimes when I'm through with him." He glanced over his shoulder at Bart who still held the other two men at gunpoint. "Tie up the henchmen, Bartholomew. You can turn Sunshine loose *after* Marsh and I stroll off for our private chat."

"I'll tell you what you want to know right where we stand," Marsh insisted frantically.

Natalie smiled wryly. "Apparently you've heard about Crow's thorough tactics of acquiring confessions. I'm glad I'm not in your shiny boots, Marsh. Having brands burned on your skin is mere child's play for Crow. He might start there but he will finish elsewhere. In case you don't survive, I wish you well while you roast in hell."

"Come along, Marsh, let's see how much pain you can endure before you pass out or die...whichever comes first," Crow said as he quick-marched his captive upstream.

Natalie listened with satisfaction while Marsh begged, pleaded and bargained for mercy. She hoped he found none forthcoming from Crow.

Bart picked up Jenson's discarded pistol, then walked over to cut the rope that held Natalie to the tree. Then he strode off to retrieve Green's weapon. She knew Bart needed her assistance tying up the prisoners because he was still nursing a mending arm. She secured Green and Jenson for safekeeping while Bart kept his pistols trained on them.

While she treated the henchmen's injuries, she heard Marsh screaming bloody murder in the near distance.

"I recommend that you two give me your statements about your involvement with Marsh," Bart advised the prisoners. "Unless you want to take your private turn with Crow."

"I hired on with Marsh in New Orleans," Jenson said readily, and then cast an anxious glance in the direction of Marsh's high-pitched howls. "He paid me to track down his runaway stepdaughter. I found out that she'd dressed in widow's digs and took the train to Fort Worth and beyond." He glanced down to watch Natalie cut open the front of his breeches' leg to inspect his wound. "We were hired to capture Natalie in Wolf Ridge, but she left town before we arrived. The hotel clerk said she got married, so we followed her."

Bart glanced at Green who cradled his injured arm against his ribs. "What about you? Do you have anything to add to Jenson's statement?"

Green bobbed his frizzy brown head. "I heard Marsh tell Jenson that we only needed three horses to chase down Natalie when she rode out of Taloga Springs—"

"Shut up!" Jenson snapped tersely.

"Hey, I'm not taking the blame for Kimball's death," he protested hotly.

Both men clammed up when another agonized shriek erupted from the underbrush.

Natalie glanced up at Bart then her gaze drifted to the place where Crow and Marsh disappeared from sight. "Do you think I should—?"

"No," Bart interrupted. "Some things are best not to watch, Nat. There are reasons why Donovan Crow has an exceptionally high rate of success in acquiring information that leads to convictions in court. I'm not questioning his methods in extreme cases like this one. Are you?

She shook her head somberly. Bart was right. Whatever Marsh received as incentive to tell the truth could never adequately compare to what he deserved for committing his vicious crimes.

Chapter Fourteen

Another half hour passed and Marsh's howls of excruciating pain dwindled to whimpers. Finally, Crow appeared from the shadows of the trees, his expression grim. "Arsenic," he murmured as he halted in front of Natalie. "Delivered in increasing doses in the meals Marsh personally served to your mother, while pretending to be a devoted, pampering husband. He has been embezzling money from your shipping company for the past few years, using the pretense of promoting the business and luring in new clients. Anything else you want to know right now or can we wait—*ooofff*..."

His breath gushed out when Natalie, so overwhelmed with anger, grief and relief leaped into his arms, causing him to stumble back a few steps before he regained his balance.

She locked her legs around his lean hips and hugged the stuffing out of him while blood-pumping tension, anger and fear that had sustained her swooshed out. Tears poured down her cheeks like falling rain. She wasn't sure how long she held on to him for dear life, letting the jumble of bubbling emotion inside her erupt like Mount Vesuvius.

Crow wrapped his arms around her and rested his chin on the crown of her head. "It's okay now, sunshine."

"I'm-m s-sorry," she blubbered then hiccupped. "I d-didn't want you t-to have to b-be the place I fell apart…"

"Take a deep breath and let it all out," he murmured comfortingly. "You were incredible this morning, did I tell you? Three-to-one odds and you held out longer, better, than most men I know."

She raised her tear-stained face and hiccupped again. "You were there watching?"

He nodded and flashed a lopsided smile. "I wanted to intrude earlier but I couldn't get a decent shot without the risk of hitting you by mistake. I figured you'd never let me hear the end of it if I did."

She teared up again and sobbed out, "They shot my horse."

"I know. I saw him. Luckily, he was back on his feet when Bart and I reached him. The bullet grazed his rump. I'll tend to him later. He'll be as good as new in no time."

"Thank you…" Natalie broke off into weeping sobs, embarrassing herself again.

She had held up under the pressure of the fast-speed chase and the dangerous confrontation with Marsh and his henchman, but now she was bawling her head off like an abandoned baby. Crow and Bart probably thought she'd gone loco, but she couldn't seem to regain her composure. Not yet anyway, not until she vented the turmoil of emotion roiling inside her.

Crow cradled her in his arms, then carried her to the stream so she could wash her face. He grabbed the monogrammed kerchief he had taken from Marsh, dipped it in water, then blotted her swollen cheek and tender lip. He was so gentle and patient with her that she broke down and cried all over again.

"Damn, sunshine, I never realized you had so much water in you," he teased.

"I'm a big sissy after all," she said, and hiccupped.

"No, you're brave and daring and amazing. Bart said something to that effect, too, while we watched you battle your enemies."

High praise from Crow was heady stuff and it helped Natalie regain control of her frazzled composure. She even managed a watery smile. "Thank you. I'm indebted to you."

"Now, take another deep, cleansing breath and expel it slowly," he instructed.

Natalie did as he suggested.

"Do you want a shot of whiskey to calm your nerves?"

"No. I had more than I'll need for a year after the first night we met."

"If we leave now, we can reach Taloga Springs by late afternoon," he commented as he blotted the swelling around her eye. "Are you up for the ride?"

Natalie nodded, then raked the wild tendrils from her face. "I'm sorry about Kimball," she murmured. "I couldn't have tolerated being married to the self-absorbed dandy but he shouldn't have died needlessly."

"I'm sorry about him, too." Crow drew her to her feet. "Marsh never intended for him to receive his fee for marrying you. In fact, Marsh hadn't planned for Kimball to leave Texas alive."

Natalie muffled a sniff, then squared her shoulders. She was bound and determined to appear strong and unrattled in the presence of the prisoners. "You will, of course, receive a generous payment for coming to my rescue today. Bart will, too. It wasn't part of our original negotiation to put you at risk by fighting this battle for me. I tried to lead Marsh's brigade away from you to protect you from—"

"Lead them away? Protect me?" His silver-blue eyes widened in disbelief and his dark brows shot up his forehead.

"Well, certainly. These men were *my* problem, not yours."

He sent her a withering glance and shook his head in dismay. "Sunshine, I can take care of myself." He curled his hand around her forearm to steady her while they walked uphill. "Don't ever put your life in danger for me again. Understand?"

For the sake of argument, she didn't reply. Nonetheless, she would do whatever necessary to protect Donovan Crow from harm. Always. Even if he didn't love her, she had fallen as deep in love with him as she could get. Although Natalie had been brave while dealing with her enemies—because her back had been against the proverbial wall and she had nothing to lose—she was the world's biggest coward when it came to telling Crow how much she cared for him. She vowed to take that secret to her grave—and she was damn lucky that day hadn't been today!

George Harper had taken only one step outside Madam Sadie's Brothel in Taloga Springs when he noticed the procession, led by Donovan Crow, riding through town. Drunk though he was, he sobered up in one helluva of a hurry. When he ducked back inside the door to prevent being seen, he slammed into his brothers, Charley and Willy, who were directly behind him.

"What the hell's wrong with you, Georgie?" Charley muttered crossly. "You stepped on my foot."

George gestured for his younger brothers to poke their heads around the partially open door to see for themselves that Crow was back in town. "That woman riding behind Crow on his devil horse must be his wife."

"I wonder if Crow received all three messages we sent to scare him before he left his headquarters in Wolf Ridge," Willy said.

"I was hoping to rattle the hell out of him and leave him wondering when and where we'd strike," Charley commented. "He's saved us the long ride to Wolf Ridge."

"We can take him by surprise right here," Willy enthused. "Maybe we can get the drop on Crow before he and the city marshal figure out we robbed the stagecoach last week while we were hiding out in no-man's-land."

George grimaced. He had masterminded the stagecoach holdup, but he'd been too drunk to sit a horse. He'd sent his younger brothers to rob the passengers for traveling money to finance the trip to Wolf Ridge so they could kill Crow. It had worked out well, he did admit. Now law officials were looking for *two* masked men not three. Plus, Crow might not suspect they were in town and that would give the Harper brothers a prime advantage.

"Look yonder at that fella named Marsh that we met in the saloon yesterday," Charley pointed out. "He was a cocky, arrogant bastard then. Look at him now. He's hunkered over his horse, *backward,* and he looks like he's had the spirit sucked outta him. I swear, Crow must've put one of his powerful Indian curses on him."

George well remembered when Crow had captured him and his brothers, then tied them backward on their horses, forcing them to stare at where they had been instead of where they were going. Made it damn hard to get the drop on that wily half-breed when you were facing the wrong direction.

"I'm more than ready to see Crow pay his due for killing Robbie, Willy said vindictively. "Then I wanna get the hell out of Texas before the marshal sics the Rangers on us again. Don't know which is worse, having Crow breathing down our necks or them Rangers hot on our trail."

Charley frowned curiously while George stared at the prisoners riding backward then broke into a grin.

"What are you grinning about, Georgie?" Charley asked, rolling his eyes in annoyance.

George inclined his shaggy head toward the woman. "We don't have to take on Crow. We'll take his bride for bargaining power and he'll come to us. We can pick him off, retrieve the hidden money from the bank robberies, then ride like hell for the New Mexico border."

Charley and Willy grinned broadly. "I like the sound of that, big brother," Willy snickered.

"I like the sound of Crow being *dead* even better," Charley added as he and his brothers watched the procession halt at the city marshal's office to quick-march the three wounded prisoners inside.

Natalie was exhausted from the ordeal with Marsh and his henchmen. The long restless night and lack of sleep had taken its toll. She was anxious to exit the marshal's office and return to her room for a relaxing bath. When she pivoted away from the cells where Crow had stashed the prisoners, Bart flung up his hand to forestall her.

"You need to file formal charges for assault and battery," he insisted. "Then Van can relay the information to Marshal Dawson that Marsh gave him."

Resigned to the delay, Natalie plunked into the battered wooden chair beside Dawson's scarred desk. The marshal, who looked to be a half-dozen years older than Crow and

Bart, inclined his broad head, then removed his sweat-stained Stetson hat from a mat of coarse black hair. The monobrow over his large hazel eyes made him look a bit fierce, but he had a cordial smile.

"I can tell by looking at you that you had a tough time with those brutes, Mrs. Crow," Dawson commiserated as he sank down at the desk. He pulled an official-looking form from the bottom drawer. "By the time I verify your battered condition and your husband gives his testimony, I can guarantee the circuit judge will have your assailants behind bars for a long time."

Natalie gave Dawson the boiled-down version of the attack, omitting her death-defying attempts to escape. She saw Bart leaning against the doorjamb between the office and the jail, rolling his eyes and shaking his head at her cut-and-dried report.

"There are other serious charges against Marsh and Jenson," Bart inserted as he pushed his drooping glass up the bridge of broken nose.

Crow ambled from the jail cells. "Come on, sunshine, you need to rest." He hitched his thumb toward Bart. "Bart is my lawyer and business agent. He can answer most of your questions about the other charges while I'm gone. After I escort Natalie to the hotel, I'll be back to finish up all the reports."

Natalie found herself hoisted from the chair and shepherded out the door to retrieve the horses. As was his habit, Crow urged her to walk *between* the horses, not *in front* of them as they moved toward the livery stable.

Crow called a halt outside the general store. "Wait here," he commanded, then left her holding both sets of reins.

He returned two minutes later to join her in between the shield of horses. Natalie recalled she had used a version of this technique when she darted under Jenson's horse, then used the animal as her armor of defense. This afternoon, however, she doubted the precaution was necessary, because Crow had locked up the prisoners that meant to do her harm. Then again, why break a good habit? This, after all, was a rough town, she reminded herself as they entered the livery stable.

When Van and Natalie entered the hotel lobby, the clerk came to attention and smiled politely. "We repaired the window in one of the rooms you rented. It's as good as new."

"Thanks. And please send up hot water for bathing in my suite," Van requested before he followed Natalie up the steps. When they reached the landing, he gestured to the left. "You'll be staying with me."

"That isn't necessary—"

"Yes, it is," he interrupted as he guided her toward his suite. "I have a few things to say to you before I return to the marshal's office."

"Can't it wait? I'd love a warm bath first."

"Sorry. No." Van closed the door behind him then rounded on Natalie. He must have looked ferocious for as brave as she was in most situations she took an involuntary step back. "You had your emotional meltdown and now I'm going to have mine," he growled at her.

She stared up at him as if she had no idea what might have set him off. So he told her sharply and succinctly. "Do not ever tie me to a bedpost and sneak off in the darkness to defend yourself against three killers," he roared, his frustration pouring out like molten lava, his voice rising with each word. "I don't care how independent you want to be and how skilled you *think* you are at survival and combat, you are no match for ruthless murderers!"

"But I—"

He made a slashing gesture with his arm to silence her. "I'm not finished yet," he snapped. "This is when I get to do all the talking and you do all the listening."

The comment didn't sit well with her. He really hadn't thought it would. She tilted her skinned chin and narrowed her dark onyx eyes in annoyance, but he was more aggravated than she was so he didn't give a damn.

"In the first place, I was embarrassed and humiliated when Bart came to speak to me last night. He had to cut me loose and he had a good laugh at my expense, thanks to you," he added, his voice dripping sarcasm.

Her lips quirked, as if she intended to smile, but he hurled a stony glare at her. "This is not funny, damn it. Besides that, it cost precious time hunting you down. The whole blessed night, while I tried to find you, I kept asking myself if you had deceived me time after time and had left the jewels and money for safekeeping so the rightful owner couldn't take it away from you."

"Rightful owner?" she scoffed. *"I* am the rightful owner."

"But I didn't know that for sure because I had only heard your side of the story. Then you stole my knife—"

"Borrowed."

"—and my boot pistol which you have yet to return to me," he said, talking over her in a loud voice.

She reached for the weapon, then slapped it into his hand. "There. Happy now?"

"Not particularly," he said, and glared at her. "When I found your ex-fiancé in the livery with a stab wound in his back, I thought you had disposed of him so he couldn't contest your story or offer a physical description of the real Natalie Robedeaux-Blair."

When she opened her mouth to interrupt Van flung up a

hand in her face. "Bart and I weren't sure what the hell was going on. You can see why we might have had our doubts after you tied me up and stole my knife. Then I stumbled over a dead man in the stall where your strawberry roan had been the last time I looked." His caustic voice rose to a shout. "I expected to be accused of killing the man!"

Van dragged in a deep breath and told himself to calm down. It didn't help. He'd been fuming all afternoon and he wanted to blow off steam—directly in Natalie's bewitching face.

"Then, if all that wasn't enough to torment the living hell out of me, while I was riding around in the dark, wondering if I had misjudged you again and thinking I was a fool, I topped the rise of ground at dawn to see three men I didn't know shooting at you."

"People shoot at you all the time," she contended. "You should be used to that."

Van grabbed another breath and gnashed his teeth as he glared at her. "I'm used to people shooting at *me,* but I nearly suffered heart seizure while bullets were flying at *you.* Then I nearly suffered an apoplexy when your horse went down and I was too far away to help you or to get a clear shot at the men who might have had good reason for trying to gun down my wife!"

He wagged his finger in her face and said, "If you want to get yourself killed, let me do it. I'll make it quick and painless and put both of us out of our misery."

Natalie shot him an agitated glance. "Are you the same man who comforted me while I made a complete fool of myself by soaking your shirt with my tears this morning? How could you be so kind, understanding and supportive this morning when you are flapping like a buzzard and picking my bones clean this evening?"

"Because you needed a place to fall apart this morning

and I was relieved to know I hadn't misjudged you. I was grateful you had survived the attack. You were incredibly brave—or stupid. I'm still trying to figure out which!"

"Thank you so much for the insult," she huffed.

He waved his arms in expansive gestures. "You are welcome. Now I'm having my say and—"

To his frustration, someone rapped at the door while he was in mid rant. Scowling, he strode beside the door—not in front of it, as was his policy—to see two tall, gangly boys toting buckets of steaming water. He directed them to the bedroom where the tub stood behind the unadorned dressing screen. He waited impatiently while they poured out the water, then trooped back to the sitting room.

When they left, Van took a good long look at Natalie and he reconsidered lecturing her. She was skinned up, bruised and she had dark circles under her eyes. He'd had his say—for the most part. He could wait until later to finish his tirade.

He tossed her satchel on the settee. "Take your bath and get some rest."

She lifted a perfectly arched brow. "You're finished chewing me up one side and down the other?"

"For now." He fished out a small dagger and handed it to her. "I bought this for you at the general store on our way over here."

She took the stiletto and tested the sharp edge. "Thank you, dear. It's the kind of wedding gift every bride loves to receive from her devoted husband."

"You're welcome, sassy minx," he said before dropping a quick kiss to the side of her mouth that wasn't swollen. Then he spun on his heels. "Enjoy your privacy."

"I'm sure I will, knowing you'll be back for part two of your scathing lecture. I'm really looking forward to it," she called after him.

Natalie huffed out an annoyed breath after the door clicked shut behind Crow. Honestly, there were moments— like this morning when he had been the very picture of gentle compassion—that she loved him so much she could hug the stuffing right out of him. Then there were times—like now—when she wanted to pound him over the head for being judgmental, domineering and cynical. How could he be so suspicious of her?

Her shoulders slumped as she peeled off her breeches that had holes in the knees and tossed them carelessly aside. She reminded herself that she had been cautious and secretive to protect herself. True, she hadn't been completely honest with Crow. Then she had sneaked off, hoping to lead Marsh, Kimball and those five goons...

She wondered what had become of the other three men who exited Rattlesnake Saloon with Marsh, Kimball, Jenson and Green last night. Maybe Marsh hadn't hired them as part of his army of assassins. She should have asked about those scraggly haired, big-boned hombres who'd had their backs to her at the saloon and were too far away to accurately identify them through the hotel window.

She would question Marsh later, she mused as she stared longingly at her bath.

"Ah, Lord, maybe I'm a hopeless tenderfoot after all," she murmured as she sank eagerly into the brass tub.

Natalie expelled an appreciative sigh while the warm water soothed her aches and pains. She was reminded of the days in her own oversize bathtub at the family mansion. Back in the day before her mother married Marsh and fell beneath his heartless scheme of greed.

While Natalie lathered herself with plain soap—not the fragrant kind she had at her disposal at home—her thoughts circled back to what Crow had said to her during their confrontation.

It cut to the core to know Crow never really trusted her and that any feelings he might have had for her were skin-deep at best. "He's a mercenary at heart and you are a fool," she chastised herself harshly. What did he need with her, other than to take advantage of the intimate privileges she'd granted him? Soon his next assignment would be awaiting him and she would be a half-forgotten memory by next weekend.

The truth stung her pride but Natalie reminded herself that she had withstood great adversity the past few months. She had survived and she had become reasonably self-reliant.

Thanks to Crow's instructions, for which she'd paid him handsomely.

Natalie scowled, then slid deeper into the tub to wet down her hair. While she was underwater, she vowed that she would head north first thing in the morning and put Crow out of her mind. She still had excitement and adventure ahead of her. She wouldn't stay where she wasn't wanted. She had the means to see the world and, by damn, she would see it all.

When that silver-eyed devil—who had turned her heart inside out and wrung all feeling from it—was out of sight she would force him out of her mind, as well.

Natalie shot to the surface, gasping for breath. Well, at least she had arrived at a sensible conclusion after soaking her head. She was going to forget Donovan Crow ever existed.

He could have the divorce he wanted. It didn't matter now anyway, she thought as she soaped her hair. Her inheritance was safe. Bart would see to that. Marsh would rot in jail or hang for two murders, embezzlement and assault. She had been vindicated and she should be thinking her lucky stars she was alive!

Chapter Fifteen

Feeling somewhat refreshed, Natalie donned the bright yellow gown Van favored. She smiled wryly, wondering if he would dispense with the remainder of his tongue-lashing if she wore his favorite dress. She doubted it, though she still hadn't figured out why he'd been so upset. Things had turned out splendidly, after all. Marsh and his goons were in jail and she would be out of Crow's hair for good by morning when the stagecoach raced off to Dodge City, the next destination for her exciting adventure.

Despite the prospect of seeing new sights, she knew she was going to miss Crow something fierce. "Think about the adventure ahead of you," she encouraged herself as she stood in front of the cheval glass, surveying her reflection.

She had acquired a bit of a tan from hours spent outdoors. The red-gold highlights in her hair had become more pronounced, she noted. Aside from a few bumps, scrapes and bruises, she had emerged from her perilous ordeal with Marsh and his death brigade in one piece. Thurston Kimball III hadn't been so fortunate. He had become Marsh's disposable pawn after he'd served his purpose.

Natalie retrieved the two-shot derringer she had reloaded, tucked it in one garter, then stashed the dagger Crow had given her in the other. Now that she had grown accustomed to wearing a shirt and breeches, she found the gown and petticoats confining. Well, she would continue her new fashion trend of breeches and boots once she set out to see the sights in Kansas and Colorado...without Crow.

Before the depressing thought took root, Natalie inhaled a restorative breath, then spun toward the door. She was determined to find out what had become of the three unidentified men she had seen hovering around Marsh and the other henchmen the previous day.

She sincerely hoped the men had cut their losses and left when news of Marsh's arrest circulated around town. Nevertheless, she planned to alert Marshal Dawson to be on the lookout for them. She didn't want them to break Marsh out of his jail cell, before he could swing from the tallest tree in Texas.

The moment Natalie emerged from the hotel lobby, she surveyed the dark street. Music from a piano and harmonica drifted from Rattlesnake Saloon, along with a customary cloud of smoke. Her stomach growled, reminding her that the dried pemmican she'd had for lunch on the trail had worn off. She was tempted to detour into a café, but decided to head directly to the marshal's office. She wasn't going to risk leaving any loose ends that pertained to Marsh.

If there was one thing she had learned about her heartless, conniving stepfather it was never to underestimate him. Then again, he had underestimated *her* ability of self-defense this morning and look where it got him.

Natalie swept down the boardwalk, ignoring the wolfish

whistles of drunken cowboys that were wandering back and forth between the Rattlesnake and Lookout saloons. She entered the marshal's office but Bart and Crow were nowhere to be seen.

Well, so much for softening up her hard-edged husband by wearing the bright yellow dress.

"Marshal Dawson?" she called out.

"Back here," he answered from the other side of the door leading to the cells.

Natalie strode through the doorway, pleased to note how good Marsh and his goons looked in a cage framed with metal bars. The only vulnerable place was the barred window that overlooked the alley. But there would be no escape attempt through the alley, not if she could help it.

She walked up to glare at Marsh who sat on a rickety stool, staring at the brick floor. "Where are the men I saw you conspiring with after you left Rattlesnake Saloon yesterday?" she asked without preamble.

"Go to hell," Marsh growled without looking up.

"You first," she countered caustically.

Marshal Dawson's thick brows furrowed over his eyes as he tugged up his sagging trousers. "What's this about other men?"

"I saw Marsh, Kimball, Green and Jenson exit the saloon yesterday with three scraggly haired, burly-looking men," she reported then stared deliberately at Marsh. "I wanted to make certain they didn't attempt to break Marsh out of jail."

"Three, you say? Not two?" Dawson questioned with sudden interest. "As I told Crow, there are two stagecoach robbers lurking in the area and a report of three stolen horses from a nearby ranch. I sent word to the Rangers a few days back, but they haven't arrived yet."

"There were definitely three men, but I only saw them

from a distance. They were dressed like cowboys in tattered shirts and breeches. They wore red bandanas around their necks. I couldn't see their faces clearly."

Dawson frowned pensively. "I better check this out. I have a description of the thieves and their stolen horses. Their mounts might be tethered to hitching posts or stabled at the livery."

Natalie cast one last glance at Marsh who looked nothing like the cocky man who had married her mother five years earlier. She liked the looks of Marsh behind bars so much better and she chose to remember him as such…*if* she decided to think about him at all in the future.

"Doctor Purcell will be back around later to check your wounds," Dawson told his injured prisoners as he walked Natalie out.

Natalie waited while the marshal locked the outside door. "No deputy?" she asked uneasily.

Dawson shook his dark head then hiked up his breeches. "My deputy was shot last week while trying to arrest a drunken cowboy fresh off a cattle drive. No one offered to take his place. This is a rough town, you know."

She nodded in agreement, then veered left while the marshal veered right to check the horses lining the street.

"Do you know where Collier and Crow are?" she called after him.

He turned back to her and shrugged. "Not for sure. Maybe they stopped at one of the saloons for a drink," he said, then continued on his way to check on the three men and their horses.

Natalie pulled a face. If she never had another swallow of whiskey, it would be fine with her. She still remembered feeling ill, befuddled and miserable after she'd had too many drinks during her business negotiations with Crow.

Lifting the hem of her skirt to hike quickly down the

boardwalk, Natalie contemplated her choices of eating establishments. She had tried the Caprock Café the previous afternoon and wasn't impressed. She decided to sample the fare at Canyon Café.

As she passed the corner by the gunsmith shop and headed for the restaurant, someone leaped from the shadows of the side alley to grab her. She didn't have time to shout for help because a man's grimy hand clamped over the lower half of her face. She bit down on a chubby finger and the man yelped in pain. Unfortunately, another hand—holding a smelly kerchief—replaced the first one. She didn't have the chance to scream at the top of her lungs.

"Hold her down, damn it," someone growled while she wormed, squirmed and kicked in vain to gain release.

Sickening dread flooded over her when she realized that three men had accosted her. They wore kerchiefs for masks, but their long scraggly hair stuck out from the rim of their hats and dangled around their disguised faces.

These were Marsh's mysterious cohorts!

Natalie fought even harder for freedom, but she couldn't lash out effectively with her feet and legs because of the confining gown. Worse, her assailants had come prepared. They jerked her arms behind her back and tied her wrists together so she couldn't claw or take swings at them.

"Now get her legs," one man ordered hurriedly.

She tried desperately to counter the attempt to bind her ankles, but she was encumbered by the dress and hopelessly outnumbered. To her fear and frustration, she found herself bound, gagged and tossed over one broad shoulder. Her captors carted her through the side alley to reach the four horses tethered behind the general store.

Her breath came out in a grunt when they dumped her on the ground, then rolled her up in a smelly tarp. One of the men carelessly tossed her over a horse, leaving her in a jackknifed position while he lashed her feet to the stirrups. Blood ran to her head, making her dizzy. She tried to rear up and throw herself backward but one of her abductors shoved the heel of his hand between her shoulder blades and mashed her chest against the horse's ribs. Another man tied a noose around her neck and secured the rope to the saddle.

She cursed herself mightily for not paying attention to her surroundings. Crow would have lectured her sternly for letting her guard down, even though she was in town. Fool that she was, she had presumed she was safe.

Safe in Hell's Fringe? What had she been thinking? Now she was practically hanging upside down, chewing on a foul-tasting handkerchief for supper and wondering if the three goons planned to hold her for ransom or for bargaining power to facilitate Marsh's release.

Natalie muttered at the very idea of Marsh escaping those iron bars that suited him so perfectly.

Her thoughts trailed off when one of her captors chuckled triumphantly. "That was easy enough."

"Wish I could be here to see the look on that half-breed bastard's face when he finds out we kidnapped his wife," the second captor sniggered.

Natalie snapped to attention—as best she could, considering she was draped over the horse like a feed sack. What did Crow have to do with these three? The thought exploded through her mind and sickening dread intensified. Surely these three men weren't the Harper brothers that had sent threatening messages to Crow.

She didn't know where she presumed the Harper Gang was hiding out, but certainly not in Taloga Springs, which was only one of several hellholes on the Texas frontier.

Good God, what rotten luck!

The third captor chuckled wickedly. "After we leave Crow another message and he walks into our trap to rescue his wife, he'll regret killing Robbie."

"Eye for an eye."

"Revenge is gonna be sweet."

"It'll be even sweeter when Crow is dead and we take our turns with his widow."

Natalie swore beneath her gag. For the second time in as many days, she worried that she might become the cause of Crow's death. She'd never forgive herself. Her future—or lack thereof—didn't look promising, either. While her captors led her down the alley in the darkness she hoped and prayed Crow had the good sense not to come looking for her. It wouldn't do either of them any good.

Van took a sip of his whiskey, then grimaced at the fiery taste burning his throat. He glanced accusingly at the bald-headed bartender in Lookout Saloon. "You doctored this tarantula juice with one-hundred-proof alcohol, didn't you?"

The rail-thin proprietor tried out his wide-eyed innocent look, but Van scoffed as he replaced his glass on the bar. "Try it again, friend. And do it right this time." He set Bart's glass beside his. "For me and Collier."

The bartender puffed up with irritation until Bart said, "Thanks, Crow. I'd like a real whiskey myself, not this throat-scorching, foul-tasting rotgut."

Alternately grumbling then eyeing Van warily, the man reached beneath the bar for a fresh bottle of whiskey. He filled both glasses to the brim. "On the house."

"You are too kind," Van muttered as he lifted the glass in a mocking toast. "We already paid for the drinks we couldn't choke down."

He sipped slowly, knowing he was procrastinating in his return to the hotel. He wanted to read Natalie several more lines and paragraphs of the riot act, but he didn't trust himself not to grab hold of her and kiss the breath out of her instead. That would only make the situation more painful for him. He knew she planned to leave on the stagecoach in the morning, headed on to the next leg of her grand adventure.

He stared into the contents of his glass and contemplated what his life was going to be like without that obsidian-eyed hellion underfoot. Damn it, he'd already forgotten what his days and nights had been like before he met her.

"I don't know about you, but I'm ready for a meal, a bath and a soft bed." Bart polished off his drink, then pivoted toward the door. "Are we inviting Nat to dine with us?"

"Yes, we'll feed her before I finish raking her over live coals for defying Marsh and his goons this morning."

Van guzzled the last of his drink, then followed Bart out the door. He frowned curiously when he saw Marshal Dawson halt behind the string of horses tethered in front of the gunsmith's shop. Then Dawson strolled over to scrutinize the horses standing in front of Lookout Saloon.

"Something wrong, Dawson?" Van asked.

Dawson hiked up his sagging breeches as he stepped onto the boardwalk. "Your wife came by earlier looking like sunshine in a pretty yellow gown." He grinned and added, "You're a lucky man, Crow. You know that, don't you?"

"Yes, I do." He remembered thinking the same thing about Nat when he first saw her in that very dress. "Did she stop by to tell Marsh where he could go and what he could do with himself when he got there?"

Dawson removed his hat and raked his beefy fingers through the coarse black hair. "Mostly she wanted to know about the three unidentified men she had seen with Marsh yesterday."

Van started, his senses on high alert. "*Three?* When did she see them?"

"She said there were three men in addition to Marsh's crew standing outside Rattlesnake Saloon in the afternoon. She thought maybe the threesome might be planning a jail-break and she wanted to stop it before it started. I decided to look for the horses described from last week's stage-coach robbery. Doubt there's a connection, but you never know. Maybe the two thieves had another man standing watch even if the stagecoach driver and guard didn't see him. Should have thought of that earlier."

Van muttered under his breath. Had Natalie seen the men while she was prowling around, trying to figure out who threw the rock through her window? Why hadn't she mentioned the men to him before? She should have…and he'd tell her so the moment he returned to the suite.

"Did she describe the men to you?" Bart questioned the marshal.

Dawson crammed the hat on his head then nodded. "Big-boned, wearing ragtag cowboy-looking clothes. Scraggly hair and red bandannas around their necks."

"*What!*" Van gasped in disbelief.

"Oh hell, you don't suppose it's the Harper Gang that hooked up with Marsh?" Bart croaked as he glanced up and down the boardwalk. "Could we be that lucky to apprehend them in the same town with Natalie's tormen-tor?"

Van sorely wished the threesome would lumber out of one of the saloons so he could pounce and be done with them.

"We better check Rattlesnake Saloon," Bart advised.

"Might try the brothels, too," Dawson suggested. "Or that fleabag hotel by the red-light district. They might be passed out and sleeping off a hangover."

Dawson's voice trailed off when he noticed three riders approaching. He grabbed his gun and pointed it at the men in ragtag clothing.

"Put away your gun, marshal. That's your long-awaited Rangers," Van smirked then stared down Montgomery, Bristow and Phelps. "I hope you delivered my two friends to the reservation unharmed and filed complaints about Lieutenant Suggs at Fort Sill."

The Rangers—all sporting several days' growth of whiskers and a layer of dust—dismounted.

"The Indian Agent is checking into the situation," Phelps reported.

Van scoffed cynically. "He might be in on the scheme. It wouldn't be the first time a corrupt agent cheated tribes."

Montgomery slapped his dusty hat against his hip then brushed off the shoulders of his shirt. "We're planning to stay on top of the situation."

"You do that, Monty, and so will I when I head that direction in the morning."

"We'd still be there but we received word about a stage-coach robbery in no-man's-land and horse thieves north of Taloga Springs," Bristow interjected as he stared deliberately at Van. "We need more Rangers to police this area and deal with a wide assortment of problems. Know where we could find a capable volunteer?"

"Don't look at me," Van said. "I have my own problems. The Harper Gang, minus their little brother I had to kill in self-defense, is in town. The brothers are out for my blood."

Phelps perked up. "If we capture them and collect the

rewards on their heads, maybe we can twist their arms a few dozen ways to find out where they hid the money from their bank robberies." He stared directly at Van. "We were told we worked cheaper than you, so you recommended that *we* track down the outlaws that escaped from jail."

Van was in no mood to rub that comment in the Rangers' faces. He wanted to find the Harpers. Now.

"I'll check the other hotels and give descriptions of the Harpers," Bart offered, then wheeled away.

"I'll check Rattlesnake Saloon," Monty volunteered. "I could use a drink anyway."

"I'll be at the livery stable looking for the horses stolen from one of the nearby ranches," the marshal said, then hurried off.

"Well, hell," said Van. That left him to check the red-light district. He wondered what Nat would say—or think—if she saw him enter the bordellos. Would she care? He reminded himself that, come tomorrow, they would part company. He had served his purpose for her. With her staggering fortune, she could buy new friends, new beaus and anything else her heart desired.

The thought put a scowl on his face as he strode toward the brothels on the west side of town.

Ten minutes later, he had questioned the harlots at the first house of ill repute, then entered the second. Madam Sadie sauntered toward him, flashing a come-hither smile.

"You're the one called Crow," she purred. "I heard you were in town and that you brought in prisoners. Perhaps you would like to unwind and relax now that you're off duty."

Van glanced down at the bosomy redhead, dressed in an off-the-shoulder red velvet gown. She flashed him a seductive smile, then rubbed provocatively against his arm. He predicted he was destined to spend the next six months—probably longer—comparing potential lovers to Natalie and finding them sadly lacking in every way imaginable.

"Thanks for the offer, but I'm looking for three men with scraggly brown hair and plain facial features. They are brothers and one is as unremarkable looking as the next."

Madam Sadie frowned distastefully. "They were here late this afternoon. One of my girls complained that the oldest one was exceptionally drunk, loud and abusive. We were glad when they left, I can tell you for sure."

"Do you know where they are staying?" Van asked urgently.

Sadie's bare shoulder lifted in a shrug. "Didn't ask. Don't care, as long as they don't come back here. They shortchanged all three of my girls before they staggered off."

Van mumbled a hasty goodbye, then exited. Knowing where the Harper brothers had been, not where they were now was doing no good whatsoever. He hoped the other men had better luck tracking the outlaws.

Ten minutes later, the men congregated in the middle of Main Street. No one reported any sightings of the bandits.

"Maybe they decided to ride out when they heard you were in town," Marshal Dawson speculated.

"Doubt it," Van said. "They promised retribution. The Harpers are around here somewhere."

"Just to be on the safe side, we better tell Natalie who those men are," Bart advised. "Knowing her, she'll decide to arrest them herself."

Van glanced up at the second story of the hotel, three windows from the left. Unease skittered down his spine when he noticed the curtains were open but no light flickered from a lantern. Then he glanced into the window of the single room on the other side of the hotel. No light glowed there, either.

"Marshal, how long ago did you say my wife stopped at your office?"

Dawson rubbed his chin pensively. "Must've been at least three quarters of an hour. She was going to grab a bite to eat."

Van sagged in relief. "Good. Since the hotel suite looks dark, that must mean she's still at one of the cafés. For a moment there I was wondering if the Harpers might have used her to bait a trap for me."

"That's one way to draw out a man without facing his deadly pistol," Monty remarked. "Better go find your pretty wife and keep track of her until we run the Harpers to ground." He glanced at the marshal. "Afterward we'll see what we can do about the two stagecoach robbers and horse thieves preying on this area."

"I'll check Canyon Café," Van said. "You Rangers can check Caprock Café."

"No sense bothering with Panhandle Café," Dawson said, shuddering. "You have to have a cast-iron belly to eat there. That's usually where I pick up meals for my prisoners. I figure they deserve it."

Van wished he'd thought to warn Natalie away from Panhandle Café when they arrived in town. Most cowboys were well into their cups when they staggered in there to eat.

"I'm ready to grab a bite," Bart insisted as he kept up with Van's swift strides. "I hope we find Nat along the way."

Bart glanced curiously at Van. "Do you still want that divorce you've been ranting about for two days?"

"Not unless Sunshine does. Hers is the only offer I'll probably ever get." Van stepped onto the boardwalk, then opened the door. He scanned the patrons at the tables but Natalie wasn't one of them. If she were here, he would have spotted that bright yellow gown in nothing flat.

"I wonder where she could be if she isn't here or in her room," Bart mused aloud.

Concern furrowed Van's brow as he reversed direction. "Maybe she decided to lie down before eating. She's had a hard day, after all."

"Could be," Bart agreed as he veered back to the café. "I'll grab something for all of us and bring it to the hotel."

Van nodded, distracted. Every minute that he couldn't account for Natalie's whereabouts intensified his concern. Not only were the Harpers lurking about, wanting Van's head served up on a silver platter, but rowdy cowboys were always causing trouble around here, too, blowing off steam before returning to their duties with the traveling cattle herds. Natalie didn't need to be roughed up again. She had been knocked around too many times this morning.

Van halted at the hotel desk to check with the clerk, who was certain he had seen Natalie leave, wearing the stunning yellow gown. He admitted that he had stepped out for a few minutes so he couldn't say for sure if she had returned.

"Damn it," Van muttered as he bounded up the steps. He hated this feeling of fear that gnawed at him. He tried to tell himself that the Harpers couldn't have grabbed Natalie. She had learned to defend herself. But what if…?

He clenched his teeth when several grim scenarios leaped to center stage of his mind. If Natalie managed to escape Marsh and his henchmen, only to meet disaster as a pawn used to lure him in, he would never forgive himself.

He unlocked the door to the suite, then called out in the darkness. Even if he awakened her from much-needed sleep he wouldn't apologize because he needed to know she was safe.

"Sunshine? Are you here?"

He lit the bedroom lantern only to see the bed hadn't been slept in and her satchel lay beside the end table. Van whirled around and hurried off to check the single room with the new glass window. Natalie hadn't been thrilled with the prospect of another long-winded lecture from him. Maybe she had gone to her own room to avoid him.

Van hammered on the door. "Natalie!"

He was met with silence. Another ripple of distress slithered down his backbone.

"Mr. Crow?"

Van whipped around to see one of the lanky teenage boys who had delivered bathwater earlier in the day.

The boy extended his hand, palm up. "I was told to give this to you tonight."

Van unfolded the note and felt his breath freeze in his chest.

Eye for an eye. One of yours for one of ours. We will tell you where to meet us in the morning. Sleep well, Crow.

In the morning? Van swore silently. He'd never last that long. The suspense of not knowing if Natalie was being abused like the harlot Madam Sadie mentioned would kill him before midnight.

And that was the idea. He was supposed to suffer all the torments of the damned, wondering where Natalie was and whether she had come to harm.

After the teenager walked away, Van slammed his right fist into his left hand, wishing he could bash in all three of the Harpers' plain-looking faces. "Damn them to hell!"

"Van?"

He lurched around to see Bart at the head of the steps, carrying a basket of food in his uninjured arm. "I picked up three supper specials. There's plenty of food… What's wrong?"

"Everything," Van growled furiously as he waved the note in the air. "The Harpers have Natalie. I'm supposed to wait until morning to find out where to meet them."

Bart glanced down at the food basket. "Suddenly I don't feel a damn bit hungry."

"I don't want food. I want to kill somebody. Starting and ending with those goddamn Harper brothers!" he raged.

"I'm sorry," Bart mumbled inadequately. "I'd gladly exchange places with her if I could."

"I *will* change places with her," Van vowed as he stormed to his suite. He halted to glance grimly at his trusted friend. "Get her out alive, Bartholomew. No matter what else happens tomorrow, promise me that she'll have the chance to enjoy the grand adventure she's dreamed about."

He didn't have to add that he would gladly become the sacrifice needed to ensure Natalie's safety.

Bart understood exactly what he meant.

Chapter Sixteen

Natalie was not surprised when she realized the Harpers had descended into the labyrinth of canyons south of Taloga Springs to hide out. The outlaws found a cave large enough to accommodate them. They removed her from the tarp and dumped her in the corner. After building a fire near the mouth of the cavern, they commenced celebrating their scheme by opening two bottles of whiskey. To her vast relief, they passed out and didn't bother her.

With her feet curled up beside her, Natalie discreetly retrieved the dagger Crow had given her. Even though her hands were tied behind her back, she was able to saw at the ropes wrapped around her wrists. She nicked her skin and drew blood but she was determined to free herself. It was tedious work and she stopped countless times to rest her aching arms. Fortunately she had all night because the Harper brothers were sprawled on the stone floor, their greasy heads propped on their saddles, snoring up a storm.

It took several hours to free herself. The golden light of dawn spilled into the cavern by the time she slowly rose to her feet. After long hours of being tied up and hanging upside down over the horse, it took several minutes before she felt steady. She removed her cumbersome petticoats, then drew the back hem of her gown between her legs to fashion makeshift breeches. Since she didn't have a belt to hold up the yards of fabric, she tiptoed over to make use of one of the holsters the men had tossed in the back of the cavern near a small tunnel. Natalie did not intend to follow it to see if it was an escape hatch or dead end. She was using the large exit—*if* she could leave without alerting the sleeping desperadoes.

Plus, she was *not* leaving without taking their arsenal of weapons with her, though she knew they had other weapons stashed on their person. But at least they wouldn't have extra pistols and ammunition to blast away at her if they awoke and realized she was gone.

She didn't want to repeat that unnerving fiasco of dodging bullets with Marsh and his goons.

When Georgie Harper rolled to his side and groaned Natalie froze to the spot. She hardly dared to breathe, for fear the sounds would echo around the cave and wake the bandits. She didn't want to fight her way to freedom as she had yesterday.

Sweet mercy! she thought as she plucked up the six-shooters and tucked them into the folds of her skirt-turned-breeches. She had crammed so much danger, excitement and new experiences into the past two weeks that it seemed like six months of living.

This is what Crow's life is like, she realized with a start. He faced perilous situations constantly. Every day tested his physical stamina, heightened his acute senses and sharpened his wits. If she could become one-fourth as capable as Crow she would be well pleased with herself.

Her thoughts scattered when Willy Harper moaned groggily and squirmed in his sleep. Natalie glanced anxiously toward the mouth of the chamber. She was as far from the exit as she could get and there were three burly outlaws standing in her way—lying in her path was more accurate. But still!

Inching along the wall, taking care not to let the spare pistols tumble from her improvised pockets and clank against the rock floor, Natalie moved along the perimeter, watching where she stepped. She stopped breathing when Charley mumbled inaudibly. She was afraid he'd rouse his brothers and the chase would be on before she had a head start.

To her vast relief, all three men remained asleep. She stepped outside to inhale a deep breath of fresh air. She would have gladly offered to purchase another two bottles of liquor for her captors if it would guarantee they'd be conked out until she was long gone.

Natalie moved swiftly down the footpath that descended thirty-five feet to the canyon floor. She did admit the Harpers had chosen an excellent fortress that provided a broad view of the crevices, arroyos and unique rock formations that towered overhead. She wanted to take time to wash her face and refresh herself in the clear spring, complete with a small waterfall that tumbled from the caprock to splatter off a stairway of limestone ledges. But time was of the essence. She had to tolerate the lingering odor of the mildewy tarp and smelly kerchief that clung to her clothing.

Her first order of business was to reach the four horses tethered near a stand of cedar trees at the base of an arroyo. She cast an occasional glance at the ridge above her to make sure the bandits didn't emerge like a swarm of angry hornets. Moving quickly, she straddled one horse bareback then grabbed the reins to the other three.

The sun cast colorful light and shadows on the rugged

rock formations as she reined north. At least she hoped it
was north. According to Crow, she had a lousy sense of
direction.

She grimaced in disappointment when angry shouts
boomed around the stone walls. She glanced up to see
Georgie Harper pumping his fist at her, promising hellish
torment and torture. Charley and Willy promptly joined
him on the ledge, calling her all sorts of foul names.

"Come back here!" Georgie bellowed furiously. "I'll
show you no mercy when we catch up with you."

"I'm gonna make you wish you were dead!" Willy
yelled.

"And I'll help him," Charley seconded. "You'll never
get out of this canyon alive!"

Natalie ignored them. She didn't have time to exchange
threats with the outlaws for she was hell-bent on escape.

From their elevated fortress, they pitched rocks at her,
startling the horses. The horses danced sideways and
threw their heads nervously while rocks pelted them. Natalie gritted her teeth and held tightly to the reins, though
her weary arm felt as if it were being stretched past its
limits.

Then the shooting started. She looked down at her
makeshift pockets, noting two six-shooters had fallen by
the wayside during her hasty descent on the footpath. Plus,
the Harpers had spare hardware tucked in the waistbands
of their breeches.

"Awk!" Natalie squawked when gunshots ricocheted
off the rock walls, pelting her face with pebbles and filling
her eyes with grit and dust.

Her eyes were watering so bad that she could barely
see where she was going. She wiped them on the sleeve
of her gown then yelped when another bullet thudded into
the boulder near her shoulder. When the horses bolted

forward and yanked on the reins, nearly jerking her arm from its socket, she gasped in pain.

"Curse it!" Natalie grumbled as she fought to regain control of the startled animals. She didn't want to release them, knowing the Harpers would chase them down on foot, then chase *her* on horseback.

Natalie instinctively ducked when a bullet whistled past her head, nearly putting a new part in her hair. She spared a quick glance over her shoulder to see Georgie blasting away with one of the pistols she had lost on the footpath. Charley had grabbed the other one. The two men fired at her again.

They were excellent marksmen, she noted. Flying bullets missed her by inches but grazed the ribs of the mount she was riding. The horse reared up on its hind legs and screamed in fright. She clamped her arms around the wild-eyed horse's neck. But without a saddle to anchor herself, she slid backward and landed on the ground with a thud and groan, twisting her ankle in the process.

She cast a frantic glance at the Harper brothers who were cursing her as they stormed downhill to capture her. Her heart hammered a hundred miles an hour as she struggled to control the prancing horses, while the Harpers fired repeatedly in an attempt to force her to release the reins.

I'm not going to make it, Natalie thought as she scrambled madly, hoping and praying she could claw her way onto one of the horses before a bullet brought her down.

One almost did. She tucked and rolled beneath one of the high-stepping horses then slammed her shoulder against a protruding boulder. She shifted before the frightened horse trampled her. Then she asked herself if it was better to be trampled than have three furious outlaws follow through on the vicious threats they hurled at her.

* * *

At dawn, Bart rapped his trademark knock on Van's door. He had intercepted another message, delivered by the second teenager who worked for the hotel. When Van didn't open the door immediately, Bart turned the latch and discovered it was unlocked.

"Van? The Harpers are holding Natalie in Phantom Canyon."

He pushed his drooping spectacles back in place as he hurried across the sitting room. He had expected to see Van pacing the floorboards, awaiting the next missive. Surely he hadn't tried to drown his troubles by downing glass after glass of whiskey. Truth be told, Bart had been tempted to guzzle a few drinks to take the edge off his nerves. But he wanted to keep his wits about him. He and the Rangers needed to assist Van in rescuing Natalie—if it wasn't too late.

Bart glanced down at the scrawled handwriting on the note that said, *If you want to see your wife alive, come alone to Phantom Canyon.*

"No chance of that," Bart muttered on his way to the bedroom. "What the hell?"

His voice trailed off when he saw Van's everyday garments scattered on the empty bed—and no sign of the headband, buckskin clothing and moccasins he always carried with him.

"Hey, Crow! Are you in here?" Montgomery called from the sitting room.

"*I'm* in here but Crow turned Kiowa during the night," Bart called to the Rangers. "He didn't bother to tell me that he wasn't waiting for the second message."

When the Rangers formed a semicircle behind him, Bart gestured to the discarded white man's clothing. "He's wearing buckskin and the beaded headband his mother gave him before she died during the army's ambush. I'd say he's gone on the warpath."

"What chance does he have against those three outlaws?" Phelps asked no one in particular.

Bart well remembered what Van had said to him last night about sacrificing himself to save Natalie. He whirled toward the door. "We need to set a fast pace. The Harpers are holed up in Phantom Canyon."

"I know where it is," Bristow said as he fell into step behind Bart.

"So does Van. It's the place where three members of his family died," he said grimly. "If there are such things as Indian spirits lurking in the Kiowas' former stronghold I hope they haunt the living hell out of the Harpers."

"He should have waited for us," Phelps grumbled as he hurried down the steps. "I know he doesn't respect the Rangers, but we can provide reinforcement if he needs it."

Bart knew Van's only concern was the safety and welfare of his wife. It reminded him of another time and place when *he* had set aside his own wants and needs to ensure the happiness of the woman who had held his heart—and still did.

Natalie scrambled madly in an attempt to control the jittery horses. She yelped when an unseen hand snagged her arm and yanked her behind the oversize boulder. She tried to scream but another hand clamped over her nose and mouth while she was dragged against a rock-hard chest. Her captor jerked the reins from her hands so fast they burned in pain.

Dear God! She hadn't realized one of the Harpers had circled around to sneak up on her. If she didn't escape now she wouldn't have another chance. She dug in her heels and pushed—hard—trying to knock her captor off balance.

"Calm down, sunshine. I'm on your side, remember?"

Natalie nearly wept at the sound of Crow's rich, baritone voice. She tilted her head sideways to stare into his grim expression. He wore the beaded headband, along with the buckskin clothes and moccasins he'd donned the day Teskee and Chulosa joined them in camp. Red, black and white war paint covered his cheeks, chin and forehead. If Natalie didn't know and love Crow to such a fierce degree, she would have been terrified. He looked as formidable and dangerous as she had ever seen him.

"How did you find me?" she whispered.

"Old Kiowa trick...and a lighted torch to follow the tracks through the dark alley. How did you escape them?"

"Old Kiowa trick," she said and managed a faint smile. "I used the dagger you gave me to cut the ropes off my wrists. Also, I relied on everything else you taught me."

Her comment prompted the slightest hint of a smile. It didn't last long. His expression turned hard as he tucked her behind the boulder for protection.

"Remember how I keep telling you to stay put, and you defy me with one flimsy excuse after another?"

She nodded her tousled head.

"This time I really mean it, sunshine."

"You and your rules," she grumbled as she waved around the pistol she extracted from the fold of her makeshift breeches. "Here I am with spare hardware and you're not letting me use it."

Smiling faintly, he dropped a kiss to her lips, then crouched so he could spring into action.

"Crow, I—" Natalie clamped her mouth shut before she did the inexcusable and blurted out that she was crazy in love with him, even when she knew she meant nothing special to him.

When he frowned questioningly, she shooed him on his way. He surged between the horses that still tugged at the reins he had clamped in his hand. Natalie shook her head in amazement as he crouched down between the skittish horses. She predicted the Harpers were going to be surprised when they raced across the canyon floor and realized Crow had materialized where she had been a moment before.

Despite Crow's orders to stay down while he took all the chances with his life and became the target to lure in the Harpers, Natalie came to her knees so she could poke her head over the boulder. Sure enough, the Harpers skidded to a startled halt when Crow expelled a war whoop and rose to his feet, while the horses circled him like a moving shield.

"Well, hell!" Georgie scowled, then took aim to fire.

"Where'd he come from?" Charley muttered sourly.

"I'll take care of him." Willy closed his left eye to take Crow's measure on the sight of the gun barrel.

What was the matter with Crow? she mused in frustration. He didn't have a pistol with him. And *he* called *her* a daredevil? Natalie raised her pistol and aimed at Willy who was trying to get a clear shot at Crow. Willy squawked in surprise when she shot him in the leg before he could fire at Crow. She didn't dare glance in Crow's direction since she had disobeyed his direct order—again.

Her mouth dropped open when Crow hooked his left arm around one of the horses' neck and tossed his left leg over the animal's back. How he kept from falling off the side of the horse she had no idea—his superior strength and practice was her best guess.

He clamped all four sets of reins between his teeth and

urged the horses forward, while George tried to shoot him twice. George yelped when Crow ran the horses straight at him, knocking him flat and sending his pistol cartwheeling through the air.

Natalie blinked in amazement when Crow maneuvered the four horses so he could kick out with his right foot to land a brain-scrambling blow to Georgie's chin.

The outlaw collapsed. He lay face up and motionless on the ground.

Natalie darted a glance at Charley who had the good sense to turn tail and run. Not that he escaped Crow's wrath. The bandit only had time to retreat ten paces before Crow and his horses plowed over him. Charley screamed his head off when Crow struck out with his right foot and slammed the outlaw's skull into the ground. Natalie winced, certain the hard blow jarred teeth and smashed Charley's nose into the dirt.

Crow's unnerving war whoop echoed around the chasm like a death knell as Willy staggered to his feet, still clutching his bloody leg. His eyes were wide as goose eggs as he hobbled back in the direction he'd come, firing his pistol erratically over his shoulder as he went. Crow ran him to ground and sent him skidding in the outwash of loose gravel at the base of an arroyo. Willy whimpered after he received a kick in the back of the head. He yelped, collapsed and lay unmoving.

While Natalie watched, Crow slid off the horse to retrieve leather strips from the pouch secured to his waist. Quick as a wink he lashed the bandits' hands behind their backs. When he spared a glance at her, his eyes were like chips of ice and his expression was nothing short of ferocious.

"Turn away," he demanded sharply. "I don't want you to see this side of me. Get up and start walking." He gestured to what she assumed was the north. "Bart and the Rangers should be here soon."

She nodded her disheveled head, then turned her back. One of the men screamed bloody murder while she limped off on her swollen ankle. Another howl rose behind her, then another.

An unholy chant rippled around the canyon walls and she realized this time it was Crow, not the outlaws. The wild, piercing sound sent shivers down her spine. Several more chants mingled with the Harpers' pained howls but Natalie kept limping in the direction Crow had sent her. Whatever was happening in the canyon seemed to be so much more than scare tactics and punishment for the bandits' crimes.

When hoofbeats resounded ahead of her Natalie ducked behind a boulder and grabbed her pistol. She peaked around the oversize slab of rock to see Bart and the Rangers clattering downhill, displacing dust and pebbles as they came.

Natalie shot to her feet. "About time you showed up. Crow is taking care of the Harpers all by himself."

All four men blinked in surprise. "Did Crow release you already?" Bart asked.

"No. I did that myself while the Harpers were sleeping off their bout with whiskey."

They gaped at her so she reached into her garter to wave the stiletto in front of them. "Wedding gift from Crow. Contrary to the consensus in New Orleans high society, diamonds are *not* a woman's best friend, a *dagger* is—"

Another bone-chilling wail echoed in the chasm. Maybe it was her imagination but she swore the sudden downdraft of wind sweeping over the caprock sounded like whispered voices.

Bemused, she glanced up at the men on horseback.

"Phantom Canyon," Phelps informed her.

"Once there was a village where Donovan Crow grew up," Bart added solemnly. "It's the place where he lost most of his family and many of his friends. The army slaughtered the tribe's horses, cattle and dozens of his clan. Those who survived were marched to the reservation in Indian Territory."

Natalie suspected the strange chants Crow had uttered were some sort of ceremonial ritual. The unholy sounds had frightened her but she imagined they had really scared the bejeezus out of the Harpers. If the lost souls of the Kiowa and Comanche were swirling around Phantom Canyon, she would not be surprised.

Bart leaned down to extend his good arm so Natalie could boost herself up behind him. "Nice breeches, by the way," he teased as she settled behind him.

"Thank you. I'm thinking of designing trousers expressly for women. Dresses are such a nuisance when you're cutting yourself loose from ropes and running for your life."

"Blair Wear?" he ventured with a chuckle.

Natalie giggled...until another ear-piercing scream filled the air. Followed by another...and another.

Phelps nudged his horse forward. "We better check on Crow and his prisoners."

Natalie looped her arms around Bart's waist and laid her head against his back. "I haven't had much sleep the past two nights. I would give a small fortune for a nap."

"You can have a nap for free, Nat," he replied, patting her hand consolingly. "I'll grab hold of you if you start to fall off."

Natalie closed her eyes, sighed tiredly and dreamed of the Kiowa warrior who had appeared from nowhere to rescue her at the precise moment she needed him most.

* * *

Van stared down at the Harper brothers, who looked the worse for wear after he had dragged them behind their stolen horses to the stream. They lay faceup, their noses and mouths barely above the water—because he had propped rock pillows beneath their heads to allow them to breathe.

Considering they smelled like stale sweat and whiskey, they were probably suffering hellish hangovers. Van was sure it was the first time in a long while the bandits had bathed—unless they had been rained on. The cool water also cleansed their wounds and that was all the medical treatment they would receive until he had the answers he wanted.

Of all the places the Harpers could have held Natalie hostage, Phantom Canyon had given the best advantage. He knew the area exceptionally well and he had accurately guessed where the Harpers had holed up.

"Now then, let's try again," Van told his prisoners. "The stolen money? You remember it, don't you? Bank robberies? Wounded bank tellers?"

"Don't recall," George snarled hatefully.

"Me, neither," Charley chimed in.

"You can go to hell, Crow," Willy sneered defiantly.

"Already been there," Van replied. "I told the devil to expect you. Even as early as today if you aren't cooperative."

He walked into the water to kick the rock from under George's head. While George struggled to keep his head above water—and couldn't—Crow stepped over him to stare down at Charley and Willy.

"Who's next, Charley? If you refuse to talk and you drown, I'll torture the information from Willy before he bleeds to death from the gunshot wound."

"You bastard—" Charley sneered before Van kicked the stone away and the bandit's face was submerged.

George lifted his head and gasped for air, but he couldn't hold himself up indefinitely so he grabbed a breath and submerged again.

Wide-eyed, Willy listened to his brothers gasp and then sink beneath the surface. "Let 'em go and I'll tell you," Willy bargained frantically. "None of us can run off after you slit our hamstrings. I got no chance anyway 'cause your wife shot me."

Van gnashed his teeth when the bandit reminded him that Natalie had openly defied him—again. Always trying to steal his thunder, the hellion. He wondered if there was any way to break her of that annoying habit. And doubted it.

He looked down at the Harpers when the two oldest brothers burst to the surface simultaneously, huffing and puffing for air. "Change your minds yet?" he asked conversationally. They glowered at him and he shrugged. "We can do this all day because you're long overdue for a good, soaking bath. I'll be here paying my respects to my departed family in Phantom Canyon. You can hear their whispering voices in the wind and their murmurs in the stream. They are chanting for me to sacrifice you to avenge their deaths."

Crow bit down on a grin when three howling voices erupted in the near distance. Maybe those Rangers weren't such a bad lot since they were playing along with his scare tactics.

"All right," Willy muttered. "I'll tell—"

"Shut up, kid," Georgie snarled on a gasping breath.

"I don't wanna be sacrificed to Injun spirits," Willy protested. "We hid the money in the cave where we stashed your wife. It's back in the tunnel that leads to nowhere."

"Damn it," Charley growled on a ragged breath. "Now he'll kill us for sure!"

Van swooped down to grab the front of Georgie's wet shirt, then slung him ashore. He did the same to Charley and Willy. "You're damn lucky I'm letting you live," he said harshly. "You wouldn't be so lucky if I had turned my wife loose on you. She wanted to shoot all of you and be done with it."

Leaving the Harpers facedown in the mud, their hands tied behind their backs and their hamstrings half-sliced so they couldn't run from the law ever again, Van hiked off to the cave where he had spent so many hours as a child. He saw the Rangers hiding in one of the ravines and motioned for them to tend to the prisoners.

When he stepped into the cavern, he noticed the empty whiskey bottles Natalie had mentioned. He also saw the frayed rope. He suspected Natalie had spent a sleepless night trying to cut herself loose and he well remembered seeing the nicks and cuts on her hands—from the sharp dagger, no doubt. Wisely, she had taken the precaution of swiping as many weapons as she could before she made her escape from the cavern.

Van shook his head and smiled. Natalie Blair was nothing if not astonishing and resourceful. "You missed your calling, sunshine," he murmured to the image floating above him in the darkness. "You should have been born Kiowa."

He crouched down to crawl into the tunnel that was only passable if a man moved on his hands and knees. He found the canvas pouches and tossed them back in the direction he'd come. Then he paused at the seeming dead end and glanced up. The escape route from the cave to the cliff above him zigzagged like a waterless river through the limestone.

Van smiled ruefully, remembering the times he and his friends had pulled themselves up by grabbing handholds in the stone to climb into the small chamber leading to a sinkhole. His smile faded, for it was in the chamber where his mother had sent him after she had been seriously wounded the day of the massacre. She had handed him the headband made from the beads his father, Mitch Donovan, had given her so many years before he vanished from their lives as if he had never been there at all.

After the massacre, Van had cut his hair and changed his style of clothing to become white. It was here that the memories of his past converged with potent intensity.

It was here, too, that Natalie could have died.

The thought struck like an arrow to the heart. The loss of his family and friends had devastated him, filled him with bitterness and resentment. If that vibrant, obsidian-eyed firebrand had died today Van wasn't sure he could have dealt with the tormenting loss.

Funny, he mused as he crawled from the tunnel. He had aptly nicknamed her. She had come to be the very sunshine in his world. If she weren't out there somewhere, he'd be stumbling around in the dark.

"Crow? Are you coming down?" Bristow called out.

Van scooped up the recovered money and walked onto the ledge. The Rangers had tied the Harper brothers to their bareback horses—backward—and secured their feet beneath the horses' bellies. Van smiled when the Rangers tipped their hats respectfully to him.

Rangers or not, he was beginning to like Montgomery, Bristow and Phelps, in spite of his earlier vow to hold the ragtag group of frontier officers in contempt for the sins of their predecessors.

Van tossed the moneybags over the ledge so each Ranger could catch a pouch in midair. "The reward for the Harpers' capture and the return of the money is yours. I have my wife back and that is payment aplenty. Oh, and don't forget to credit the Harpers for the stagecoach robbery and horse thefts. Wouldn't want to shortchange them."

Monty tipped his head back to peer up at him. "You coming with us, chief?"

"I'll be along later."

Van stared over the spectacular canyon that was once a Comanche and Kiowa stomping ground. It was time to make peace with the demons that haunted him, he mused as he watched the Rangers lead the bandits away. Van would always be Kiowa at heart, but the old days and the old ways were forever beyond his grasp. He recalled what Natalie had said about being alone in the world and leaving her past behind to chase her dreams of adventures.

He sank down cross-legged on the cliff and inhaled a restorative breath. From his bird's-eye view, he stared over the chasm, as if looking through the window of time. He could visualize the peaceful village of teepees, grazing cattle and herd of horses that he and his friends took pride in training.

He realized he had never really come to terms with his grief, just stowed it away and carried it with him for more than a decade. He had joined the white's world and had taken from it to compensate for the loss of tribal lands and sacred ground. The money from his assignments didn't lessen the blow to Kiowa pride or self-respect, but he had symbolically regained what his clan had lost—one assignment at a time.

Van said goodbye to his tormented past and tucked away the good memories in his heart. He mourned the clan he had loved. It struck him suddenly that all the bandits he had brought to justice weren't the only ones locked away. *He* had been a prisoner of his past and he had built confining walls around himself because of his anger and resentment.

He smiled faintly, knowing that he had learned much about himself through Natalie. The mentor had become the student. The time had come for *him* to look forward, not backward.

It had required great courage for Natalie to strike off into the unknown and the unfamiliar to create a life that made her happy.

"And I hope you do find happiness, sunshine," he murmured as he lifted up his face and arms to the Great Spirit that watched over the Earth, the seas and the endless blue sky. "I will remember you always...."

Chapter Seventeen

Natalie tossed aside her yellow gown, which had suffered irreparable damage during her abduction and escape. When she sank into the bathtub in Crow's suite, she expelled a weary sigh. She was more than ready to wash away the unpleasant ordeal with the Harpers and put the experience behind her.

An hour passed and Crow never appeared. She wondered if that was significant. Then another hour passed and she took it as a sign. Crow had concluded his assignment. He was ready to move on to the next job that awaited him. Natalie knew it was best to part company without awkward farewells. Besides, she was in no mood for another dressing-down because she had disobeyed Crow's orders in Phantom Canyon.

The man didn't seem to understand that she loved him wholeheartedly. Therefore, she was compelled to provide whatever reinforcement needed when he faced lopsided odds. He could scold her a dozen different ways but she would protect him if she could. Always.

Natalie stepped into the stylish lavender gown she had

stashed in her satchel. Her next order of business was to purchase a ticket for the morning stagecoach headed to Dodge City.

It is best if I'm gone when Crow returns, she told herself sensibly. If not, she might become overly sentimental and blurt out her affection—as she'd nearly done this morning. She predicted that confessing her love would make Crow uncomfortable. She would be humiliated while he fumbled about, trying to overcome his blunt, straightforward manner to attempt to let her down as gently as he could.

Natalie packed her satchel and tattered carpetbag. She smiled slightly, remembering how gentle and considerate Crow had been when she fell apart after the ordeal with Marsh. However, he had been biding his time until they were in the privacy of his suite. He hadn't minced words when he jumped down her throat for sneaking off at night to lure Marsh and his death brigade away from him.

The familiar signal rap at the door assured her that Bart had arrived, not Crow. It had been more than three hours and still there was no sign of him. Pasting on a smile, she opened the door for Bart.

He stared at her and then at the luggage by the door. "You're leaving?"

"I have time to catch the coach to Dodge City. This is the day I planned to leave," she reminded him. "If Crow still wants the divorce—"

"He doesn't," Bart cut in then glanced around the sitting room. "He isn't back yet?"

Natalie shrugged casually, though her heart ached. "No, but it's better this way. I paid him in full for his services. If either of you need to get in touch with me, you can contact my lawyer in New Orleans. I will send him telegrams until I return home to check on my estate and shipping business."

She walked over to the small desk to jot down the information Bart needed. "You will be generously compensated for seeing that Marsh receives severe punishment for his crimes."

"I'll do it for free," he assured her without hesitation.

"Nevertheless…" Her voice trailed off as she handed him the lawyer's name and address and pressed a kiss to his cheek. She inhaled a determined breath as she picked up her luggage. "It has been a pleasure knowing you, Bartholomew. Please let me know through my lawyer what happens with Marsh and the Harper brothers' court trials and sentencing."

Bart took the luggage from her hands and accompanied her down the hall. "I'll go with you to purchase your coach ticket. I'm going to miss your misadventures, Nat," he said teasingly. "They were more interesting than most of my court cases in Wolf Ridge. But I have to say that I hope the next phase of your grand adventure, as Van calls it, isn't plagued with so many mishaps."

On the way down the steps, Natalie kept hoping Crow would suddenly appear so she could savor the sight of him one last time. On the other hand, not seeing him was easier. She wouldn't have to pretend that going her separate way wasn't killing her, bit by excruciating bit.

"Will you be returning to Wolf Ridge immediately?" she asked as they hiked down the street to the stone-and-timber depot that sat on the east side of town.

"Doubt it. Van is headed to the reservation to make certain Lieutenant Suggs faces criminal charges. I thought I might be of help."

Natalie didn't mention that she had made a mental note to do what she could to improve the conditions for Teskee,

Chulosa and their clans. Besides, arranging to send supplies would keep her occupied. She definitely needed to keep busy so forgetting Crow would become easier with each passing day.

The clatter of hooves and jingle of harnesses demanded her attention. She glanced east to see the stagecoach roll toward the depot, bringing a cloud of dust with it. Attendants scurried forward to replace the team of horses for the next leg of the journey across no-man's-land to Kansas.

"You have your dagger and derringer, right?" Bart questioned as she pivoted toward the depot to purchase her ticket. "You'll need them in that rowdy town. Or so Van says. I haven't been to Dodge yet."

She nodded and patted the pocket sewn into the side seam of her lavender gown. "I haven't been to your town of Boston," she remarked. "Are there sights I might like to see after my tour of the West?"

Bart's expression sobered. "Of course, Nat. Much history was made there. High society is alive and well there, too."

She didn't have time to ask, but she sensed from his comment there were drastic reasons why Bart had pulled up stakes and moved to Texas. The sparkle had disappeared from his alert green eyes in nothing flat. She suspected she would loose the sparkle in her eyes, too, when someone mentioned Crow.

Which made her wonder if the tortuous memories Bart had stashed away from the world had something to do with a woman who meant a great deal to him.

When she returned from purchasing her ticket, the Rangers were waiting with Bart. After a quick round of fare-thee-wells, Bart assisted her into the coach.

"Be careful, Nat," Bart warned.

She leaned out the window to smile playfully at the four

men. "And miss all the excitement I'm used to? Where is the fun in that?"

Bart snickered. "Ah yes, I forgot. You live for thrills and danger these days, don't you?"

The Rangers and Bart were still smiling at her when the stagecoach pulled away, taking Natalie to her future. She glanced out the window to wave her final goodbye, then looked toward canyon country. Still, Crow was nowhere in sight.

It doesn't matter, she told herself as she settled back on the padded seat to share the confined space with two men who looked to be wastrels or gamblers, judging by the cut of their clothes.

She carried with her the image of Crow for he had taken up permanent residence in her heart and in her soul. He had turned out to be a little *too* perfect as a husband. Letting go of her deep-seated feelings for him was going to take the longest time, she predicted.

Natalie frowned pensively, wondering if putting a hundred miles between them would make the lonely ache in her heart easier to bear. But honestly? She doubted one mile or a thousand miles would make the slightest difference.

Van rode Durango into town and caused a commotion because of his war paint and clothing. But once the bystanders on the street realized who he was, they went their own way. Leaving his gelding at the livery, with instructions to brush him down and give him an extra portion of feed, Van headed for the hotel. The cleansing ritual he'd performed at the creek in Phantom Canyon served as a bath, but the war paint had to go.

Van stopped in his tracks when he opened the door to his suite and felt the empty silence sweep over him. When he walked into the bedroom to pour water into the basin so he could wash his face, he saw the discarded yellow gown draped over the end of the bed. Natalie's luggage was gone. Had she moved back to the single room he had rented for her when he thought she had lied to him about the money and jewels she carried with her?

Van scrubbed off the war paint, then quickly changed into his everyday clothing. He strode down the hall to check on Natalie. She deserved another lecture for poking her head above the boulder to blast away at Willy when Van already had the situation well in hand. Damn it, she could have gotten her gorgeous head shot off, since all three Harper boys had been packing pistols. But had she listened to his instructions? Had she ever? She just kept thumbing her nose at his commands.

The thought annoyed him as he rapped loudly on the door. He was met with silence. "Natalie? Open the door so I don't have to break it down."

"She isn't there."

Van spun around to see Bart exit from his suite. "Then were the hell is she? Getting into more trouble?"

Bart shook his head, then readjusted his wire-rimmed spectacles. "She took the stagecoach to Dodge over an hour and a half ago. Since we skipped breakfast this morning I thought you and I might have lunch together."

"She's gone?" The word echoed around the hollow place that suddenly opened inside his chest.

"The Rangers stopped to say goodbye and we put her on the coach. I'd say that is about as gone as a woman can get."

She had time to tell everyone else fare-thee-well, but not me? he thought, incensed. *Is that all I am to her? A paid employee whose services are no longer needed?*

His pride stinging, Van swore under his breath. He

should be relieved she was gone. He'd gotten along just fine without that misfit plunging from one mishap to another. He'd come to her defense—without hazard pay, mind you. Though being kidnapped by the Harpers really wasn't her fault, he did admit. She'd been at the wrong place at the wrong time.

"Lunch sounds like a good idea." Van lurched around and moved swiftly toward the staircase. "I'm starving."

Bart fell into step beside him. "I'd like to accompany you to the reservation. I might be of help with formal charges against the theft ring preying on your clan."

"Glad to have the company." Maybe Bart's presence would ease the frustration of Natalie riding off, as if there was nothing left between them.

There isn't, he reminded himself. *How did you think this was going to end? She wants to see the world and you have seen far too much of it. She is practically royalty and you come from lowly beginnings. You should be glad she's gone.*

When they veered into Caprock Café Van ordered a double plate of food. Bart arched an amused brow when two plates of steak and potatoes arrived.

"You think extra food is going to satisfy your hunger?" Bart inquired.

He dug in like a field hand. "I was up all night tracking the Harpers and I spent the morning performing purging rituals," he explained between bites. "Nothing wrong with a healthy appetite."

"Certainly not, but I can tell you from personal experience that the gnawing ache won't go away as easily as you might expect."

Van halted with his fork in midair when he noted the tormented expression in Bart's eyes. "What are you talking about?"

"Did I ever tell you why I left Boston?"

"No, did I ever tell you how I survived the army massacre when most of my family didn't?"

"No, and I'd like to hear about it when you're ready to discuss it."

Van frowned curiously. "Does that mean we're discussing Boston over lunch?"

Bart nodded. "Watching Nat leave town brought back memories of a decision I've begun to question lately."

"Is there a moral to this story that has something to do with a woman?" Van questioned warily. "If you're trying to apply it to Sunshine's departure, then forget it. You know as well as I do this is best. She's who she is and we both know what I am. So...case closed, as you are so fond of saying when you wrap up a trial."

"Nice closing argument." Bart pursed his lips. "But you're making the same mistake I did."

"Really? Then you and I have more in common than I do with Nat."

Bart sipped his coffee, then eased back in his chair. He crossed his arms over his chest and stared somberly at Van. "I was in love with my older brother's fiancée."

Van grimaced. "This doesn't sound good."

"You're right. It turned out badly. My brother put me in charge of escorting Elizabeth to social functions while he was called away to New York to argue a high-profile case that took more than six weeks. The more time we spent together, the closer we became."

Bart glanced over Van's shoulder, staring into space. It was a moment before he continued. "She fell in love with me, too. We both felt we had betrayed Thomas, who had everything to offer Bet. I was an upstart attorney looking to open my own practice and I knew I couldn't be a partner in my brother's law firm. Seeing him with Bet and pretending I didn't love her would have been too painful."

Van continued eating and wondered how it would feel to ache for a woman who was slated to marry his brother—not that he had one, but he figured it was like his friendship with Bart. He also knew what betrayal felt like because there was a time not too long ago that he thought Natalie had betrayed his trust and used him. Those feelings had cut to the quick.

Bart expelled an audible sigh. "I had to leave Boston. I was determined to outrun the bittersweet memories and find a place to settle that was unlike my home in the east."

"And Wolf Ridge was the best you could do?"

"It was the end of the tracks. Hundreds of miles from my former life and the only woman I've ever really wanted. I couldn't shame my family or cause a scandal that might affect them and my brother's prestigious law practice." He leaned forward, forearms on the table, and stared directly at Van. "It's been eight years but when I close my eyes I can still see her face. I remember her smile, her scent and her touch. I'm telling you here and now that if you have feelings for your wife you had better do something about it…. Do you?"

"Do I what?"

Bart cast him a withering glance. "Being deliberately dense doesn't suit you, Van. If you care about Nat—"

"*She* left *me*," he interrupted in a harsh tone then clamped his mouth shut before he called unnecessary attention to himself.

"Maybe she was waiting for you to ask her to stay, but you didn't show up until she was long gone," he ventured. "That didn't send her an encouraging message, you know."

Van focused on his second plate of food. "I'm sorry about your Elizabeth," he said quietly.

Bart gnashed his teeth. "She isn't mine and her daughter isn't my child." Clearly, Bart's noble decision still haunted him. "Now here I am in the middle of nowhere, stuck with you. It's too late for me, but you have a chance to be happy," he said intently. "If you think you don't deserve her or that you aren't good enough because her family descended from titled nobility, then you're wrong, my friend."

Although Van anticipated years of tormenting memories, he refused to chase down Natalie. Bart had taken the moral high road and Van wasn't going to hold Natalie back. She was ready to spread her independent wings and fly. She had earned it.

"I'm leaving for Fort Sill and the reservation this afternoon," Van said, then washed down his meal with coffee. "You'll be deeper into the middle of nowhere if you come with me."

"Stagecoach or horseback?"

"Horseback. We'll travel light." He had to. He had burden aplenty. The excessive weight—of missing Sunshine until hell wouldn't have it—was bearing down on his heart like an anchor.

Three days later, while Bart was pestering the fort commander about court-martial proceedings against Suggs, Van made the rounds visiting extended family and friends, who bent his ear with plenty of complaints about the corrupt lieutenant.

Van half turned when he heard a commotion behind him. He frowned, bemused, as two wagons, laden down with stacks of supplies, halted in the center of the teepee village. Whoops of excitement filled the air as men, women and children rushed forward to unload the bountiful goods.

Van ambled over to the driver and guard who sat atop the first wagon. "Is this army-issued?"

"Nope. We came down the military supply road from Fort Dodge to Fort Supply, then to here," the young private reported. "This is a private donation sent by Mrs. Crow."

Van's jaw dropped open wide enough for a pigeon to roost. Natalie was furnishing supplies for his people? On second thought, he shouldn't be surprised. She knew exactly how it felt when someone took advantage of her, how incensed she became when Marsh tried to steal her inheritance after he had killed her mother. *She* hated that oppressed feeling, as all Indian tribes did. As *he* did.

While Van watched his people distribute goods that doubled what he'd sent a month earlier, Bart strolled from the commander's office, smiling triumphantly.

"Did you have Suggs and his ring of thieves locked in the stockade?" Van asked curiously.

"I didn't have to do anything." Bart watched in satisfaction while families carried off supplies to their teepees. "A certain Louisiana senior senator contacted a Texas senior senator and Kansas senior senator who demanded a full investigation of military practices concerning Indian reservations."

"Louisiana, huh?" Van said.

"Apparently the Robedeaux-Blair family has connections in high places." Bart hitched his thumb toward the military compound. "Proceedings to court-martial Suggs and two other soldiers suspected of cheating Indians for their own personal profit are already underway. And yes, our man Suggs is in the stockade, eating the spoiled food he gave the Kiowa and Comanche and complaining to high heaven about it."

Bart glanced at Van. "Shall I contact Nat's lawyer in New Orleans to pass along your gratitude for her crusade to right the wrongs against your people? Or are you going to thank her in person?"

"I don't know where she's gotten off to by now." Van stared into the distance, telling himself that Little Miss Sunshine was living the life she had designed for herself and she no longer needed him.

Bart smirked in amusement. "You managed to track her to Phantom Canyon after dark with no help from anyone else. Did you suddenly forget your tracking skills? Damn, that's going to limit future assignments, if that's the case."

Van scowled at his smart-alecky friend. "That's enough from you."

"Always glad to be of help," he replied too cheerily.

Van stood there for the longest time, studying the relieved expressions on his people's faces. For years he had remained suspended between the Indian and white worlds, unsure who or what he was. Only recently had he accepted what he couldn't change. His half-white heritage had allowed him precious freedom. Because of it, he had been able to do many things for his people that he couldn't have done if he lived on the reservation with them.

He couldn't do as much as Natalie Blair, high and mighty heiress of a shipping fortune, of course.

The thought of her generosity provoked mixed emotions. He could do as Bart suggested and correspond with her Louisiana lawyer or he could—

"Well?" Bart said, breaking into Van's conflicting thoughts.

"Well what?"

"I asked if you wanted to head home or stay the night here," Bart prompted.

Home? Back to the suite he had shared with Natalie after they negotiated their marriage and he slept by her side…until she rode out of his life without a proper goodbye. Now his hotel headquarters were filled with the sweet, tormenting memories of her lingering presence that would likely drive him as close to loco as he ever wanted to get.

It was bad enough that he was carrying around the tattered yellow gown she'd left behind, as if it were his security blanket, or some such ridiculous nonsense. No one had considered him a sentimental fool in all his thirty-two years of existence. So why had he tucked the garment in his saddlebag?

Damned if he knew.

"Do what you want," Bart said impatiently when Van didn't respond. "I'm going back to Wolf Ridge. I still have a law practice and clients who depend on me. Let me know where you are and I'll send a telegram with a list of potential assignments and the contact people."

Bart swung into the saddle. "If by chance you happen to cross paths with Nat, give her my fond regards." He smiled wryly. "Too bad she didn't ask *me* to marry her. I'd have packed up and gone on her grand adventure with her."

With a playful salute, Bart reined his horse south. And still Van stood there as if he'd grown roots. He watched his best friend disappear from sight and then stared at the village of teepees near the fort. His gaze swung northwest, wondering if his wayward wife had learned enough defensive techniques and survival skills to stay out of trouble.

Or perhaps she had hired a guide to lead her into the mountains she was anxious to explore.

Natalie alone in the wilderness with another man? The distasteful speculation soured his mood in one second flat.

Wheeling around, Van walked off to find Teskee and Chulosa. He damned well needed someone to distract him from his troubled thoughts.

Chapter Eighteen

Two weeks after Natalie left Taloga Springs she halted in the high meadow in the magnificent Rocky Mountains. The afternoon sun splattered over the towering ridges and rugged peaks. Admiring the panoramic view, Natalie dismounted from her newly purchased black gelding with its white stockings and a white blaze down its nose. The horse had been an impulsive buy in Colorado Springs because it reminded her of Durango.

Her new breeches and shirt had been special-made by a talented seamstress in Dodge City. As was the tailored jacket that boasted concealed pockets galore. Her unique style of dress had drawn puzzled glances in each town she entered during her travels, but when she gave her name at hotels, no one seemed surprised that she was a bit eccentric.

"After all," she had overheard several people remark, "she is married to Donovan Crow and that explains everything."

Her new oversize saddlebags held another set of clothing, boots and secret compartments where she carried

spare bank notes to pay her way across Colorado. She had
contacted Wells Fargo to return her family jewels back to
New Orleans for her lawyer to place under lock and key.
She had acquired a pathetic-looking pack mule in Pueblo
because the poor thing needed a friend. The animal was
laden down with food supplies to last her for a week, along
with a tarp to fend off inclement weather.

A woman on an adventure didn't bother with tents when
tarps, makeshift stakes and tree limbs served her well. She
had learned that recently—but she chose not to recall who
taught her because it triggered memories that still hurt too
much to resurrect. Perhaps after a few months she would
allow herself to remember a lopsided smile, silver-blue
eyes and shiny raven hair. But not now. Not yet.

Natalie cupped her hand over her eyes, then stared up at
the rocky crest thirty feet above her. She intended to make
the climb, just because the peak was there and she needed
to focus on one challenge after another to fill the empty
loneliness that had become her constant companion.

Tethering her horse, Natalie began her ascent, using
footholds in the rocks. She paused once or twice to catch
her breath. Eventually she reached the summit that provided a spectacular view of a canyon filled with jagged
rocks, tall timber and an eagle soaring in the cloudless
sky. The bird screeched and the haunting sound rippled
through her aching soul until tears filled her eyes.

Natalie inhaled a deep cleansing breath of mountain air.
She told herself that she had learned pride of accomplish-
ment and self-confidence the past month. She had seen
amazing sights and she had only begun her adventures.
Yet, something vital was missing. Even her prize horse,
the majestic views, her custom-made wardrobe and unlim-
ited freedom didn't satisfy the gnawing ache inside her.

Perhaps in a month.,,or three...who would allow herself to admit what was missing from her life.

She sank down on the cliff and dangled her booted feet over the edge. She leaned back, bracing herself on her hands and closed her eyes. Yessirree, she was living her dream—

"Nice view, sunshine."

Crow's amused baritone voice came from out of nowhere.

"Awk!" Natalie was so startled that she jerked upright quickly—and she nearly catapulted herself off the cliff.

Crow clamped his hand on the nape of her shirt and yanked her backward before she nosedived into a broken heap.

"Sorry. Didn't mean to startle you," he murmured against her ear.

Those gone-but-not-forgotten sensations assailed her when he sank down behind her and pulled her against the hard wall of his chest. He settled her between his legs and rested his chin on the crown of her head so he, too, could dangle his legs over the ledge and admire the breathtaking view.

"Where did you come from?" she questioned, her voice nowhere near as steady as she would have preferred.

"Back side of the peak," he informed her. "Taking the Cheyenne footpath is easier than climbing up the stone face of the crest."

"How did you find me?"

His quiet chuckle reverberated through his chest and echoed through her suddenly sensitive body. Odd, she'd felt dead for two weeks—adventures or not—and suddenly she felt happy and wildly alive.

"You might be surprised, but people pay me an

exceptional amount of money to track missing persons all over creation…if the price—"

"—is right," she finished for him. "Yes, I know, Crow. I was one of your customers." She glanced over her shoulder at him, noting he'd cut his hair short and his ruggedly handsome face was clean-shaven. "So why are you here? Are you off to another high-priced assignment?"

"More or less."

She rolled her eyes in exasperation. "Since when did you become so vague? I could always count on you to be blunt and to the point…. Oh wait, I remember now. Since I didn't stick around for your lecture on following your orders of staying put, you're here to rake me over the coals. Right?"

"You're right, sunshine. You didn't stick around…to say goodbye. Rather rude behavior for the high priestess of the shipping world."

"So you are here to jump down my throat for disobeying you," she concluded, hugely disappointed.

"Actually, Bart wanted me to send along his kind regards and Chulosa and Teskee wanted me to thank you for your generosity. Suggs and his cohorts are serving jail time, thanks to you."

Natalie tilted sideways to stare into those hypnotic silver-blue eyes fanned by long thick black lashes. "You came all the way to Nowhere, Colorado, to relay the messages?"

"No, I brought you a gift that you didn't wait around for me to give you." He reached into his pocket to display a compass. "Didn't want you to wander so far off course that you couldn't find your way back."

She accepted the gift and blinked back the infuriating tears that threatened to spill from her eyes. Natalie was trying to remain nonchalant so her feelings wouldn't show. She was not going to throw herself at Crow and beg him to take her with him on his next assignment, even if she had to promise to stay put when he told her to. Well, she amended, she would *try* to follow orders. That's all she could promise. She couldn't and wouldn't stand aside and see him hurt. Ever.

"Also, I wanted to give you this," he murmured, reaching into another pocket.

Natalie gasped when he held up a silver wedding band embedded with two oversize diamonds and two sapphires that reminded her of the colorful depths of his eyes. Her heart twisted in her chest and she barely found enough air in her deprived lungs to draw breath.

"It's beautiful," she whispered as he removed her mother's gold band from her left hand and replaced it with his expensive gift.

"So are you, sunshine." He dropped a tender kiss to her cheek. Again, he reached into his pocket. He fished out a role of large denomination bank notes that—dollar for dollar—looked suspiciously like the ones she had used to pay him. "I'm prepared to pay you generously to take an assignment for me."

She stared at his chiseled lips—that she wanted to kiss so badly that she could barely stand it. Her gaze dropped to the money rolled up in his fist. "What do I have to do?"

His expression softened. "Stay married to me for all the right reasons. Don't go haring off without me. I can't stand myself when I'm not with you, sunshine. Nothing has been the same since you left me behind."

And that is the honest truth, Van thought to himself. He had been miserable and lost—and cranky, according to Bart.

He watched her dark eyes widen in disbelief and her

jaw say against the collar of her crisp linen shirt. His attention dropped to the full swells of her breasts and the trim indentation of her waist. Gawd, but she was a welcome sight to behold! He thought he'd never track her down. She had been on the move like a tumbleweed blowing wherever the restless wind took her.

"The right reasons?" she repeated, bewildered.

Van gathered his nerve and bared his heart. "First off, because I'm in love with you. And secondly, you are perfect for me." How many times had she said those last words to him and made him feel ten feet tall?

Her eyes rolled back in her head and she wilted sideways before he could grab her. He did manage to latch on to her knee before she tumbled off the ledge. Sweet mercy, she had fainted on him?

Fainted? he thought as he came to his feet to hoist her up so he could cradle her in his arms. Was this the same daredevil who defied murderers and thieves and fought her way out of some of the worst scrapes imaginable? *Now* she fainted?

He would never understand this wife of his—but he'd like to spend the rest of his life trying.

While her head dangled off the side of his arm and her flaming auburn hair waved in the breeze, Van carried her to the spot where he had followed the footpath to the peak. He sidestepped down to the meadow and circled to the stone face of the summit. He chuckled when he noticed her new horse bore a striking resemblance to Durango, just as her clothing reminded him of the garments he favored. She had become the female version of her gun-for-hire husband, he mused wryly.

Knowing her, she would hire herself out for assignments after she tired of sightseeing and began to yearn for a different kind of adventure and excitement. He was afraid the thrill of defying danger had seeped into her blood. There would be no holding back this spirited beauty now.

Van eased Natalie onto the plush grass, then grabbed his canteen to dribble water on her peaked face. She came to with a sputter and a cough then shook her head to clear her dazed senses.

"Did you say what I thought you said?" she chirped.

Van couldn't help himself. He angled his head to savor the long-awaited taste of her lips. Two weeks of starvation, he mused. It was a wonder he had survived this long without her.

"You mean that you are perfect for me? Yes, that's what I said."

She flapped her arms dismissively. "No, the *first* part."

"The part about loving you?" He smiled into her upturned face. "I didn't know what love was until you, sunshine," he told her softly and sincerely. "I merely existed until you blew into my life like a cyclone and touched off so many emotions I didn't know how to control any of them. I don't expect you to love me back so I'll gladly pay you—"

His breath exploded from his chest when she lunged at him, knocking him off balance and leaving him flat on his back. She hovered over him, while flaming red-gold strands of her hair danced in the breeze. Tears flowed from her eyes and tumbled onto his cheeks.

"*Pay* me?" she said brokenly. "You'd have to pay me *not* to love you back, Crow. Even then, I couldn't *not* love you. You might as well ask me not to breathe. I love you so much it hurts and I've been miserable all these lonely days and nights without you. I've wanted you beside me each time I've gazed at a panoramic sight. Something was always missing and that something was *you*."

The uncertainty he'd carried with him for a fortnight, wondering if his confession from the heart would be well received, gushed out with his ragged breath. He reached up to brush his thumbs over her cheeks, rerouting her tears…and he felt an unfamiliar mist in his own eyes.

"I never realized I needed anyone or anything until I spent two hellish weeks without you, sunshine."

He gestured toward the gown he had draped over Durango's saddle. Natalie giggled in delight when she realized he had purchased a new yellow gown to replace the one damaged during her ordeal with the Harpers.

"If I can't kiss you first thing in the morning and the last thing at night then I'll have no life at all," he murmured. "I love you like crazy, sunshine."

"I love you, too. More than simple words can ever express." She brushed a tender kiss over his mouth and his heart melted down his ribs. "Where do we go from here, Crow?"

"Wherever you want, for as long as you want. I want to see the spectacular sights of the West through your fresh set of eyes." He shrugged casually. "After that, we could take a few assignments of a less dangerous nature."

"You mean it?" A pleased smile settled into every bewitching feature of her face.

"I've never been more serious in my life."

She grinned impishly as she unbuttoned his shirt to splay her hand over his chest, making him sizzle with desire in less than a heartbeat. "Ever made love in the mountains, Crow?"

"I never made love at all until there was you," he whispered as he removed her shirt and skimmed his hands over her satiny flesh.

She laughed and said, "If you keep saying all the right

things, Donovan Crow, you can have whatever your heart desires."

He cupped her smiling face—surrounded by a cloud of frothy auburn curls—in his hands. "All I want is you. If this isn't paradise, then I'm as close as I'll ever need to be."

Then he cherished her body with his hands and lips and his own aching body. He made a solemn vow that he would love his wife with all his heart and all of his soul beyond forever.

And he did.

They are together still...walking hand in hand on a mountaintop overlooking Eternity.

* * * * *

COMING NEXT MONTH FROM

HARLEQUIN®
HISTORICAL

Available August 30, 2011

- **GOLD RUSH GROOM**
  by **Jenna Kernan**
  (Western)

- **VICAR'S DAUGHTER TO VISCOUNT'S LADY**
  by **Louise Allen**
  (Regency)
  Second in *The Transformation of the Shelley Sisters* trilogy

- **VALIANT SOLDIER, BEAUTIFUL ENEMY**
  by **Diane Gaston**
  (Regency)
  Third in *Three Soldiers* miniseries

- **SECRET LIFE OF A SCANDALOUS DEBUTANTE**
  by **Bronwyn Scott**
  (1830s)

You can find more information on upcoming
Harlequin® titles, free excerpts and more at
www.HarlequinInsideRomance.com.

REQUEST YOUR FREE BOOKS!

 HARLEQUIN® HISTORICAL:
Where love is timeless

2 FREE NOVELS PLUS 2 FREE GIFTS!

YES! Please send me 2 FREE Harlequin® Historical novels and my 2 FREE gifts (gifts are worth about $10). After receiving them, if I don't wish to receive any more books, I can return the shipping statement marked "cancel." If I don't cancel, I will receive 6 brand-new novels every month and be billed just $5.19 per book in the U.S. or $5.74 per book in Canada. That's a savings of at least 17% off the cover price! It's quite a bargain! Shipping and handling is just 50¢ per book in the U.S. and 75¢ per book in Canada.* I understand that accepting the 2 free books and gifts places me under no obligation to buy anything. I can always return a shipment and cancel at any time. Even if I never buy another book, the two free books and gifts are mine to keep forever.

246/349 HDN FEQQ

Name	(PLEASE PRINT)	
Address		Apt. #
City	State/Prov.	Zip/Postal Code

Signature (if under 18, a parent or guardian must sign)

Mail to the Reader Service:
IN U.S.A.: P.O. Box 1867, Buffalo, NY 14240-1867
IN CANADA: P.O. Box 609, Fort Erie, Ontario L2A 5X3
Not valid for current subscribers to Harlequin Historical books.

Want to try two free books from another line?
Call 1-800-873-8635 or visit www.ReaderService.com.

* Terms and prices subject to change without notice. Prices do not include applicable taxes. Sales tax applicable in N.Y. Canadian residents will be charged applicable taxes. Offer not valid in Quebec. This offer is limited to one order per household. All orders subject to credit approval. Credit or debit balances in a customer's account(s) may be offset by any other outstanding balance owed by or to the customer. Please allow 4 to 6 weeks for delivery. Offer available while quantities last.

Your Privacy—The Reader Service is committed to protecting your privacy. Our Privacy Policy is available online at www.ReaderService.com or upon request from the Reader Service.

We make a portion of our mailing list available to reputable third parties that offer products we believe may interest you. If you prefer that we not exchange your name with third parties, or if you wish to clarify or modify your communication preferences, please visit us at www.ReaderService.com/consumerschoice or write to us at Reader Service Preference Service, P.O. Box 9062, Buffalo, NY 14269. Include your complete name and address.

HH11B

New York Times *and* USA TODAY *bestselling author*
Maya Banks presents a brand-new miniseries

PREGNANCY & PASSION

When four irresistible tycoons face
the consequences of temptation.

Book 1—*ENTICED BY HIS FORGOTTEN LOVER*

Available September 2011 from Harlequin® Desire®!

Rafael de Luca had been in bad situations before. A crowded ballroom could never make him sweat.

These people would never know that he had no memory of any of them.

He surveyed the party with grim tolerance, searching for the source of his unease.

At first his gaze flickered past her, but he yanked his attention back to a woman across the room. Her stare bored holes through him. Unflinching and steady, even when his eyes locked with hers.

Petite, even in heels, she had a creamy olive complexion. A wealth of inky-black curls cascaded over her shoulders and her eyes were equally dark.

She looked at him as if she'd already judged him and found him lacking. He'd never seen her before in his life. Or had he?

He cursed the gaping hole in his memory. He'd been diagnosed with selective amnesia after his accident four months ago. Which seemed like complete and utter bull. No one got amnesia except hysterical women in bad soap operas.

With a smile, he disengaged himself from the group

around him and made his way to the mystery woman.

She wasn't coy. She stared straight at him as he approached, her chin thrust upward in defiance.

"Excuse me, but have we met?" he asked in his smoothest voice.

His gaze moved over the generous swell of her breasts pushed up by the empire waist of her black cocktail dress.

When he glanced back up at her face, he saw fury in her eyes.

"Have we *met?*" Her voice was barely a whisper, but he felt each word like the crack of a whip.

Before he could process her response, she nailed him with a right hook. He stumbled back, holding his nose.

One of his guards stepped between Rafe and the woman, accidentally sending her to one knee. Her hand flew to the folds of her dress.

It was then, as she cupped her belly, that the realization hit him. She was pregnant.

Her eyes flashing, she turned and ran down the marble hallway.

Rafael ran after her. He burst from the hotel lobby, and saw two shoes sparkling in the moonlight, twinkling at him.

He blew out his breath in frustration and then shoved the pair of sparkly, ultrafeminine heels at his head of security.

"Find the woman who wore these shoes."

Will Rafael find his mystery woman?
Find out in Maya Banks's passionate new novel
ENTICED BY HIS FORGOTTEN LOVER
Available September 2011 from Harlequin® Desire®!

Copyright © 2011 by Maya Banks

HDEXP0911

Harlequin®

Desire

ALWAYS POWERFUL, PASSIONATE AND PROVOCATIVE.

NEW YORK TIMES **AND** *USA TODAY*
BESTSELLING AUTHOR

MAYA BANKS

**BRINGS YOU THE FIRST STORY
IN A BRAND-NEW MINISERIES**

PASSION & PREGNANCY
*When irresistible tycoons
face the consequences of temptation.*

ENTICED BY HIS
FORGOTTEN LOVER

A bout of amnesia…a mysterious woman
he can't resist…a pregnancy shocker.

When Rafael de Luca's memory comes
crashing back, it will change everything.

*Available September
wherever books are sold.*

www.Harlequin.com

SD73120R

Harlequin® *Romance*

**Discover small-town warmth and community spirit
in a brand-new trilogy from**

PATRICIA THAYER

*Where dreams
are stitched...patch
by patch!*

Coming August 9, 2011.

Little Cowgirl Needs a Mom

Warm-spirited quilt shop owner Jenny Collins promises to
help little Gracie finish the quilt her late mother started,
even if it means butting heads with Gracie's father,
grumpy but gorgeous rancher Evan Rafferty....

The Lonesome Rancher
(September 13, 2011)

Tall, Dark, Texas Ranger
(October 11, 2011)

www.Harlequin.com

HRI7745

ROMANTIC
SUSPENSE

NEW YORK TIMES BESTSELLING AUTHOR

RACHEL LEE

The Rescue Pilot

Time is running out...

Desperate to help her ailing sister, Rory is determined
to get Cait the necessary treatment to help her fight
a devastating disease. A cross-country trip turns into
a fight for survival in more ways than one when their plane
encounters trouble. Can Rory trust pilot Chase Dakota
with their lives, and possibly her heart?

**Look for this heart-stopping romance in September
from *New York Times* bestselling author Rachel Lee
and Harlequin Romantic Suspense!**

Available in September wherever books are sold!

www.Harlequin.com.

RSRL27741

Harlequin®
Super Romance®

Love and family secrets collide in
a powerful new trilogy from

Linda Warren

the **Hardin Boys**

Blood is thicker than oil

Coming August 9, 2011.
The Texan's Secret

Before Chance Hardin can join his brothers in
their new oil business, he must reveal a secret
that could tear their family apart. And his
desire for family has never been stronger, all
because of beautiful Shay Dumont.
A woman with a secret of her own....

The Texan's Bride
(October 11, 2011)

The Texan's Christmas
(December 6, 2011)

www.Harlequin.com

HSR71723